INDELIBLY YOURS

A Tasty Temptations Novel

MONICA MYERS

Published by Rosewood Books

ISBN (eBook): 978-1-83756-091-2
ISBN (Paperback): 978-1-83756-092-9
ISBN (Hardback): 978-1-83756-093-6

PROLOGUE

Move it or lose it, Zel.

I glanced at the clock on the dashboard and smacked the center of the steering wheel. The horn cut through the morning tranquility of the suburban cul-de-sac and several drapes twitched. I cursed. This was the third time I'd sounded the horn. Zel had been riding to work with me for two weeks while his car was in the shop, and I couldn't recall a single occasion when he'd been ready on time.

Most people on the business end of three horn blasts might have looked flustered, but not Zel. He walked jauntily down the path like a ray of obnoxious sunshine—a big grin on his face and a travel mug in each hand.

Zel was my best friend and I loved him. All the same, everything from the bounce in his step to the rainbow tie-dye on his shirt felt perfectly crafted to irritate me. I opened the door and he slid into the passenger seat, taking care to keep the travel mugs upright.

"Happy Monslay, buddy! Today's the big day. Got your game face on?"

I glared over the rims of my aviators.

"Two strikes, Zel."

"What?"

I rested my hands on the steering wheel and twisted my neck until the muscles crunched.

"Monslay is third on the list of words you're never allowed to use in my car, and you're late. Again."

"Well, excuse me for taking two minutes to add an extra sprinkle of love to your mochaccino."

He held out one of the mugs. Still glowering, I took it from him and cracked the lid.

"Pretty sure that's called cinnamon, but ok."

He'd even drawn a smiley face in the brown-speckled foam. Zel removed the top from his own coffee and sighed dramatically.

"I know there's joy in that leathery old heart somewhere. I'm going to keep digging until I find it."

"You do that."

My phone buzzed and I fumbled one-handed with the screen lock. When I saw it was a message from Crystal, my jaw tightened. Normally, I didn't mind hearing from my cousin, but I knew what this was about. In her endless crusade to prevent me from 'turning into a bitter, crusty old man,' Crystal had been trying to set me up with her friends. I'd even been on a couple of excruciatingly awkward dates, just to shut her up. All this week she'd been bending my ear about her friend Brooke who was 'just my type.' This probably meant Brooke had one, maybe two tattoos. I wasn't prepared to sit through another evening with a vapid ex-cheerleader who couldn't wait to show me her tramp stamp.

"Who loves ya, baby?" Zel asked, bringing my attention back to him.

I took in his outfit once more. "It's the 90s. They want your shirt back."

"For your information, tie-dye is in right now."

"Yeah, right."

I hit send on my terse reply to Crystal, put my coffee in the cup holder and restarted the car.

"Think I see why the studio isn't getting any business," I said sourly.

Zel sipped his coffee and eyed me pointedly.

"Hm. I have some theories about that too, Mr. Grumpy. But if you insist on making a pitstop to the 90s to drop off my shirt, can we leave your nasty attitude there too?"

"What's my nasty attitude got to do with the 90s?"

He shrugged.

"Probably nothing. But we sure as hell don't need it here."

"Ever thought about taking the bus to work?"

I pulled out of the cul-de-sac and onto the main drag.

Zel chuckled.

"You'd miss me. Anyway, I'd never abandon you in your hour of need."

I gave him a sidelong glance.

"My what?"

Zel twisted in his seat and stared intently at my profile.

"Joel, I love you. You are a big, beautiful man with a big, beautiful heart."

"You're free to stop talking at any time."

He continued as if I hadn't spoken.

"Inside this prickly shell, there's a sweet squishy center, and I know it's hurting."

"Seriously. Are you and Crystal in this together?

"Of course not. You are *prickly* this morning. You're like a suspicious little rambutan."

"How many times do I need to explain that I'm not interested in dating? I have problems enough of my own without taking on someone else's."

Besides, no one with any sense would ever hitch their wagon to mine.

We were closer to the city center now, just hitting the

dense morning traffic. I drummed my fingers on the wheel as we slowed to a crawl.

"You've been walking around like a bear with a stick up its ass for weeks," Zel continued. "It's obvious what's going on."

"My business is going down the toilet and I'm carpooling with Bozo the Clown?"

"We are not going down the toilet. We're just in a slump. Things will pick up. This new building is going to make all the difference."

"Building's not ours yet," I said. "They haven't officially accepted our offer."

"That's just a formality. Positive thoughts, remember?"

My scowl deepened. It was hard to share his confidence.

Ever since graduating from art school, I'd dreamed of owning my own tattoo studio. Cutting the ribbon on Sailor Joey's had been the proudest moment of my life. Five years down the line my dream had started to resemble a nightmare. In the last 18 months, business had dwindled. Sailor Joey's had gone from making a slim profit to barely breaking even. My aunt and uncle had lent me the money for the deposit. For a while, I'd been able to put money aside each month to pay them back. Now I was regularly dipping into that fund just to survive. Aunt Loretta and Uncle Jeff never said a word, but I felt terrible. After Mom died, they'd taken me in and raised me. Forcing them to scrimp and save when they should have been enjoying their retirement was a shitty way to pay them back. I needed a miracle.

And then I found one.

Investing in a bigger property when business was on a downswing seemed like craziness, but I was convinced this place could turn things around. I'm not a superstitious guy but when I saw that building for sale, I got a *feeling* about it. Lots of room, prime location, plenty of foot traffic. And there was so much potential. With a space like that, we could be more than just a tattoo studio. I'd gotten into art school because someone recognized my talent and took a chance on me. Now, maybe I could give other people that chance. There were so many kids who thought they had no better use for their artistic skills than tagging walls. With a bigger space, I could finally get involved in some community outreach. Our offer had been provisionally accepted and the bank defied all my expectations and approved the loan. It felt too good to be true. We were expecting final confirmation from the realtor today. Despite Zel's insistence that it was 'just a formality,' I was sweating.

As soon as we arrived at the studio, I knew something was off. For one thing, Lily was working. At this time of the morning, my teenage apprentice usually had her ass in a chair and her head in her phone. The sight of her tidying the reception desk gave me the urge to pinch myself.

"What's gotten into you?" I asked.

She shrugged.

"Nothing. I was a little early, so I figured I'd do something useful."

She shuffled a pile of consent forms and glanced over her shoulder.

"I wanted to make sure everything was ***in position*** for when ***you arrive***."

"Why are you shouting? I'm right—"

"Surprise!"

The door at the back of the studio banged open. I stared dumbstruck as an avalanche of balloon-wielding relatives poured out. Aunt Loretta, Uncle Jeff, Crystal, and all three of her kids. Cody and Kelvin's shoving match in the doorway was descending into a full-blown fistfight and Georgia was balanced on Crystal's hip, singing an off-key rendition of "Baby Shark." It was far too much chaos on far too little coffee.

I accepted Aunt Loretta's hug and glanced furiously over her shoulder at Zel and Lily. How many people had been in on this? Loretta stepped back and began brushing invisible lint from my shoulders. My family gathered around me, grinning excitedly and somehow taking up even more space than usual. I gave myself a mental shake.

"W-what are you all doing here?"

"It's your big day," Loretta said, smoothing a crease from my shirt. "We wanted to be here when you opened the letter. We were hoping Dustin could be here too, but he's working a double shift."

I swallowed and licked my dry lips.

"But I haven't even checked the mail yet. It might not be—"

Before I could finish speaking, Lily bounded from behind the desk and thrust a white envelope under my nose. Uncle Jeff chuckled wheezily.

"We had a hard time stopping her from ripping it open."

I glanced down at him and forced a smile. He sounded bad today. Jeff had been a powerful-looking guy when he was younger, but these last few years, he seemed to have crumpled in on himself. Thirty years working demolitions had chewed up his lungs and he was diagnosed with COPD soon after retirement. No matter how much time passed, I couldn't get used to that weird, wet rattling when he breathed, or to the sight of the wheelchair and oxygen tank.

Wiping my hand on my pants, I took the envelope. I felt their eyes on me as I fumbled with the flap. Having my family here to share the moment should have made me happy but the weight of their expectations only added to the tension squirming in my stomach.

It was always weird when my aunt and uncle came to the studio—two worlds colliding. And now that business was bad, it drove the guilt home extra hard. I unfolded the letter and a stone dropped into my stomach. I read it three times from beginning to end but it refused to make sense. The words swam before my eyes in a confused jumble. I barely reacted when Zel plucked it from my fingers.

"We've been outbid."

It was such a short sentence, but it broke the silence like a brick through the window.

Why does it sound more real now he's said it out loud?

Aunt Loretta looked between us helplessly.

"I don't understand. You'd applied for that special grant, and the owners were really excited when you told them about your plans."

Zel's mouth moved wordlessly as he scanned the letter again.

"There's not much to understand really," he said. "Someone came along who had the money upfront, and they offered to pay over the asking price."

"Let me look at that."

Aunt Loretta held out a hand for the letter and rummaged in her purse for her reading glasses. We all watched silently as she studied it. Even the kids were quiet.

"What the heck is Sticky Treats?" she said eventually.

Crystal's eyes widened.

"No way! I know that place. They did some catering for Belinda's bachelorette party."

"Their cakes have bathroom parts on 'em."

Silence descended again. Cody chewed on the neck of his t-shirt and looked around the room, delighted with the effect of his bombshell. My aunt frowned.

"Did I hear that right?"

Crystal composed herself with visible effort, channeling her explosive laugh into a cough.

"They're an erotic bakery, Mom."

"A what?"

"It's a...specialist bakery. It's like on those Netflix shows where they make cakes in the shape of dragons and stuff. Only difference is these cakes look like—"

"Butts!"

"Among other things," Crystal said, glaring at her son.

"Butt-cakes!"

Kelvin took up the chant. Soon they were shouting it in unison like a war cry. Even little Georgia joined in. Crystal pinched the bridge of her nose. It was hard to tell whether she was embarrassed or trying not to laugh.

Eventually, the kids were silenced on pain of losing their allowance. Zel ushered them to the other end of the studio, promising to get out his face paints later if they behaved. He was a body painter, and his face painting skills were the stuff of birthday party legend.

"They must be doing pretty well to have that kind of money upfront," Crystal said. "This building is much bigger than their old place."

Thanks. That makes me feel much better.

Aunt Loretta shook her head.

"To each their own, I guess."

Crystal smiled slyly.

"You should place an order, Mom. It'd be guaranteed to liven up the church bake sale."

"I imagine it would. Might put an end to some people."

"At least it'd be a happy ending."

Crystal ducked her mother's swat without missing a beat. Thirty years of being a wiseass had honed her reflexes.

"Cinderella had a happy ending when she married the prince."

Somehow Georgia had toddled back over without us noticing. The kids were on fire today.

"Do you think that hurts?" Lily asked, waving her phone at us.

She'd already found her way onto the Sticky Treats Instagram page. Her screen displayed a photo of some cake pops that featured extremely personal piercings.

My aunt swiped the phone from Lily and looked at the screen. After a moment, she pursed her lips and put her head on one side.

"You know," she said. "Might not be my cup of tea, but whoever made these knows their way around buttercream."

"Seriously? Is this what family loyalty is supposed to look like? Can we forget about the porn cakes for a second and focus? These people swooped in, like the slimy, over-privileged jackasses they are, and stole my dream. I was gonna do things with that place. But apparently, the world needs cake pop titties more than youth outreach programs."

I realized I'd been shouting and closed my mouth with a snap. It was the first time I'd spoken since opening the letter and they all stared at me apprehensively. My cheeks burned.

"Hey!" said Zel, a little too brightly. "Why don't I take everyone down the street for some coffee? Magda usually has a fresh batch of breakfast scones right about now."

There was a muted chorus of approval and everyone except Aunt Loretta trickled out of the studio. Crystal gave my arm a squeeze on her way past and Lily mouthed a silent "Sorry." Once I was alone with my aunt, I slumped in a chair at the desk and put my head in my hands.

"I'm sorry, Joey. I know you had your heart set on this."

I winced. Whenever she called me Joey, I felt like a little boy again. That was the last thing I wanted right now. Suddenly it was like I had something stuck in my throat.

"Sorry," I said. "I'm just—"

"Disappointed. I know."

"I was hoping that expanding the studio might be a way to pay you back faster."

"Honey, you know we don't care about—"

"Well, I do!"

I hadn't meant to bite her head off, but the gnawing guilt was too much to bear. They'd taken me in and treated me as a son even though they had two kids of their own. In return, I'd brought them misery and hardship. The fact that everyone had been on hand to witness my latest failure made it even worse. When they offered to help me start my business it had taken a lot of cajoling before I'd take their money. I only found out afterward that they'd remortgaged their condo to get it. They knew I'd never have accepted it. Discovering the neat stack of bills in my aunt's bureau hit like a gut punch. Because of me, they now had to juggle mortgage payments *and* Uncle Jeff's Medicare premiums.

I'm a fucking curse.

"Listen," she said sternly. "Your uncle and I have never regretted what we did. You needed that money to start your business. We were just happy there was something we could do. I know that building seemed perfect, but life throws curve-balls all the time. You'll find somewhere else eventually."

"I guess."

"I just wish you didn't insist on shouldering all these worries by yourself."

"Not this again."

I sat up and began shifting things around the desk. Now that Lily had 'tidied' nothing was where it was supposed to be.

"Yes, this again. You're doing it right now. Every time something goes awry you snap and growl and push everyone away. You're all closed off like some crusty old barnacle."

"Crusty?"

She sank into the only vacant chair, suddenly looking very old and tired.

"Look," she said gently. "You're a great guy, Joel. I hate seeing you alone."

"Alone is how I like it."

It's better for everyone that way.

CHAPTER ONE

Olivia

Oh, God! Who died?

I groped for my phone, wincing as half the items on my bedside table clattered to the floor. The chirpy trill of my ringtone had yanked me from a deep sleep, and I shook with adrenaline. Five a.m. calls rarely meant good news. I eventually reached my phone by performing some undignified gymnastics that I was grateful no one was awake to see. Peering at the screen, I frowned when I saw my brother's name. Nolan was never awake this early, and Erin wasn't due for months. I pressed accept and stifled a yawn.

"Hello?"

"Liv! You *are* home. Thank fuck!"

It was tempting to point out that I was unlikely to be anywhere else at 5 a.m., but his flustered tone stopped me. I sat up straighter, panic fluttering in my chest.

"What's wrong? Is it Granny? Has Erin gone into labor?"

Catastrophic scenarios sprouted in my mind like toadstools. I was already assembling a mental to-do list by the time Nolan replied.

"What? No! It's nothing like that. I just need a favor."

I slumped back against the pillows. My panic receded and I began to remember that I should have been asleep.

"Do you have any idea what time it is?"

"I woke you up, didn't I?"

"No. You dragged me up kicking and screaming. What do you need?"

"I need you to drive to Sticky Treats with your spare keys."

"Huh?"

I scrubbed a hand over my face. My eyes were hot and itchy.

"Sticky Treats," Nolan repeated. "Jayden's lost his keys, and Erin—" He paused delicately. "Erin's rather attached to the bathroom right now."

"Morning sickness?"

I grimaced sympathetically. When I was pregnant with Abby, the second trimester had been pure hell.

"Yeah. Not sure whether to call for a doctor or an exorcism. I know it's a big ask, but I don't want to leave her, and the re-opening is tomorrow. They need to start piping profiteroles for the croquemballs."

"Don't you mean croquembouche?"

"Nope. It's actually really clever. They've filled them with this creamy—"

"It's ok. I get the idea."

I needed at least one cup of coffee before I was physically and emotionally ready for cream-filled balls. Not that edible body parts were a novelty anymore.

Everyone (including me) had been delighted when my brother fell head over heels for Erin Donovan. After a string of disastrous relationships, he'd finally settled down with the woman of his dreams. It was typical of Nolan that the woman of his dreams also happened to own and run an erotic bakery. My brother was allergic to anything normal.

"Anyway," he said. "If I can't get someone to let him in,

she'll try to go in herself. I don't think that would be good for her, or her vehicle upholstery. I could ask Granny, but—"

I sat up straight again.

"Nolan Reid, if you drag our grandmother out of bed—"

"I wouldn't worry too much," he said dryly. "She's the reason Jayden lost his keys in the first place."

"She is?"

Finally accepting that I wasn't going back to sleep, I swung my legs over the side of the bed and slid my feet into my cozy bunny slippers.

"Yep. They went out for cocktails last night. She drank the poor kid under the table."

"Sounds about right."

People were frequently weirded out by the friendship between my 80-year-old grandmother and Erin's 20-year-old assistant, but it made sense. My grandmother (Granny V to most of the world) lived according to the mantra that 'growing older is inevitable, growing up is optional.' She had more energy than a lot of people half her age. Apparently, even Jayden was struggling to keep up. I stood up and stretched.

"Let me throw some clothes on and drag Abby out of bed, then I'll head right over."

"Thanks, Liv. You're a saint!"

"I know. Hug Erin from me."

I threw on jeans and a sweater and stumbled downstairs to turn on the coffeemaker. Persuading Abby out of bed was going to take some persistence. Might as well make sure my caffeine drip was ready.

I had two projects due today and Abby had karate class. Technically, I could skip the PTA meeting, but I wasn't sure I could cope with the political fallout on four hours of sleep. It was bad enough that I still hadn't RSVP'd Marsha about her daughter's birthday. I hated being 'that parent' (especially to the head of the PTA) but a makeover party just didn't feel appropriate for seven-year-olds. I needed a tactful way to bring this up that didn't end with Marsha calling me 'girlfriend' and telling me to 'chillax.' As if 'chillaxing' was easy. We couldn't all be super-mom. I glanced at the schedule on the refrigerator and winced. The next few days were a frantic explosion of red pen and post-its.

You sure pick your moments, Nolan!

I'd manage. I always did. It wasn't as if I had a choice.

"Olivia's so capable."

"...a saint."

"...don't know how she does it."

"...never had to worry about her."

You hear something enough times, and it sinks into your bones, becoming part of who you are. Single parenthood, career, busy schedule; I took it all in my stride and I made sure I was there to pick up the pieces when my family needed me. If there was one thing I hated, it was letting people down.

Peeking into Abby's bedroom, I couldn't help but smile. As usual, she'd thrown the covers off. Now she was lying on her front, spread out like a softly snoring starfish. She had her Olaf plushie tucked under one arm, and the other rested on a hand-held console. I needed to start confiscating that thing before bed.

Thanks, Alana. Thanks bunches!

Alana was my brother's PA and probably the only reason he ever made it to any of his meetings or appointments. She also happened to be a close family friend and Abby's favorite babysitter. The latter likely had something to do with the fact that Alana had pink hair and lots of colorful tattoos. According to Abby, Alana and her girlfriend Jess were 'the coolest people in existence.' The last time she had stayed with them for the weekend, they had introduced her to retro gaming. She came back with a Nintendo 3DS and an obsession with *The Legend of Zelda*.

I sat down on the edge of the bed and brushed Abby's red

curls from her cheek. When she didn't stir, I gently shook her shoulder.

"Hey," I whispered. "Time to get up."

She made a muffled, grumpy noise and pulled Olaf closer to her chest.

"Come on," I said, combing my fingers through her hair.

"But Pumba hasn't beeped yet."

I threw a guilty glance at her *Lion King* alarm clock.

"I know, baby. But I need you to get up a little earlier today."

"I'm still sleepy."

She squirmed away from my caress and burrowed further into the pillow. I eyed her handheld, struck by inspiration.

"Uncle Nolan has an important quest for us."

She stopped wriggling immediately. One green eye winked open.

"What kind of quest?"

"It's, uh—a rescue mission."

Abby raised herself onto her elbow and blinked at me blearily.

"Are we rescuing a princess?"

"Maybe. Does Jayden count?"

She gave me a hard look.

"No."

"Why not?"

"Because he's a jerk."

This seemed to settle the matter. She flopped back onto the bed and put the pillow firmly over her head. We'd had a lot of discussions on the qualifications needed to be a princess. Whilst we had concluded that princesses could be boys, apparently, they couldn't be jerks. I tried a different tactic.

"How about Auntie Erin? We're rescuing her too."

"We are?"

Abby's interest rekindled. Erin had made the cakes for

Abby's last two birthday parties, and she ranked high on the list of her favorite people.

"Auntie Erin's feeling really sick this morning," I said. "So, she needs us to take some keys to Sticky Treats and let Jayden in. Otherwise, they won't be able to make all the cakes in time for tomorrow. You remember why tomorrow is important, right?"

She nodded solemnly. For months, Erin had been frothing with excitement over her grand re-opening, and the hype was infectious. Sticky Treats had been a runaway success from the moment it opened, and they were finally expanding. Erin had found the perfect building. Not only could she sell her bespoke treats, but she could expand into serving coffee. She'd also confided that she wanted to use the extra space to support other artists in the alternative community. She was even talking about using some of the upper rooms to open a gallery. It was a lot to take on with a baby on the way, but Erin was driven and ambitious and Nolan had been incredibly supportive. We were all happy for her. She was a sweet, lovely person who deserved her success, especially given what she'd gone through to get the money.

"That's why we need to accept this quest. Auntie Erin and Uncle Nolan need us to step up and be the heroic saviors of the party."

Abby bit her lip.

"Ok," she said eventually. "What's the reward?"

"Reward?"

She eyed me shrewdly.

"When Link does a quest, he gets a reward, like weapons or rupees...or sometimes bugs."

I guess I did this to myself.

"Well, I don't have any rupees, but how about Pop-Tarts for breakfast?"

"Yay!"

Her face lit up and she bounced out of bed. I didn't usually approve of that kind of reward, but I had dragged the poor kid out of bed at 5:30. She was only seven. I still had a few more years where I could preserve the illusion that good deeds are rewarded and the hero always wins. One of the guilty pleasures of parenthood was seeing the world through your child's eyes and indulging the fantasy that life was simple.

But life was never simple. Abby herself was proof of that. She was the best thing I ever did, yet she came out of the worst decision I ever made.

My chest tightened as I watched her digging through her dresser, no doubt looking for her brightest, pinkest t-shirt. Whatever happened, I was determined I would never let her down.

As usual, our epic quest began with utter chaos. I should've known that juggling a sleepy child and a hot cup of coffee was above my skill level at 6 a.m. By the time we got in the car, my sweater was sporting an ugly brown stain and I was seriously frazzled.

I knew something was amiss as soon as I put my foot on the gas. A downward glance confirmed my suspicions. Two fluffy white faces stared innocently back up at me. I muttered under my breath and Abby's eyes widened. Parenting 101: no matter how quietly you curse, your kid can always hear you.

Really killing it this morning, Olivia.

I looked at the clock on the dashboard and bit my lip. It wasn't like they weren't safe to drive in. Besides, who was likely to see me at this hour?

CHAPTER TWO

Joel

Ok. One more look, then I'm done.

I took the long way to the studio after leaving the donut shop. A route that just so happened to run right past Sticky Treats. Parking my car on the opposite side of the street, I leaned on the steering wheel and glowered at the building. It was practically finished now. I looked through the big windows into the spacious shop floor.

So much fucking potential...for someone else.

Some finishing touches had been added to the exterior. The shop sign was now adorned with a frosted donut, suggestively skewered by an elegant finger.

Cute. Real cute.

I expected to feel the familiar flash of rage, but it didn't come. Something heavy settled in my chest and I just felt depressed. As the deadline to the opening counted down, my mood had plummeted. Things had come to a head yesterday when I snapped at Lily. I'd arrived at the studio to find her in her usual position—feet on the desk, eyes glued to her phone. When she'd pointed out that 'it was no big deal because there was no one here anyway,' I'd lost my temper. I told her if she wasn't interested in working, she knew where the door was.

Lily fled to the back room in floods of tears and Zel gave me one of his dressing downs. This happened so rarely that it never failed to hit its mark. He hit me in the face with everything I knew but couldn't admit. The main thing being that I'd taken it out on Lily because I felt guilty. The studio accounts were looking bleaker than ever and the thought of having to let my apprentice go was tearing me up. After a miserable night of staring at my bedroom ceiling, I'd driven out at 5:30 a.m. to soothe my conscience with a gigantic box of apology donuts.

I was on the point of driving away when an SUV pulled up in front of the shop and a slim redhead jumped out. I watched her as she hurried to the door and fumbled in her purse. Putting a shape to the person who had elbowed me aside kindled something inside me. Seeing her, so sweet and complacent in her stupid pink sweater, made my anger flare up; I almost welcomed it. Depression made it hard to do anything, but anger galvanized me. I'd always pick movement over inertia, even if it propelled me straight to Bad Idea Town.

On this occasion, it propelled me over the street. Before I realized what I was doing, I was standing in front of Sticky Treats, watching my nemesis fumble with her keys.

My nemesis had a nice ass. Round, toned, and perfectly hugged by tight jeans. I dragged my gaze upwards, but that just drew my attention to her hair. It was a vibrant red and it tumbled over her shoulders in shining waves. I had the crazy urge to run my hand through it, imagining the way the silky strands would feel between my fingers. I should have left. Just turned around and walked away. Unfortunately, my mouth had other ideas. It wanted to compensate for my traitorous, ass-fancying eyes.

"Gotta say, you're not what I was expecting."

"Excuse me?"

She turned around. I might have hated this woman on principle, but I couldn't deny she was stunning. Clear skin, gorgeous green eyes, a cupid's bow mouth that begged to be kissed and the cutest fluffy bunny slippers.

Wait...what?

I took a second look to make sure I wasn't dreaming. One ear flopped at an angle and an eye hung loose from a thread. They were old and ratty but in a cozy way. It might have been less surreal if she hadn't been glaring down her nose at me. She looked way too dignified for someone whose footwear had whiskers. Questions stacked on my tongue like Jenga blocks while my brain subjected me to a psychedelic medley featuring a disturbing mash-up of Lewis Carroll and Jefferson Airplane.

Ask her if she's late...for a very important date.

I realized my gaze had lingered too long. Furious with myself, I folded my arms and averted my eyes, opting to glare over her left shoulder instead. I had every reason to be pissed and refused to be derailed by bunny slippers.

"Didn't expect the soccer mom get-up," I grunted. "I mean it's obvious you're not open for business, but I assumed you'd be expected to show more flesh."

I felt a savage stab of satisfaction when her mouth fell open.

"How dare you?"

"Now you're offended. You think anyone who meets you doesn't automatically think of titties on a stick?"

She blinked.

"Is this some lame attempt at a pick-up line? I feel I should tell you that aggressive misogyny isn't the turn-on you think it is. Three out of ten. Try harder next time."

"Why three?"

She smiled bitterly.

"Because sad as this sounds, I've actually heard worse. Now, this has been delightful, but I have to flee now. Would you like my fake phone number, or should I jump right to macing you?"

Is she for real?

"Don't flatter yourself, princess. You're not my type. Doubt I'm yours either. Bet you're used to a guy with a bigger—"

She raised a hand and closed her eyes.

"I'd advise you not to finish that sentence. I wasn't kidding about the mace. And don't call me princess."

"Hey, I was going to say bank balance. Some of us don't always have our minds in the gutter."

Her hands flew to her hips, sending her red curls bouncing over her shoulders. A flash of déjà vu hit me out of nowhere. She reminded me of someone, but I couldn't put my finger on it. I barely had time to register the new feeling before she snapped me from my reverie.

"And where was your mind, exactly?" she asked. "Polishing your guns? Planning your next blog post on Chads Anonymous: 'Gangsta ink for meathead posers'?"

My eyes had drifted downwards. In my defense, my attention had initially been drawn there by the stain on her sweater. It looked like she'd spilled a cup of coffee and hadn't had time to change. But once I was down there, I couldn't help noticing the swell of her breasts, and the outline of perky nipples through the thin fabric. It should've taken a lot to distract me from a view like that, but 'gangsta ink' was just too much. My head snapped upwards like someone had jerked a wire. Who did this judgmental bitch think she was?

"Well, that's just typical, isn't it?" I snapped. "You take one look and think you know all about me. Here, what do you think this is?"

I thrust my forearm under her nose. Reluctantly, she glanced at my arm and shrugged.

"A weird fish skeleton thing?"

"Wrong! But thanks for playing. This is a Yōkai. Know what a Yōkai is?"

"No. But I don't see how that's—"

"A Yōkai is a spirit from Japanese folklore," I interrupted. "This happy little fellow is a bake-kujira. A ghostly whale spirit. The tattoo was designed to mimic a school of Japanese painting popularized in the late Edo period. In short, this is art. Not quite as a high brow as a chocolate wang, but—"

"I like that one. It looks like a Pokémon."

We turned in unison. We'd been joined by a little girl with wild red curls—an adorable miniature of the woman standing next to me. The woman's eyes darted between me and the kid. Her cheeks had flushed a pretty pink that made the green in her eyes look even brighter. She smiled through gritted teeth.

"Sweetie, what are you doing out here? I told you to wait in the car."

The little imp looked unabashed. She put her hands on her hips in a perfect imitation of her mother and tossed her curls.

"I got bored," she said. "And hungry. When can I have Pop-Tarts?"

"This your kid?"

A minute ago, I'd been fired up with righteous fury. Now I felt uncomfortable and ashamed—like I'd grown three feet and morphed into a big stomping brute.

"Yes," said the woman, tucking a stray hair behind her ear and crossing her arms. "This is—"

"I'm Abby."

To my surprise, the kid approached me without a trace of fear and stuck out her little hand. I took it carefully in my much larger one and shook it.

"We're on a quest," she continued. "And I'm supposed to get Pop-Tarts at the end."

I raised my eyebrows.

"A quest, huh? Sounds like fun."

She bit her lip.

"It was fun until I had to wait in the car. That was boring. Then I saw you and Mommy arguing and I thought you might be the boss battle. You look like a boss battle."

"Abby!"

My lips twitched. I glanced at my bulging muscles, the

colorful tattoos, and the chains hanging from my jeans. Maybe the kid had a point.

"That's ok," I said wryly. "I've been called worse things."

I dropped to one knee so I was at eye level with Abby.

"Bosses drop loot, right? Can't claim to have Pop-Tarts, but I've got a big box of donuts in the car. Want one?"

Her face lit up.

"Yeah!"

"No!" the woman cut in firmly. "It's very kind of you, but we don't accept gifts from strangers."

She addressed the last remark to Abby, glaring at her meaningfully.

"Aw! Mom! Please?"

The little girl's lip quivered, and her eyes got big and round. She knew how to turn the cute up to 11. It was super-effective.

"Seal on the box is intact," I offered. "I'm not out to poison anyone."

The woman looked between me and her daughter and huffed out a breath.

"Ok!" she relented. "Just this once."

"Yes!"

Abby punched the air and launched into an adorable little victory dance. As I jogged to my car, I wondered what the hell I was doing. This encounter was not following the damn script. Abby's eyes went wide when I cracked the lid on the box of donuts. I expected her to take a long time choosing, but she immediately homed in on the glazed jelly filled.

A girl after my own heart.

While I was holding out the box, I felt the woman's curious eyes on me.

"Abby," she prompted. "Say thank you to Mr..."

"Morris. Joel Morris."

"Thank you, Mr. Morris," said Abby thickly, jelly dripping down her chin.

"Yes," said the woman briskly. "Thank you very much, but now we should be—"

"Wait." My irritation rose again. "You don't recognize my name, do you?"

She frowned.

"Should I?"

Unbelievable.

"The realtor didn't even tell you the name of the guy you edged out, huh?"

"Ah. I think you've made a—"

"You pushed to the front of the line with your big wad of cash and bought the whole damn building for your stupid little bakery."

Abby's face darkened.

"Mommy, why is Mr. Morris being mean about Auntie Erin?"

"*Auntie* Erin. You're not the—"

"Maybe I should introduce myself," said the woman frostily. "I'm Olivia Reid. I would offer to pass on your compliments to my sister-in-law, but I'm actually quite fond of her."

Oops.

CHAPTER THREE

Olivia

I was aware of him before I saw him. While I rooted for my keys, I experienced that weird tickle that goes up your spine when you feel someone standing behind you. Glancing to my right, I saw him reflected in the windowpane. A tall, toned snack in a sleeveless shirt and black jeans. He had an undercut, shaved at the sides, long on top and pulled into a bun at the back of his head. I couldn't see his face clearly, but I could make out a strong jaw with a healthy growth of scruff, and heavy dark eyebrows. But the thing that really caught my attention was the muscles. He looked like he'd been sculpted. Somehow the tattoos made them even more impressive.

He didn't get any harder on the eyes when I turned around and looked at him properly. The dark eyebrows contrasted sharply with intense stormy grey eyes. The scruff on his jaw was almost black, but his hair was honey colored. He reminded me of a Viking—if Vikings shopped at Hot Topic and wore really sexy cologne.

Heat rushed to my cheeks and my mouth went dry. I crossed my arms over the stain on my sweater and tried to pretend my feet didn't exist. I'm not usually the 'thirsty' type, but it had been a while. Dating as a single parent was a minefield. The idea of disrupting Abby's life with a series of failed relationships had always felt unacceptable. This meant plenty of nights with only Netflix for company and a permanent shortage of batteries. Maybe my stellar impression of a hot mess was a blessing in disguise.

Then he opened his mouth and shattered the beautiful illusion.

On behalf of women everywhere: It'd be nice if Mother Nature would stop putting such pretty wrapping paper around total douchebags. You'd think by this point I'd be able to see them coming.

He managed to tick every obnoxious box. Everything from aggressive creepiness to calling me princess. And the soccer mom dig was just unfair. I'd purchased the SUV for safety and convenience. How else do you ferry an entire karate class to a pizza party? Admittedly the Japanese art lecture went a little off script.

When Abby showed up, things got even weirder. There was my instinct to protect her. But also, a strange embarrassment, like she'd walked in on me doing something unspeakable. Then Hagar the Horrible upended all my expectations for the second time. He was incredibly sweet with her. They vibed. Watching them together, I couldn't help smiling. Hopefully, she wouldn't walk away with the expectation that all strangers dropped loot.

I could've left while he was retrieving the donuts and told Jayden to meet me elsewhere. Abby wouldn't have been happy. It might have required an emergency application of 'mom voice' but the opportunity was there. For some reason, I stayed. I couldn't even claim I was staying for Abby. If I'd been on my parenting game, I should've been teaching her not to be fooled by the handsome guy who sweeps in with cool tattoos and grand gestures. Having said that, the sight of him kneeling in front of her with the box of donuts was adorable. It was like

Prince Charming presenting the glass slipper to a mini-Cinderella.

I was just starting to think that I'd been wrong about him, when he dropped the bomb. I wasn't sure whether he was more or less of a jerk once I knew what his deal was. It was certainly satisfying to watch his face go slack when he realized his mistake.

"*Auntie* Erin. You're not the—"

"Maybe I should introduce myself. I'm Olivia Reid. I would offer to pass on your compliments to my sister-in-law, but I actually quite like her."

He threw his head back and closed his eyes.

"I saw you with the keys and I—"

"Assumed?"

He folded his arms and looked away.

"I guess, yeah."

There was an uncomfortable pause. His tongue made a little bulge as it poked the inside of his cheek. Out of the corner of my eye, I saw Abby glancing curiously between us as she munched her donut.

"I suppose I should apologize, maybe," he said grudgingly.

I raised my eyebrows.

"But you have to admit it was a reasonable assumption, given that—"

Unbelievable.

"Ok," I said slowly. "So, digging through that and assuming there was an apology buried in there somewhere: What you're actually saying is that you're sorry you were a jerk to me and not my sister-in-law?"

Still refusing to meet my eye, he made a convulsive movement with his head. It was probably as close as I'd get to a nod.

I crossed my arms and pressed my lips together.

"Do I have to explain how this doesn't endear you to me?"

I'd slipped into the tone I used with Abby when I had to explain to her why her behavior was unacceptable. Kicking ass in my bun-bun slippers was a challenge. Luckily, parenting had blessed me with one or two super-powers. If I could brazen it out when Abby asked every member of my grandmother's sewing circle if they enjoyed their menopause, I could tough this out too. Judging by his blush, my tone hit home. He picked up the box and held it out sheepishly.

"Donut?"

Resisting the smile tugging at the corners of my mouth, I bit my lip.

"Hate to break it to you, but *I'm* not seven. You'll have to do better than that."

"Maybe you should try seeing this from my perspective?" he said. "I was all set up to buy this place—poised to sign the damn papers. Then your sister-in-law comes in and—"

"Are you trying to say you were here first? Are *you* seven?"

His fingers tightened on the donut box.

"I'm just trying to say I wasn't being a jerk."

"You called me a soccer mom!"

"What about you?" he shot back. "You threatened to mace me!"

"You should both say you're sorry and make up."

We looked down. Abby was staring between us with her hands on her hips. Joel reddened and I felt my own cheeks getting hot.

Dammit! Foiled by my own parenting.

Joel took a deep breath and gritted his teeth.

"I'm sorry, pr—Olivia. I made a mistake."

Abby raised her eyebrows at me expectantly. I rubbed a hand over my forehead, torn between wanting the ground to swallow me up and the desire to burst out laughing.

"I'm sorry too, Mr.—"

"Joel," he insisted. "It's weird when people call me Mr. Morris."

"Ok. I'm sorry, Joel."

"Now shake hands," Abby ordered.

Joel held out his hand obediently. I bit my lip and stared at it uncertainly.

"Afraid I'm gonna bite?"

He quirked a dark brow and smirked. The faintest hint of a challenge glinted in his eyes. I wasn't sure what game we were playing, but I wasn't going to let him win. Sticking out my chin, I reached out and grasped his hand. It was warm and just a little rough. His grip was strong, but not crushing. My stomach flipped and I felt my tongue darting out to lick my lips.

"Sorry we're late, dears!"

We jumped in unison, and I dropped Joel's hand like it was hot. I hadn't noticed my grandmother's car pull up.

"Granny V!"

Abby launched herself at my grandmother and hugged her. I smiled. Anyone would think it'd been two months rather than two days since she'd last seen her. Granny blew me a kiss over Abby's shoulder, and I waved.

"We'd been wondering where you'd gotten to," I lied, praying she wouldn't notice how flushed I was.

"We had to make a couple of emergency pitstops."

I raised a suspicious eyebrow.

"Do I want to know?"

"Probably not."

My grandmother's hand flew to her throat, and she glanced back at the car. Jayden emerged from the front seat like a turtle poking its head out of its shell. He wore dark glasses and looked extremely pale. It didn't contrast well with the lime green of his man-bun.

"I thought he'd be fine," my grandmother said anxiously. "He's got a young person's constitution after all. Turns out those slippery nipples go down too easily."

Joel cleared his throat, and my grandmother finally registered his presence. Her face slipped from worry to not-so-innocent curiosity.

"And who's this strapping young man?" she asked, looking him up and down approvingly.

I cringed as she eagerly leaped to all the wrong conclusions. When my grandmother enters matchmaking mode nobody is safe. She might have been right about Erin and Nolan, but she was way off base with this one. I gritted my teeth and forced a smile.

"Granny, this is Mr.—"

"That's Joel. He and Mommy were fighting because he thought she was Auntie Erin. But he's nice really. He gave me a donut."

Thanks, Abby.

My grandmother looked at me and smiled knowingly.

"I can see we've got some catching up to do, Olivia."

I never thought I'd be so happy to hear poor Jayden retching. He'd disappeared behind the car, but the wet gagging sounds told us everything we needed to know.

"So," I said, pushing my hand through my hair. "It's less than 24 hours until the grand opening and both bakers are down for the count. This doesn't look good for the croquemballs."

"The what?"

Joel tilted his head and frowned. My grandmother grimaced.

"You might want to avoid saying croquemballs," she whispered. "That was the cause of pitstop number one."

"Great! That's just great. Erin's going to have a total meltdown."

"Depending on how stocked that kitchen is, I can whip up a pretty good hangover cure."

My eyebrows shot up. I'd expected Joel to be reveling in this. He'd made his feelings about Sticky Treats clear. I was still staring at him when my grandmother leaped forward and seized him by the elbow.

"Well, aren't you just a lifesaver! Let's get you inside and see what we can do for the poor boy. Hand me the keys, Olivia, and go check on Jayden."

"Sure," I said, rolling my eyes.

There'd been no noises for a while, but he hadn't appeared from behind the car. I wasn't daunted. When you've been a parent for seven years, puke will be among the least scary things you've had to deal with. Jayden squatted miserably behind the car, glasses askew. I rubbed his back and made vague soothing noises, all the while wondering what the hell Joel was up to.

CHAPTER FOUR

Joel

My morning had taken a bizarre turn. I'd gone out for apology donuts and ended up in a strange kitchen trying to find the ingredients for a prairie oyster.

Most of the food and equipment were still packed in boxes. Jayden was no help, so I had to rummage. I couldn't even have said why I was doing it.

Obviously, it had nothing to do with Olivia. Or if it did, it was only because I felt bad about the mix-up. She was attractive—anyone with eyes could see that—and she had a certain feisty appeal, but I wasn't looking to score points. I had zero interest in dating. I had even less interest in dating suburban moms in rabbit slippers.

The best I could come up with was curiosity. After weeks of glaring at the place, getting a look inside was too tempting to pass up. I had to admit I was impressed. Rooting through random boxes for pepper, I came across a black binder. It was similar to the folders we used to showcase tattoo designs and I couldn't resist peeking. I'd only intended to take a quick look, but it sucked me in. The pictures were mind-blowing. Creating such complex and lifelike sculptures from cake and chocolate took serious talent.

"All set?"

I whipped around. 'Granny V' was hovering in the doorway. I'd been so absorbed in flipping through the album that I hadn't heard her come in.

"Well," I said. "We're good on eggs, and I found some pepper. Probably shouldn't expect to find hot sauce."

"You might be surprised by what you find. They're very experimental here."

"So I gathered."

My face twisted into an awkward smile. Her eye fell upon the book, and I fought the urge to squirm.

"I came across it when I was looking for ingredients."

"Ah! You found my wedding cake!"

Whatever I'd been expecting, it wasn't that. I looked at the picture of the four-tiered fairy orgy and then at the sweet little old lady standing next to me.

"I designed it myself," she said proudly.

So many questions, none of them appropriate.

"In fact," she continued, "they might—"

She stepped away from the counter and searched through boxes.

"Ah! Yes. Here it is. My original concept. Erin insisted on framing it."

It was a beautiful colored-pencil drawing of the fairy cake. The discrepancy between style and content was striking. Suddenly I was imagining a weird alternate universe where Beatrix Potter had illustrated the *Kama Sutra*.

"You drew this?"

She chuckled.

"Yes. I was an illustrator when I was younger. I'd forgotten how much fun it could be. Are you an art lover, Mr. Morris?"

"It's Joel. And, uh, yeah. You could say that. I have a tattoo studio."

I expected her to disapprove, but she didn't turn a hair.

"We all have our preferred mediums, and with a canvas like that, who could blame you?"

She looked me up and down and threw me a sultry wink. My cheeks burned.

"I don't know about that, ma'am."

I rubbed at the back of my neck and looked away.

"Now, now, don't get bashful on me. Our bodies are nothing to be ashamed of, young man. Someone in your profession should know that. And nobody calls me ma'am. It's Granny V."

I liked this woman. She had a sense of humor and zero tolerance for bullshit.

"So," she said suddenly. "Were my old eyes deceiving me, or did I see some sparks fly between you and my Liv?"

By this point, I'd found some hot sauce. As luck would have it, I was carefully sprinkling a few drops into a glass when she launched her surprise attack.

"Damn!"

The bottle slipped and half the contents glugged into the tumbler.

"Well," Granny said. "You *did* say this would wake him up. That might be going a bit too far though."

She plucked the glass of hot sauce from the counter and handed me a fresh one.

"Thanks. And. No. No sparks. Not like that anyway. We, uh, had a misunderstanding."

She raised an eyebrow and smiled suggestively.

"Like Elizabeth and Mr. Darcy?"

The egg plopped into the glass and floated like a bright yellow island on a red-tinged sea.

"Nope. More like Jayden and the slippery nipples if I'm honest."

"Wow! Just when I thought you couldn't get any more charming."

Olivia leaned on the kitchen door frame, staring at me coldly.

"I didn't hear you come in," I said feebly.

"Came in to see if you needed any help finding things. But I can wait if you'd like to finish telling my grandmother that I make you want to barf."

Grimacing, I clasped my hands behind my head and addressed the ceiling.

"You're taking this too literally. I just meant we were a bad mix. Personality-wise."

"I agree. I'm not a fan of jerks. You done with that?"

Her eyes seemed to flash an even brighter shade of green when she was angry. She stepped up to the counter and nodded at the prairie oyster.

"Yes, but if you'd let me explain—"

"There's nothing to explain, really. I'd better get back to Jayden. I left Abby playing doctor and I'm not sure how much more he can take."

Seizing the glass, she turned on her heel and stalked out of the kitchen. I braced both hands on the edge of the counter.

"I think that proves my point." I sighed.

Granny V smiled enigmatically.

"Actually, I think we just proved mine if I know my granddaughter. And it just so happens that this is your lucky day."

"What do you mean?"

"My friend Ruth has been waiting to get her bunions done for five years, and would you believe, they up and changed the date of her surgery?"

I blinked. I needed a map for this conversation.

"I can see you're as shocked as I am," Granny continued, misreading my expression. "But there's no use crying over spilled milk. What it does mean is that she can't come to the opening tomorrow."

She reached into her purse and brought out an envelope.

"You should come along. It'd be the perfect chance to make it up with Olivia."

I stepped back and held out my hands, forestalling her.

"This is very kind of you. But I meant what I said. I'm sure your granddaughter is great, but I'm equally sure we'd be a terrible mix. I'm also not looking to date right now."

She shrugged and held out the envelope.

"In that case, treat it as a thank you for rescuing Jayden. Be a good boy and indulge an old woman."

Somehow it was impossible to say no. I accepted the invitation with a sigh.

"Ok. No promises, but I'll see if I can come along."

I will?

Why did I say that? I'd rather stick glass up my nose than go to the opening of the business that'd outbid me. On the drive back, I told myself that I only said I'd go to be polite. It wasn't as if there could be any other reason. Anyway, there was no way I was actually going.

The first thing I registered when I stepped into the studio was a pair of sculpted green buttocks. Zel was applying a base coat to his latest canvas and Lily was at the reception desk, flipping through a magazine.

"Where are the donuts?" Zel asked. "You lured me in early with promises of donuts."

"Shit!"

I'd left them in the kitchen at Sticky Treats. Zel shifted to the side of his model, applying the airbrush to a muscular thigh.

"If you don't have the donuts, where've you been all this time? We were about to send out a search party."

"I wasn't gone that long."

"Your 9 a.m. called to cancel, *Mr. Morris.*"

Lily addressed me coldly, pointedly keeping her eyes fixed on her magazine. I grabbed the spare chair and scooted up next to her.

"Look," I said ruefully. "I'm sorry I was a dick yesterday, ok?"

"You're always a dick."

She turned a page, still refusing to look at me.

"I know I've been kinda moody lately. How can I make it up to you?"

She closed the magazine and bit her lip.

"There's a dude coming in this afternoon for some really simple flash."

I narrowed my eyes. I knew where this was going.

"Can I just do the outline? Pretty please!"

I wrenched my gaze away from her puppy dog eyes and shook my head.

"I don't think you're ready yet," I said firmly. "Your linework's still too sloppy."

Lily folded her arms and spun in her chair.

"I'm tired of inking skulls on bananas." She pouted.

"I get it," I said, ruffling her teal tresses. "How about I let you have a go on my leg later? I've got some spare real-estate on the back of my calf. Do a good job on that and I'll think about letting you at the customers. Now, go take your break before our 11 a.m. gets here."

She rolled her eyes and flounced off, but it felt like she'd cheered up. Once she was out of earshot, Zel threw me a sidelong glance.

"Gonna fess up?"

"About what?"

"About where you really went."

"I was at Sticky Treats."

I picked up Lily's abandoned magazine, trying to look casual. Out of the corner of my eye, I saw Zel's shoulders slump. Sighing, he put down his airbrush and straightened up.

"You know what," he said, addressing his model. "Why don't you take five, man? Just try not to touch anything."

He came and stood in front of the desk, looming over me. I pretended not to notice.

"You need to tell me everything," he said quietly. "And if this story involves rat poison or glitter bombs, then it is officially time for an intervention."

"Fine!"

I spun in the chair and recounted everything, reciting the story to a poster on the back wall. When I got to the part about Abby, Zel snorted with laughter.

"I think I'd like this kid. Which is saying something, as she ate my jelly donut. So, did Olivia forgive you once she realized what an idiot you were?"

"I think she was about to, but—"

"Oof!" Zel exclaimed. "I do not like the sound of this. Lemme guess. You managed to put your big size 12s in it again?"

I crossed my arms and clenched my jaw.

"That about sums it up."

"So, then you left?"

"No. Then her grandmother showed up and invited me to the opening tomorrow."

The room spun unpleasantly as Zel grabbed my chair and swiveled me around.

"Ok," he said, standing in front of me and clasping his hands like he was praying. "I think you skipped a few steps in this story, but in the circumstances, I'll let it slide. Please, please, please tell me you're going."

"No, I'm not."

I swung the chair out of his grip, put my feet on the desk, and retrieved the magazine. A second later it was yanked from my grasp. Zel threw it over his shoulder, narrowly missing his startled model.

"Why the hell not?"

"For starters, I really don't want to, and secondly, this

woman only invited me because she's trying to set me up with her granddaughter. Which is ridiculous. I mean—"

"Ah, ah!" Zel looked at me severely. "Can we leave you, your issues and your penis out of this for one second? Think what this could do for our business."

I frowned.

"What do you mean?"

Zel made an exasperated noise.

"Come on, Joel. Use your imagination. Do you think there's no crossover between people who like naughty cakes and people who want tattoos? This is a chance to go schmooze."

"Schmooze?"

"Yeah! It's easy. I imagine it going something like this..."

He twisted his face into a scowl and affected a gravelly voice.

"Hi, I'm Joel. Aren't the banana butt-muffins simply divine? Oh, by the way, here's my business card.

"Just think about it," he pleaded. "Don't shoot us in the foot on this."

I closed my eyes and pinched the bridge of my nose. I hated it when he was right.

CHAPTER FIVE

Olivia

"Stop it."

Granny V blinked at me owlishly.

"Stop what, dear?"

We'd been at Erin's launch for nearly an hour, and she hadn't stopped glancing at the door. Every time the bell rang, she started up.

"Looking out for him. He's not going to show up, and what's more, I don't want him to."

"You don't?" she asked innocently. "I thought he seemed nice."

"You weren't there when he was making witty remarks about soccer moms and titties on a stick."

I absent-mindedly nibbled the end of some penis shortbread. Suddenly aware of what I was doing, I took it from my mouth and snapped it in half. Granny eyed me smugly over the rim of her coffee cup.

"I may be old, but I'm not blind. I know chemistry when I see it."

"Yeah. The kind that causes explosions, bad smells, and 3rd-degree burns."

"Abby seemed keen on him."

We edged our way through the bustling crowd. Finally, we managed to locate a relatively quiet corner. I sighed and leaned against the wall.

"Abby is seven. She's too easily seduced by sugar."

That was part of the reason why she wasn't here today. Supervising her in this crush would be next to impossible and I'd rather not expose her to the temptation of wall-to-wall treats. Fortunately, Alana and Jess were giving it a miss too. They'd been fans of Erin since before we'd even met her, but Jess didn't cope well with crowds. They were more than happy to babysit, and Abby's excitement at seeing them was enough to make her forget I was cake-blocking her.

"Don't sell Abby short," Granny said. "Kids have good instincts when it comes to people. She never had any time for her dad, even when he showed up all smiles with gifts coming out of every orifice."

I smiled bitterly.

"Yeah, he was good at that. Charles is an excellent example of what happens when I let myself make impulsive decisions."

He had never shown much interest in being a parent, but he occasionally tried to show up and play at being 'daddy.' As if the latest 'must have' toy and a few dresses would compensate for abandoning her before she was even born. Apparently, our disastrous relationship hadn't taught him that you can't buy forgiveness with big gestures.

"Anyway," I continued. "It doesn't matter. I know why you invited Joel and I'm not interested. I don't care if he's a saint or the mayor of Ass-Ville. My answer would be the same."

"But why?"

A server floated by with the croquemballs, and my grandmother plucked two pods from the sticky mass.

"I know you had a bad experience with Charles," she said, licking her thumb and offering me a ball. "But not all men are like that. It's possible to start again. You just have to make sure you're home when love comes knocking."

Her gaze shifted across the room. When she spotted her husband Russ investigating the chocolate fountain, she smiled dreamily. Granny V and Russ had been married for a little over a year. He was only 61 and she affectionately referred to him as her toyboy. The two of them still acted like lovesick teenagers. It was adorable. A little sickening sometimes, but still adorable. Granny's big ambition in life was to see her beloved grandchildren as happy as she was. With Nolan, she had gotten her wish. I was likely to be a more challenging project.

"It doesn't matter," I said, turning the sticky pastry in my fingers. "I don't have the time. I'm already raising a kid and running a business. How am I supposed to manage a relationship on top of that?"

"Relationships aren't something you *manage*, sweetheart. Get it right and you have someone else to shoulder half of life's burdens."

I snorted.

"Not with any of the men I've met."

"Well..."

Granny peered over the heads of the crowd and smiled triumphantly.

"Every now and then people surprise you."

I followed her gaze and my eyes widened. Joel had just edged through the doorway. Even in the vibrant surroundings of Sticky Treats, he stuck out. For one thing, he stood head and shoulders above everyone else. The fact that it was a crowded room made him seem even bigger. Then, of course, there were the tattoos and the fact that he was probably the sexiest man I'd ever seen. When he saw me, his face froze. Heat raced up my neck. Within seconds it felt like my cheeks were glowing.

"You're looking a little flushed, dear. Are you feeling alright?"

"I'm fine. It's just hot in here."

Joel was still watching me, but his face had darkened into a scowl. Our eyes met again, and he nodded curtly. When I caught Granny's knowing smile, I rolled my eyes.

"I'll get us some more coffee," I said, seizing my chance to duck into the crowd.

It didn't help. Everywhere I went, I was aware of his eyes on me. Even when I couldn't see him, I could *feel* him. It made my skin tingle. I swallowed. What was it about this guy that had gotten under my skin so much? So what if he was gorgeous? So what if his face popped into my mind at an extremely inconvenient moment last night?

I'd been feeling a little pent-up when I got into bed, so I turned to one of my tried-and-true methods of stress relief. Then, out of nowhere, Joel sprang up in my head like an irritating jack-in-the-box. I tried to push him down, but my libido had other ideas. Suddenly, I was imagining how his scruff would feel against the delicate skin of my inner thighs. I pictured him looking up at me from between my legs, grey eyes twinkling wickedly. I could practically feel his hot breath caressing my dripping folds.

Through all my years of singledom, I'd had one constant companion. It was purple, it vibrated, and it lived in my nightstand. Last night I was so wound up that my purple friend never made it out of the drawer. All I'd needed were my fingers and my fevered fantasies.

I blinked and gave my head a little shake. Thinking about last night was a mistake. Now I was standing in the middle of a crowded room, cheeks flushed and pussy throbbing. What I needed was a serious reality check. I elbowed my way through the throng, searching for Joel. It was vital that I found him and reminded my raging hormones what a jerk he was.

He wasn't difficult to locate. I found him standing at a corner table, examining a tray of expertly painted sugar cookies.

"I wondered when you'd come over," he said, not bothering to look at me.

"Think you're that irresistible?"

"Nope."

He spun around and folded his sculpted arms over his chest.

"I'd rather you just came right out with whatever has your panties in a bunch. Maybe then you'll stop staring at me with a face like curdled milk."

My irritation flared. Of all the obnoxious, arrogant...

"I have n—I mean, I'm not saying I didn't notice you. You have to admit, you stick out."

"Stick out?"

"Well, yeah. You're big and colorful, like a peacock, or a parrot."

He arched a dark eyebrow.

"That almost sounded like a compliment."

"Well, it shouldn't. Have you ever heard the noise a peacock makes? And parrots, well, they're just the assholes of the bird kingdom."

Ok, you're rambling. Back it up, back it up.

Joel frowned.

"The assholes of the bird kingdom? Where the hell are you getting this?"

I flushed.

"Well, they are," I protested, rifling my brain for corroborating evidence. "They bite and swear and they...hang out with pirates. Plus, in the movies, they're always jerks—look at Iago."

"From *Othello* or *Aladdin*?"

"There are no parrots in *Othello*, genius."

"Says the woman who didn't recognize a bake-kujira."

I opened and closed my mouth, temporarily stumped for a retort. Joel smirked.

"I think we're getting side-tracked," I said testily. "I was just trying to say that I wasn't the one staring. If anything, it was you who was the...starer."

Joel tilted his chin in a silent challenge.

"If you weren't looking at me, how did you know I was staring at you?"

"Because...because I could feel you broadcasting dick waves."

I officially withdraw my own speaking privileges.

He thrust his hands into his pockets and looked at me appraisingly. The bastard stood there letting 'dick waves' hang in the air. He was probably enjoying watching me squirm.

"So you came to tell me to stop waving my dick around?"

My mouth twitched and I bit the inside of my cheek. I refused to laugh.

"Essentially, yes," I said, with as much dignity as I could scrape together.

"Relax. I'm not here for you."

"Well, good," I said jerkily. "Because I don't know what my grandmother's been putting in your head, but I'm not interested."

He turned back to the table and began inspecting the cookies again.

"So, you fought your way across a crowded room to tell me you're not interested in talking to me?"

"No! I'm here to support my sister-in-law. I came over to make sure you weren't planning to be a douchebag. Of course, it seems to come naturally to you, but—"

"Would you like a cookie?"

He swiveled around and held out a pair of breasts tightly squeezed into a yellow polka dot bikini. I gave him a withering look.

"First donuts, now cookies? Are you about to offer some cheesy line about sweetening me up?"

"No," he said levelly. "Just figured the fastest way to get you to shut up would be to stick something in your mouth."

CHAPTER SIX

Joel

"Figured the fastest way to get you to shut up would be to stick something in your mouth."

Time froze as I stood there like an idiot, holding out the boobs.

A boob with some boobs. It's boobception.

Thank God I hadn't offered her the enormous dick with the rainbow cock ring. But now the image was in my head, and I couldn't shake it. I pictured that gorgeous mouth sliding over my cock, soft and torturous. Then I imagined running a hand through her thick, red hair as she swallowed me to the root. Something stirred in my crotch.

It was bad enough that I hadn't been able to take my eyes off her. I wasn't doing it on purpose; she just materialized everywhere my gaze happened to rest. I don't know if it was her hair or a trick of the light, but she looked brighter than everyone around her. It was like someone had cranked up her saturation. It was so distracting that I panicked when she came over to talk to me. Then I overcompensated with a double dose of dickishness.

The awkward silence stretched on forever. Despite having told her to shut up, I prayed she'd say something. Anything.

Even some crazy nonsense about parrots. Eventually, she raised her eyebrows and blinked.

"Wow," she said. "That's impressive. You successfully lowered the tone in every way imaginable."

Ok. She can shut up again now.

Feigning nonchalance, I took a big bite of the boob cookie. It was maddeningly delicious. Sweet and buttery with a subtle hint of lemon. By this point, I'd reached critical salt. I was looking for a way to bail out gracefully when we were accosted by a woman carrying a tray of cupcakes.

"Olivia!" she said breathlessly. "Granny V was looking for you."

Olivia smiled, and I was caught off guard by a strange feeling in my chest. I wished I'd taken a smaller bite of cookie. All my saliva had mysteriously vanished.

"Thanks, Erin. I'd gone to get coffee and I got sidetracked by something *really annoying.*"

She turned and glared at me, emerald eyes flashing. I swallowed hard. My throat felt like it was lined with sandpaper.

So this was Erin. I'd imagined meeting my nemesis a couple of times. I hadn't pictured a tiny brunette in chef's whites. She looked like I could fling her across the room with a violent sneeze. I chanced another glance at Olivia. She pointedly turned her back on me and addressed Erin.

"How's the launch going?"

Erin shifted the tray to her other arm, and I noticed there was one area she wasn't so tiny. Her stomach was slightly swollen, straining the buttons on her jacket. She looked about five months along if Crystal's pregnancies were anything to go by.

"It's been crazy. I haven't had a single moment to—"

She paused, noticing me for the first time.

"I'm sorry!" she said. "I'm being so rude. Introduce me to your friend."

"I'm—"

"He's not—"

Erin blinked and looked between us. Olivia recovered first.

"Erin Donovan, this is Joel Morris."

Light dawned on Erin's face.

"Oh! Of course. I've been meaning to thank you."

"Thank me?"

"Yeah! You came in clutch with that prairie oyster. I had no idea those things actually worked."

I rubbed at the back of my neck.

"Honestly might have just been a placebo effect," I said modestly. "There's some theory that an amino acid in the egg yolk helps the body break the bad stuff down faster, but you'd be hard-pressed to find medical evidence. Having said that, my uncle's special recipe never failed me yet."

Olivia gave me a look that made the back of my neck heat up. Meanwhile, Erin beamed.

"Well, anyway. You were our hero. Jayden wanted to rename the croquemballs in your honor."

I winced.

"That's not necessary."

"Oh, I don't know."

Olivia glanced at the platter of profiteroles. It had been extensively picked over and the formerly impressive phallic dimensions had wilted.

"Seems fitting to me."

Ouch.

Erin glanced back and forth and swiftly changed the subject.

"Your tattoos are amazing by the way. So vibrant."

"It's nice to meet someone who appreciates alternative art," I said, staring meaningfully at Olivia. "Some people look at tattoos and all they see is a poser or a gangster wannabe."

Erin looked stricken.

"Really? That is *so* closed-minded."

"I know, right?"

By this point, Olivia's mouth was a thin, angry line. She folded her arms across her chest and her fingers drummed restlessly against her biceps.

"You're so right," she said tightly. "It's annoying when people are judgmental like that. *Some* people see a sensible sweater and an SUV and assume I must be some vapid stereotype of a suburban soccer mom."

Erin's gaze darted between me and Olivia like someone watching a tennis match.

"Um. Granny V said you worked as a tattoo artist. Is that right?"

"Yeah," I said. "Me and a buddy own a studio together. He's a body painter."

Erin's eyes lit up.

"Cool! I think this must have been fate."

"Fate?"

"Yes," she said earnestly. "I'm looking to develop the Sticky Treats brand. I don't want people to look at us and just see some smutty gimmick."

I happened to catch Olivia's eye over Erin's shoulder. She raised a sardonic eyebrow. I shifted from foot to foot, hoping the ground would swallow me up. Erin burbled on, oblivious.

"I see our products as alternative art, just like your tattoos. I'm interested in collaborating with other artists in the community. Maybe even do some charity events. It's important that art has a social conscience, don't you think?"

I opened my mouth to respond, but she raced on.

"Look, I don't have time now, but can I leave my card?"

"A-ah, yeah, sure."

"Great! Better get moving."

Once she was out of earshot, Olivia smiled smugly.

"Hard to hate, isn't she?"

"Yeah, she is."

I flipped the card repeatedly against my palm, bracing for the next barb.

"Thank you."

Huh?

"Thanks for what?"

"Not being a jerk."

I snorted.

"Didn't expect me to rein in my natural impulses?"

"Something like that."

She faced me squarely and her shoulders dropped a little.

"Look," she said softly. "I don't know why you came here today, but you should give some thought to working with Erin. Not sure why I care but you seem like the type of person who'd let pride get in the way of a good deal. Sticky Treats has a lot of traction, and it could help grow your business."

Once again, irritation popped up in my skull like a scaly red monster.

"Who said I need help?"

Her eyes widened and a look of hurt flickered briefly over her face.

"That's not what I—"

She squeezed her eyes shut and pressed her fingers to her forehead.

"You know what? Forget it. I have to get back to Granny."

And with that, she vanished into the throng. I clasped my hands behind my head and stared at the ceiling.

I felt like a prick. My temper wasn't a monster, it was a rat, gnashing angrily at the ankles of anyone who came near before fleeing into the shadows. I looked around at the chattering crowd, suddenly hating everyone and everything.

What the fuck am I doing here?

Desperate to escape, I pushed toward the door. I didn't catch sight of Olivia again, not that I was looking for her, of course.

I threw myself into the front seat of my car and yanked my seatbelt on. This had been a dumb idea. Zel should've known I wasn't cut out for networking. Plus, every time I was in the same room with Olivia, I managed to make a total ass of myself. The woman rubbed every nerve in my body the wrong way. I stared at the Sticky Treats business card for a moment, before ripping it neatly into four. With a final shake of my head, I dropped the pieces out of the window and drove away.

CHAPTER SEVEN

Olivia

Ferris wheels and funnel cake do not mix.

This was my new personal mantra. Family visits to the county fair are synonymous with puking; it's an American tradition. But if anyone was going to get queasy, I'd expected it to be Abby, not me. This was another reminder never to listen to my brother when he said things like, 'it'll be fine' and 'you worry too much.'

To give Nolan his due, he did redeem himself by taking charge of the kiddo while I recovered. He took Abby to see 'the world's smartest chicken' while Erin and I sat at a picnic table with some questionable coffee—decaf in her case.

Erin watched Nolan leave with Abby on his shoulders.

"He's so good with kids," she said, smiling serenely.

I snorted.

"That's because he *is* a kid. His toys just got bigger and more expensive."

She chuckled and ran a hand over her stomach.

"Maybe. But you can't say he's not great with Abby. He's crazy about her. I think he's going to be a good dad."

"I think so too," I agreed. "For one thing, he knows I'll kick his ass if he's not."

"Get in line."

Our eyes met and we tapped our coffee cups together. Sometimes it was easy to forget how strong she was. And she'd gotten even stronger in the past year. I sipped my coffee and wrinkled my nose. Questionable was an understatement. We had two more pots of creamer and we'd grabbed some extra sachets of sweetener. I seized one now and tore the end off.

"It's still kinda weird, to be honest," I said, dumping the white crystals into my coffee. "The idea of Nolan as a dad blows my mind."

"Why?"

I let out a long breath.

"I've been taking care of him since I was Abby's age. I love him, but he's always been my dumb little brother. He'd get himself in trouble and I'd step in and fix things. Even now he's an adult, I'm still looking over his shoulder, waiting to bail him out. Probably drives him crazy."

I stirred my coffee vigorously, creating a whirling vortex in the center of the dark liquid. Erin put a hand on my arm and squeezed.

"I think it's nice you're so protective. He appreciates it too."

"I'm not so sure."

The sweetener had taken the rough edge off. I took a long sip and frowned.

"I spent a long time trying to keep a tight rein on both of us so Granny would never have to worry. It's—it's a tough role to step out of. Even now when he's got you and a baby on the way, I'm still poised for him to screw up."

Erin gave me an understanding smile.

"I know it's hard to let go, Liv, but you need to relax. Focus on yourself for once. You spend all your time worrying about other people. When was the last time you let yourself have any real fun?"

I gave her a sidelong glance.

"Look who's talking, Miss Workaholic."

"Doesn't count. My job's fun."

"Web design can be fun."

"I meant something a little spicier."

She eyed me suggestively over the rim of her cup.

"What about that hottie I saw you with at the launch?"

I covered my face with my hands and groaned. What was it with happy couples and their obsession with pairing everyone off? I rested my elbows on the table and pushed my hair back from my face.

"Joel *is* hot," I conceded. "But I don't think he's my type."

"Are you sure? Looked to me like the two of you were vibing."

I rolled my eyes.

"Everybody keeps saying that. I'm starting to think I might have been out of the dating game too long. I didn't realize 'vibing' involved wanting to strangle someone several times a minute."

Erin burst out laughing.

"Was he really that bad?"

I shrugged.

"Ok. Maybe I was exaggerating—but not much. He's so abrasive and grumpy. I don't think I could be with a guy who was always that salty."

Erin raised an eyebrow and smirked.

"Some women like a salty snack."

"We're talking about dating, not pretzels," I said, shooting her a withering look.

"Did somebody say pretzel? I could go for a pretzel."

Nolan and Abby had snuck up while we were talking. Abby had acquired a helium balloon shaped like a pink alpaca and a large stick of cotton candy.

"I guess I might be ready to contemplate food," I said, draining the last of my coffee. "Abby definitely needs something that's not loaded with sugar or swimming in grease."

"Are you feeling better now, Mommy?" Abby asked.

She shuffled up next to me on the bench and offered me a sticky hug. That was when I noticed her arms. From elbow to wrist, they were a hideous clashing mural of temporary tattoos.

"What's all this?"

"We went to the tattoo place we saw earlier," said Abby innocently. "You said I could have one."

Abby had been obsessed with tattoos ever since that morning outside Sticky Treats. When I picked her up from Alana and Jess the next day, I found they'd indulged her by drawing all over her in sharpie. It was harmless and (mostly) washable. She'd accepted she couldn't have one until she was 21, but that didn't stop her from drawing endless dinosaur- and unicorn-themed designs. When she spotted the temporary tattoo booth at the fair, her face lit up and she was only enticed away by the prospect of chocolate funnel cake and a pony ride.

"I said you could get *one.*" I glared at Nolan. "I've told you before about spoiling her."

Nolan shoved his hands in his pockets and shifted guiltily.

"She couldn't decide which cutie mark she wanted. Are you trying to claim you could've chosen between Pinkie Pie and Rainbow Dash?"

I huffed out an exasperated breath.

"You're not the one who has to persuade her to take a bath tonight."

"They don't come off in the—"

"*Or* make sure she's presentable for school on Monday."

"You're not supposed to talk about me like I'm not here," said Abby, pouting.

Nolan sat down heavily.

"Sorry, Abbster," he said. "I forgot Mommy was queen of the no-fun zone."

I narrowed my eyes and Erin kicked him under the table.

Despite the fact that I'd just scolded her, Abby leaped to my defense.

"Mommy is fun sometimes. She had dessert last night, even though she wasn't on her period."

There was a long pause. I could practically hear the crickets. Erin bit her lip trying not to laugh and Nolan went red. I rubbed at my temples. The dull promise of a headache throbbed behind my eyes.

"Abby," I said patiently. "Do you remember that conversation we had about periods?"

"Yes! You said they're a perfectly natural part of a woman's life and nothing to be embarrassed about."

Dang! Why did I let her get so smart?

"She's got you there." Nolan giggled. "Where's Jayden and his popcorn when you need it?"

"Jayden has tattoos," Abby announced, seizing the chance to revert to her favorite subject. "So does Alana. They don't have as many as Joel though. His are the coolest."

She paused to take another bite of her cotton candy.

"Alana told me Uncle Nolan has a tattoo on his butt."

Now it was my turn to laugh, and Erin snorted into her coffee.

"I'd forgotten about that," I said, nudging my brother with my foot. "I think we have a teachable moment here. You should tell her what it is."

Nolan winced and rubbed his leg.

"When did you start hating me?"

"When you said I was no fun."

"Fine. It's a hot-dog."

"And what does it say underneath?"

"Sun's out, buns out."

Abby frowned and licked pink wisps of cotton candy from her lips.

"Why did you get that?"

Nolan shot me a dark look and then addressed Abby.

"Sometimes even grown-ups do stupid things. Especially when they're on vacation with their fraternity and they've had a tiny bit too much to drink."

"I think it's cute," Erin assured him, patting his knee.

"You see, Abby," I said. "The thing about tattoos is that they're permanent. You have to be super sure about what you want. Otherwise, you might end up with something silly that you're stuck with forever. That's why only grown-ups are allowed to get them."

"What would you get if you were getting a tattoo?" Abby asked.

Before I could answer, Nolan sniggered.

"I don't think that would happen, Abby."

"Why not?" I asked, suddenly annoyed.

"Well," Nolan said sheepishly, "you're just not that type of person. You're the sensible one, remember?"

And whose fault is that?

The bitter thought bubbled to the surface of my brain unexpectedly. Yes, being 'the sensible one' all the time was exhausting. But I didn't have a choice; people needed me.

When was the last time you had any real fun?

It had been a long time since I'd done something just for me. Besides, I wanted to teach Abby that it was ok to step out of her comfort zone and take risks now and then. Maybe it was time to do something brave.

Abby could only be persuaded to get into the bath after I'd covered her forearms in saran wrap. To an outside observer, it might have seemed a ridiculous indulgence, but I believed in picking my battles. After tucking her in and loading the dishwasher, I flopped onto the couch and typed out a message on my phone.

Olivia: Evening.

Alana: Hey, nena. How was the fair?

Olivia: Crowded, queasy, oil drenched. The usual. You got a minute?

Alana: Sure, what's up?

Olivia: I was wondering where you go to get your tattoos.

CHAPTER EIGHT

Olivia

Olivia: I'm not sure this is such a good idea.

Alana: Good! That means it's a great idea. This is fear talking, nena. We don't listen to that asshole, remember?

I bit my lip and stared at my phone. I'd been sitting in my parked car for 10 minutes. I always left early for appointments. It allowed time for traffic and questioning my life choices.

Olivia: I'm not even sure why I'm doing this.

Alana: Because Nolan pissed you off?

Olivia: Yeah, that sounds like a stellar reason.

Alana's reply was instant. Lord knows how that woman typed so fast.

Alana: I'm kidding. It wasn't the reason. It was the catalyst. You're doing this for you. And it's going to look beautiful.

Olivia: I wish I shared your confidence.

Alana: You're in good hands, I promise. Joey's not much of a people person, but he's crazy talented.

I leaned an elbow on the window and fisted a hand in my hair.

Olivia: You're not going to talk me out of this, are you?

Alana: Nope. Gtg. Good luck xxx.

The first glimpse of the studio didn't inspire confidence. It was on one of those narrow side streets where the buildings seem too close together. I remembered Alana's initial description.

The place doesn't look like much, but it's awesome. One of those best-kept secrets kinda deals.

Sailor Joey's was nestled between a barbershop and a place that sold bongs and novelty t-shirts. Out of place didn't even begin to cover my feelings. I hovered outside for a couple of minutes before I worked up the nerve to step through the door.

The first thing that hit me was the strong smell of cleaning fluid. The studio was well-lit and reassuringly spotless. If it hadn't been for the artwork on the walls and the weird taxidermy sculptures, it could've passed for a dentist's surgery. Sadly, my relief didn't last long.

My mouth fell open when I saw a familiar Viking hipster. Joel sat with his feet on the desk, thumbing listlessly through his phone. He looked up when I entered, and his grey eyes widened.

"What're you doing here?"

I bristled. It had taken a lot to come in here and this wasn't the welcome I had anticipated.

"Well, if this is how you greet your customers, I'm not surprised this place is empty."

He blinked and swung his feet from the desk. I was struck by how long and graceful his legs were. He moved like a panther.

"Customers? You're my 11 a.m.?"

I couldn't blame him for being surprised. I was the last person who expected to see me here too. But drawing attention to it was a dick move.

"Yes, but I'm starting to think this was a bad idea."

I was ready to nope out of this situation. I had a first-class ticket on the nope train. Joel leaned back in his chair and smiled smugly.

"Gonna chicken out? Can't say I'm surprised."

"What's that supposed to mean?"

My hands flew to my hips of their own volition, and I stared him down. I longed to wipe that complacent smirk from his stupidly handsome face. He shrugged.

"You don't seem the adventurous type."

"Jesus!" I exploded. "Why does everyone keep saying that? Just because I'm capable of acting like an adult from time to time."

By this point, I was out of breath and my cheeks burned. I probably looked like my head was on fire. But once I started, the words kept tumbling out.

"Because sometimes someone has to act responsibly, and for some reason, that someone is always me. And what thanks do I get? It's always like, there goes Olivia, queen of the no-fun zone!"

Mortified, I took a deep breath and rubbed my hands over

my face. Joel didn't say anything for a long time. He just stared at me impassively, rubbing a hand over his chin.

"I don't know if I'd call you a *queen,* but you're definitely a royal pain in my ass."

He plonked a spare chair in front of me, and gestured to it with exaggerated politeness.

"Can I offer you a seat, your majesty?"

"A seat?"

I stared at him, my brain struggling to catch up. There was something magnetic about those eyes.

"You haven't left yet. So, unless you've succumbed to my charm and animal magnetism, I'm guessing you still want that consult."

Walking out was still tempting. I hadn't committed to anything, and nobody but Alana knew I was here. He arched an eyebrow, and I bit the inside of my cheek. Fuck! Every time we met, I sensed him throwing down a gauntlet. I never could back down from a challenge. I clicked my tongue irritably and sat down, making sure to turn to the side, angling my body away from his.

"My email was answered by someone named Lily. Why can't I 'consult' with her?"

"Because Lily's my apprentice."

He swung his feet back onto the desk and picked up a pen. It was a clicky top. The invention of Satan himself. To my immense irritation, he began rapidly clicking the end of the pen.

"Anyway, she's out sick today, and Zel's at a convention until Monday. So, it's just you and me."

"Lucky me."

The clicking stopped. He put the pen down and rolled it up and down the desk. The shrill vibration of plastic against wood sounded way louder than it should have. I crossed my arms and jiggled my foot.

"How did you find us?" he asked suddenly. "Don't recall

placing an ad in the PTA newsletter."

"How did you know I was—?"

"Lucky guess."

I cast a suspicious eye at the spotlights embedded in the ceiling. It was weirdly hot in here. My cheeks were warm and sweat prickled between my shoulder blades.

"You came recommended," I said stiffly. "Apparently you're 'crazy talented.' I'm going to kill Alana."

The last part was muttered under my breath, but he caught it anyway. His eyebrows shot up.

"Alana? Really?"

For some reason, his ears were very pink.

"What? I'm not supposed to have friends now?"

He blinked and gave his head a little shake.

"'S not that. I just didn't expect you to have those kinds of friends."

I rolled my eyes. I wasn't even going to try and unpack what that meant.

"So, how is this supposed to work?" I asked. "So far, I've walked in and you've insulted me for," I consulted my watch, "10 minutes. Is this part of your 'crazy' talent?"

"Nope. That's a special bonus just for you. Basically, you tell me your concept and I try to turn it into a tattoo design that won't look like crap."

"Charming."

"That's me. So, what sort of thing do you want?"

I shifted uncomfortably. I knew what I wanted. I had it with me. The pages were neatly folded in my purse. Suddenly, I couldn't bear to show him. It was too intimate. A fragile, secret part of myself I wasn't ready to share. Especially not with him. What if he laughed? Stalling for time, I smiled slyly.

"You seem to know me so well, I shouldn't need to. Why don't you guess?"

He stuck the pen behind his ear and puffed out his cheeks.

"I dunno," he said. "Figured you'd go with something super-generic. A rose. Maybe a cute little heart with 'mommy' inside. Am I close?"

"Not in the slightest."

He rocked back in his chair and clasped his hands behind his head. The move made his triceps bulge impressively. A school of dolphins swum up one arm while a mermaid basked on the other.

"I suppose there's always a crown."

I narrowed my eyes.

"Rabbits," I said. "I want rabbits. And if you mention bunny slippers, I walk now."

"Rabbits?"

"These rabbits."

I rummaged angrily in my purse and dumped the folder on the table. Then I looked away, cheeks flushing. I heard the soft flap of the folder opening and chanced a glance out of the corner of my eye. Joel studied the pages, brows drawn together. Looking at the faded drawings, I felt my heart lurch. Three familiar bunnies scampered across the pages. Of course, I'd looked at them last night when I dug the folder out, but this was different. Watching someone else look at them was strange.

Why do I feel like he's seeing me naked?

Joel's was surprisingly gentle as he turned the pages. His hands were large, and—like the rest of him—covered in tattoos, but I saw for the first time how long and tapered his fingers were. He went through all the pages several times before looking up.

"What is this?"

I folded my hands in my lap to stop myself from picking at my cuticles.

"It's a story. Granny V made it for me and my brother when we were kids. She wrote it out and she drew all the pictures. I know it seems twee, but—"

"It's beautiful."

I looked up sharply. His face was completely open. We held each other's gaze for a fraction too long. We weren't sniping at each other anymore. We'd both taken our eye off the conversation and allowed it to drift somewhere...weird. Suddenly, there was an awkward intensity that almost felt like a physical ache. He cleared his throat and brushed a stray hair behind his ear.

"She's uh, she's a talented artist," he said gruffly.

"Yeah, she is," I agreed, relieved that one of us had spoken. "Must run in the family. Abby's been drawing tattoo designs since we first met you."

"Really?"

His face softened, and he gave me a genuine smile. It was amazing how much it transformed his face. The weird ache tweaked at my chest again and it was my turn to clear my throat.

"Yeah. You made quite an impression."

"Never underestimate the power of donuts."

I chuckled.

"They helped, but I don't think it was just that. Watching you with her made me wonder if you had any kids."

He rubbed the back of his neck and laughed nervously.

"No! No. I do like kids, though. There's no bullshit with them. Always know where you are."

I nodded.

"That's definitely the case with Abby. Her teachers tell me she's 'assertive.' Pretty sure that's code for bossy."

"Wonder where she gets that from."

He looked at me from under his dark brows and his eyes twinkled. I couldn't prevent my lips from flickering into a smile.

"I don't know," I said, feeling the flush creep up my neck again. "Sometimes I think she could give me a lesson in people skills."

"I think she schooled us both."

Another awkward pause. This time the air crackled with all

the things we weren't saying. This was probably the closest either of us would get to a real apology. I relaxed back into my chair, shoulders dropping a little. He glanced around the small studio as though seeing it for the first time.

"Feel like I should offer you a drink or something—just as a customer service thing," he put in hastily. "Afraid we're not fancy enough to have a coffee machine, but we could order in. There's a place down the road. It's good coffee...if you drink coffee. Zel's gotten really into kombucha recently, but I don't see the big deal."

"It's ok. I'm fine."

His fumbled attempts at solicitude were endearing. His hands twitched back to the folder, and he thumbed through it again.

"This story about you?"

"Me and my brother, yeah. And Granny. She's the white one."

He tilted his head and scratched his temple with a forefinger.

"So, why is one of the little bunnies—"

"Blue? Nolan wanted to be a blue bunny. He tried to insist that I had to be pink because pink was for girls. But I hated pink. Granny said it didn't matter. The magic of stories was that you could be anything you wanted to be."

He looked at me thoughtfully, chin on his hand.

"You're saying you could've been any color you liked, and you chose to be brown? Way to think inside the box."

I made a high-pitched noise of outrage.

"First of all, that's chestnut. And yeah, I couldn't decide so I chose something that let the picture hang together."

"Very accommodating."

I gave him an appraising look. His tone was wry but there was no malice.

I shrugged.

"I guess even back then, I found it hard to—"

I paused, knotting my fingers together. I'd inadvertently touched on something painful. Something I didn't quite feel able to put words around. Now I really did feel naked.

"Hard to what?" Joel asked, staring at me intently.

God! Those eyes did things to me. Hot squirming things, lower down my belly than I cared to admit. They reminded me of a frothing ocean or massing storm clouds. Only now there was a hint of something warm and gentle.

"It's nothing," I insisted. "I was just rambling on. So, do you think you can use them?"

He coughed.

"Yeah! Yeah. I can do that. Can't exactly match your grandmother's style, but I think I can come up with something you'll be happy with. How big do you want to go?"

The question caught me unawares. I hadn't given any thought to it at all.

"I-I'm not sure. Not too big?"

"Not saying you have to get a full back piece, but if you go too small you risk ending up with blobs rather than bunnies. These drawings have so much life, so much character. It'd be a shame to lose that."

"I guess I'll put myself in your hands then."

I'd spoken without thinking. Now I was thinking too much. Imagining my body, quivering and pliant, in his strong hands.

"Sounds good. Where do you want it?"

Right here. Over the desk. Pound me hard until I come apart on your cock.

I rubbed my fingers over my eyes and gave myself a little shake.

"The tattoo? Oh, um. I hadn't thought about it. I'm not sure I want other people to be able to see it. Not all the time, anyway. And I don't want it to be too painful."

I expected him to roll his eyes and call me a princess or a diva, but he didn't. He put his head to one side and looked at me critically. My hand flew to my throat and fiddled with the slender gold chain around my neck.

"Belly's a good place. Looks really pretty on a woman."

I bit my lip.

"I don't know."

He raised his eyebrows.

"Well, the other relatively painless option is your ass, but I thought you'd take it the wrong way if I suggested that right off the bat."

Shut up, ovaries! Nobody likes you.

"I don't understand why people get tattoos on their butts," I said. "Why go through all that hassle and expense for something you can't see without a mirror?"

"Fair. I only started in on those areas when I ran out of other room. Are you sure you don't want this on your belly? It's a nice flat canvas."

My mouth twisted.

"Not so flat after having a kid, trust me. And that's the problem. Abby was a caesarian."

"That's not a problem," he said casually. "I can avoid it. Or I can go over it. I've done plenty of cover-up work."

My hand drifted instinctively to my belly.

"I don't think I want it covered," I said thoughtfully. "It's part of my story now, and Abby's. But if you're sure you can work around it—oh, shoot!"

My phone chirped. We must have been talking for over an hour. Where the hell did that time go? I jumped up hastily. Joel looked taken aback.

"What's wrong?"

"Ugh! I didn't realize it had gotten so late," I said, furious with myself. "I have to pick Abby up from gymnastics."

"Ok."

Joel picked up the folder.

"If you're happy to leave this with me, I'll draw up a design and send it to you. I can email you. Or—"

He flushed again.

"If you give me your number, I can message you."

"Sure."

I pulled a notelet from my bag and scribbled my number, wondering why I felt so bashful. This was probably completely normal tattoo protocol. I slid my number across the table and hurried out of the studio, Joel's eyes burning into my back.

CHAPTER NINE

Olivia

"What can I get you, hon?"

I blinked at the menu above the counter. The place looked more like a Victorian laboratory than a coffee shop. There were gears, cogs, and goggles everywhere. Even the coffee maker looked like it could double as a time machine. It smelled right, though. The oily aroma of roasting beans was unmistakable.

The barista was a plump, middle-aged woman with short spiky black hair and a faded Iron Maiden t-shirt. A lot of her tattoos reflected the steampunk décor, so it was a reasonable guess that she owned the place. She should have been formidable, but she exuded welcoming warmth. I nibbled on my lip.

"I'll have a hazelnut macchiato and..."

I paused, suddenly embarrassed.

"I don't suppose you know what Joel usually has. He owns the tattoo place down the street."

"Yep."

The barista retrieved a pad from her apron and a pencil from behind her ear.

"Comes here every day. *Very* particular about his coffee.

Dark roast with a double shot of espresso and a drizzle of honey. I call it a black-eyed bee."

She gave me a sidelong glance as she grabbed two cups and flipped on the machine.

"First time someone other than Zel or Lily has picked it up for him though."

My cheeks burned.

"Oh, w-well, he drew such a great design for my tattoo, and I remember him saying that he didn't have a coffee machine, so...I thought it might be nice."

"I've been on at him about that before," said the barista, raising her voice over the gurgle of the machine. "Not sure why as I'd be robbing myself of a good customer, but..."

She trailed off with a shrug.

"I'm Magda by the way. Everyone calls me Mags."

"Olivia. I've gotta say, I'm surprised you gave Joel business advice. You're a braver woman than me."

I remembered him storming off at the launch. For some reason, it still stung. Magda flapped her hand dismissively.

"Eh! He doesn't scare me. A smart artist knows better than to piss off their caffeine supplier. Anyway, his bark's worse than his bite. Here."

She reached into the glass case under the counter and brought up a tray of lemon bars.

"Take two of these on the house. They're his favorite."

Her conspiratorial smile made me blush all over again. I tried not to feel self-conscious as I walked down the street with the cups. This was no big deal. It was just coffee. His customers probably brought him stuff all the time.

My hands were full, so I had to nudge the studio door open with my shoulder. Nobody looked up when I edged inside. Joel sat on the padded bench with his shorts rolled up, while a young girl with rainbow braids tattooed his thigh. He was frowning and watching her hand movements intently.

I couldn't help staring. His leg was a long, tapered expanse of sculpted muscle. Like the rest of him, it was an impressive canvas of tattoos. Most of his thigh was taken up with an old-style treasure map, while a mass of tentacles writhed up his calf.

"Stay inside the line, Lily. What d'you think the stencil's there for?"

The girl yanked the needle away from his skin and huffed petulantly.

"I'm trying, but it's impossible! And your stupid leg has a weird bump in it!"

"That's a thigh muscle, quite a common occurrence in the leg area. And coloring inside the lines isn't impossible, it's preschool. Don't make faces, just concentrate. See, there ya go."

So this was his apprentice. He sounded like a demanding teacher. I felt a pang of sympathy for Lily as she bent over his thigh, muttering mutinously. But I could see what she couldn't. When he praised her, his face lit up with a proud smile. I couldn't help wondering if he'd ever allowed her to see it. Her or anyone else.

I was startled from my thoughts when a door opened at the back of the room. A tall man in lime green shorts and a tie-dyed purple t-shirt strolled in, holding a jar of paintbrushes. He caught my eye with a friendly wink and turned to Joel.

"Hey, Joel. You got a customer, man."

When Joel caught sight of me, he went through a rapid series of expressions. It was like his face didn't know what to do with itself and it was cycling through its default options.

"Oh, um. Yeah. Hi. Sorry. Little teaching session. Lost track of time."

"It's fine. I can wait."

I adjusted my stance. I wanted to look more like a nonchalant customer in a tattoo parlor and less like a waitress who'd lost her table.

Why did I think this stupid coffee was a good idea?

"Shouldn't be too long. What'd you think of my design?"

"I liked it."

'I liked it' actually translated to I downloaded the file and I cried. It was stunning. He'd drawn the bunnies sleeping in a wooded glade. They were all cuddled up together with the blue and chestnut bunnies using the white bunny as a pillow. Most significantly, the chestnut bunny wasn't chestnut anymore. He'd emphasized the red hues in the brown fur until it was closer to fiery auburn. It was...perfect. Somehow, he'd plucked at a naked, tender nerve I hadn't even known was there. A nerve that made my eyes fill up and my chest ache.

"I thought adding some green foresty backdrop would make the bunnies pop a little more. I know I took some liberties with the pose, but I re-read the story a couple of times before I got to work. It felt a lot like your grandmother was kinda your safe space, so I wanted to make sure I conveyed that."

Ooh boy! There's that nerve again. How is he doing that?

"Yeah," I said hoarsely. "She was."

He looked at me shyly. More for something to do than anything else, I raised my coffee to my lips and took a generous sip. I realized my mistake immediately. My mouth filled with acrid bitterness, and I scrunched up my face.

"Ugh! Oh, God!"

I stuck out my tongue and shook my head vigorously. My eyes were screwed shut, but I heard a rumbling chuckle. If I hadn't been too busy contemplating the untimely demise of my tastebuds, it would have occurred to me that this was the first time I'd heard Joel laugh.

"Bleh! Here."

I took a cleansing sip of macchiato and thrust the other cup at Joel.

"I brought you a coffee."

He was still grinning. His teeth were white and even and he had an adorable dimple in his cheek.

"That's thoughtful of you. But after the face you just pulled, I'm not sure I want it."

"If you don't like it, I'll have a bone to pick with Magda. Supposedly this is (and I use the term literally) your poison."

"You brought me a black-eyed bee?"

He sounded surprised. Maybe even touched.

I shrugged.

"I just thought that—"

"Ow! Dammit, Lily!"

Joel seemed to have forgotten that his apprentice was still working on his leg. He hissed in pain and clutched his thigh.

"Oops! I think I drove the ink in too hard."

"This is why we don't let you touch the customers."

"I'm sorry."

She slumped back on her ankles and hung her head mournfully. Joel sighed.

"It's no big deal," he said, his tone softened. "Everybody makes mistakes when they're learning. You're getting better, though."

"No, I'm not."

He gave her a soft punch on the shoulder.

"Sure you are. If you'd let me take a photo of that wobbly ass line you did on that banana peel a few months ago, you'd be able to see how far you'd come."

"I guess."

She smiled shakily.

"I think donuts are in order!"

I jumped. I'd almost forgotten the other man was in the room. He wiped his hands on a rag and clapped Lily on the shoulder.

"Why don't I take our young Padawan out for a sugar fix and leave you in peace with your customer?"

Customer? Oh, yeah.

I'd been so caught up in watching Joel with Lily—and watching Joel generally—that I'd forgotten why I was here. I swallowed and bit nervously at my thumbnail. So far, I'd managed to blank out the fact that a bazillion tiny needles were about to force ink through my skin. Alana had assured me it wouldn't hurt that much, but was she a good judge? I'd seen the implements that hung on the back of her bedroom door.

Once Zel and Lily left, I felt awkward and shy. I'd drunk my coffee too fast, and it sloshed queasily in my stomach. Joel handed me some medical forms and bustled around noisily, assembling tools and bottles on a trolley. Occasionally I stole a glance at him. He never caught my eye, but the back of his neck was suspiciously red.

The consent form had a staggering list of medical questions, none of which helped my nerves. I could confidently state that I'd taken no hard drugs in the last 24 hours, but I'd had a glass of dry white wine after dinner. Did that count? I could just ask, but I didn't want to look stupid. Time for Dr. Google. Reaching into my purse for my cellphone, I encountered a lumpy paper package. Of course, Magda's lemon bars. I cleared my throat loudly. Joel looked up from scrubbing his hands in the sink.

"Compliments of Magda," I said, waving the bag. "Apparently they're your favorite."

Joel snorted and shook his head.

"I gotta have words with that woman. We should probably keep them until after the tattoo. Don't want you going into body shock on me."

"Is that likely? I ate like you said."

I cast an anxious glance at the medical forms.

"Relax. This isn't my first rodeo."

Despite the sarcastic tone, there was something reassuring in his gravelly rasp. Or maybe that was the comforting part. It was unsettling when he was being all sensitive and perceptive. Now he was back to being a jerk. Nice and familiar. Definitely safer.

"Now I just need you to pop your shirt off and we can get this show on the road."

Ok, less comforting now.

I took a deep, shaky breath. Why was I being so stupid? It wasn't as if he could tattoo me through my clothes. This was no different than undressing at the doctor's office...an incredibly public doctor's office with an unreasonably sexy doctor. My fingers felt big and clumsy as I fumbled with the buttons on my shirt.

Fuck!

I might have been playing it cool, but my nipples had zero chill. They had scrunched into tight, aching points that strained against the fabric of my cups. If that wasn't enough, some unholy force had compelled me to put on my thinnest, laciest bra. The underwear gods had forsaken me.

I stood in the middle of the room clutching my shirt against my stomach. When Joel looked back at me, I felt a molten flush spread from my chest and up my neck, warming my cheeks to a rosy glow. A muscle flickered in his jaw and his throat bobbed convulsively.

"Perky...I mean peachy."

He cleared his throat loudly and blushed.

"If I can just get you to hop up on the bed here, I can see what kind of space I'm working with."

I lay down on the raised bed, shivering as the cold leather touched my skin. My nails dug into my palms as I clenched my hands into tight fists. Joel pulled up a stool next to me and peered at my stomach. He was so close that the scruff on his jaw almost tickled my skin. He smelled good, like crisp fresh apples, chocolate, and woodsmoke. I wondered what shampoo he used. His fingers ghosted over my belly, and I inhaled sharply, my stomach muscles contracting under the gentle touch.

"All good?" he asked, glancing up at me.

I nodded. I didn't trust my voice.

"Hm. These jeans sit quite high. Could I get you to unbutton them, push them down your hips a little?"

I stiffened.

"Do I have to?"

Joel looked at me thoughtfully.

"Is this about the scar?"

He needs to stop reading my mind. It's extremely rude.

No matter how many pep talks I gave myself, I still felt self-conscious about my scar. It wasn't as if it looked that bad, and no one saw it outside of bikini season. But the birth had been...dramatic. Granny always joked that it was the only time in Abby's life that she'd had stage fright. The result had been more than worth it, but it had been the most uncomfortable 54 hours of my life. Every time I looked at that thin, puckered smile, I pictured myself in that hospital bed, half-naked, sobbing, and terrified. It made me feel vulnerable. I gave a non-committal shrug.

"If it makes you feel any better, I can guarantee I've seen worse. Tattoo artists deal with bodies in all shapes and sizes. I've tattooed lingerie models and guys with big hairy beer bellies. Cover-ups are also a specialty of mine, so I've seen some pretty gnarly scars."

"O-ok."

Reluctantly, I undid the buttons on my jeans and pushed them below my waist. Then I lay on my back staring fixedly at the ceiling.

"There. Perfect. I drew the design with a low transverse incision in mind, and yours is super neat. I should be able to avoid it entirely."

I blinked. He truly had put a lot of thought into this. And he was so professional and matter of fact. I was touched.

"Thank you," I muttered. "I know I shouldn't get so embarrassed about it."

"I get it. But, like you said, it's part of your story."

He'd been examining my skin as he spoke. Now, he lightly

traced the pad of his finger along the incision. His touch went through me like an electric jolt, and I twitched.

"God! I'm sorry. Don't know why I did that."

"No, no. It's fine."

Fine wasn't the right word, but I wasn't unhappy. It had taken all my willpower to keep my hips on the bed.

"Anyway. Still sorry."

He shook his head and pulled his trolley closer. After wiping down my skin with some foamy soap, he picked up a razor. I frowned.

"What's that for?"

He raised an eyebrow.

"Never used one of these before?"

"Haha! You know what I mean."

He shrugged and slid the plastic cover off the blade.

"Need you completely smooth before I start."

"But I don't have any hair there," I protested, clamping a hand reflexively over my stomach.

He rolled his eyes.

"Vellus hairs. Everybody has them. Now behave yourself and hold still."

After brushing over my skin with the razor, he squirted a generous quantity of lotion into his palm. I tensed and screwed my eyes shut, expecting it to be cold. It was, but it soon warmed up. He flattened his palm and rubbed the lotion into my skin with soft, circular movements. It felt weird. Soothing and stimulating at the same time. The gentle pressure on my belly transmuted into a spreading warmth that went straight to my pussy. I fought the urge to squirm as I felt myself getting slick and swollen. Flushing, I clasped my arms in front of my chest. I couldn't do anything about my flaming nether regions, but I could at least conceal the tiny erections on my boobs.

"Ok," Joel said. "Just need to apply the stencil, then we can get started. Feeling nervous?"

"No."

Just embarrassingly aroused.

"Atta girl. No big deal, right?"

He gave me a reassuring smile and a wink. My insides melted like warm butter.

"It gets a little uncomfortable after a while, but it's really more of a prickle than a stab."

Are we still talking about tattoos here?

"Gonna need you standing to apply the stencil. It's a skin movement thing. Hop off the bench and try to stand as naturally as you can."

Simple tasks like 'standing naturally' are surprisingly complicated when you're half-naked and achingly turned on. The studio was warm, but my skin was stippled with goosebumps. Joel knelt in front of me with the stencil and I had the surreal experience of towering over him. After smearing my skin with a thin layer of strongly antiseptic smelling fluid, he spent a long time fiddling with the placement of the stencil transfer paper. He talked me through what he was doing, but I barely took in a word. I didn't know what to do with myself. A gorgeous man at eye level with my crotch was not a standard feature of my Wednesday afternoon.

My mind scurried off to dangerous forbidden places. I imagined the soft rustle of fabric as he yanked my jeans and panties down to my knees. My mouth falling opened as he greedily delved into the moist molten folds of my pussy. Legs buckling as his tongue flickered over my clit. His grey eyes smoldering as he looked up from between my legs.

"Still with me?"

"Huh?"

I swallowed.

"Sorry. Think I zoned out for a second there."

"Well, now you're back on planet earth, look in the mirror and tell me if you're happy with the stencil placement."

My legs were like Jell-O as I tottered towards the full-length mirror on the left side of the studio. When I saw my reflection, I cringed. My hair fell over my shoulders in disordered waves and my cheeks were crimson. I looked like a hot mess—literally. I scowled disapprovingly at my breasts. My nipples were still making a determined bid for freedom. At least the stencil looked good. The purple outline of the tattoo covered the right side of my abdomen from belly button to hip.

"Happy?"

Joel stepped up behind me. His intense grey eyes stared out from the mirror and my heart leaped into my throat.

I nodded jerkily, hardly daring to breathe. How on earth did I get here? Half-naked, heart-pounding, pussy throbbing. What had I gotten myself into?

CHAPTER TEN

Joel

Wow. Check out Beauty and the Beast.

There was me, tall, scowling, covered in tats, and then there was her. The top of her head barely reached my chest. Standing in front of my bulk, she looked tiny and fragile. Her creamy skin contrasted sharply with the fiery hair tumbling over her shoulders in beautiful waves. Eyes bright, cheeks flushed, she was...

Damn. She was beautiful.

I could smell her shampoo. She smelled like strawberries and coconut. I watched her watching herself, watching us. Her lips were parted, and her nipples strained against her bra. My mouth watered. I imagined wrapping my arms around her, sliding my hands up her belly, and cupping her tits. I wouldn't even take her bra off. I'd rub my thumbs ever so gently over her nipples, teasing her through the lace until she begged for more. Then I'd brush my lips over her neck, nuzzling and nipping at the tender skin behind her ear. Thinking about it was enough to make me hard as rock.

I was furious with myself. I was supposed to be a goddam professional. Prepping her skin had been bad enough. When I rubbed the lotion on and she started squirming, it was all I could do to keep myself together. Baseball didn't get the job done. I had to pull out the big guns. I thought about Zel saying 'Monslay,' and Crystal's birthing tapes. Then I thought about that Sunday school teacher with the coffee breath who had somehow convinced herself my name was Jonathan. It wasn't even like we had another Jonathan in the class. All those thoughts combined were barely enough to get my rebellious dick under control.

This woman pricked at every nerve in my body. We'd only met a handful of times, yet she could get under my skin like no one else. She made me want to tear my hair out. And I couldn't stop thinking about her. Ever since that stupid launch party, my mind kept drifting back to her.

She'd invaded my dreams too. I'd be somewhere—work, the grocery store, Aunt Loretta's bridge club meeting. She'd show up and we'd be at each other's throats as usual. She'd snipe and hiss at me until I grabbed her and claimed her mouth. No matter where it started, the dream almost always ended the same way—cutting her off mid-rant by kissing her breathless. Then I'd wake up, sticky with sweat and diamond hard. The day she walked into the studio I was briefly convinced I'd dozed off in my chair.

The worst dream had been the night before last. It was one of those dreams where you're going about your regular business despite being naked. I was alone in the studio when Olivia came in, wearing nothing but a smile and a set of floppy, chestnut bunny ears. She walked up to me with a sexy sway in her hips and laid her palm on my chest. Pushing gently, she propelled me toward the tattoo bed, and I lay down. I watched transfixed as she leaped up and straddled my hips. Her pussy was hot and wet against my rigid length, and I pressed against her with a grunt. She threw me a sultry wink and leaned back, bracing her hands on my thighs. Then she rocked her hips and slid back and forth, grinding her pussy against the shaft of my cock, whimpering when the head bumped her clit. Growling with frustration, I felt my hands fly to her buttocks to pull her against me. Only where I expected to find firm, hot flesh, there was a fluffy puff of bunny tail.

I should never have read that story before bed. I'd inadvertently turned something sweet and innocent into an HD surround-sound sex dream. I was already feeling guilty. I'd been a complete dick to her when she'd turned up at the studio. But I didn't know how to explain myself. "I was a complete ass because you're the reason I've had to jerk it in the shower every morning for two weeks straight," probably wouldn't have gotten me very far.

Reading the story showed me a new side of her—a sweet, vulnerable side that I wanted to protect. That was why I'd drawn the bunnies in that sleeping pose. It was my way of putting her somewhere safe.

My feelings were all over the place. Whatever was happening, I needed to clamp down on it hard, stamp it out.

After she confirmed she was happy with the stencil placement, I turned my back on her, mindful of the suspicious bulge in my shorts. Fortunately, plastic aprons cover a multitude of sins. While I prepped the needle, she lay on the bed, staring nervously at the ceiling.

"Remember to tell me if you need a break."

She nodded. I hoped once we got started, I'd sink into the zone. There's something soothing about the repetitive precision of tattoo work. Ink, wipe, ink, wipe. I thought she'd squirm and fidget, but she was a surprisingly good subject. There was just an occasional twitch when I caught a sensitive spot.

Whoever you're dealing with, there's a certain intimacy to tattoo work. Depending on the piece, you could end up spending 12 hours straight with someone. That's a long ass time if you're not good with small talk. Usually, I liked the quiet ones. They came prepped with music or audiobooks and tuned me out. I could focus on the job and let my mind go blissfully blank. It was different with Olivia, though. I kept glancing at her, wondering what she was thinking. Getting inked is a strange kind of pain. Hot and tickly. Some people get off on it. Was she biting her lip because she was in pain or...?

Put those thoughts back where they came from or so help me!

"What got you into tattoos?"

It was such an effort to keep my brain from wandering down inappropriate tracks that I was relieved to hear her speak. I dunked my needle in the rinsing cup and carefully dipped it into the cap of green.

"Other than being a meathead poser, you mean?"

She rolled her eyes.

"*Yes*. Besides that. You don't seem like a people person, but what you do forces you to work with people."

"Fair point."

I smoothed Vaseline over her belly, and she shivered. My cock twitched.

"I wanted to make art that can't be turned into a thing. You paint a picture—someone can buy it, sell it, or let it gather dust in a vault. It becomes like any other object. Tattoos are different. It's not about what something's worth. It's about people expressing themselves."

I felt her eyes roam over me, and the hairs prickled on the back of my neck.

"What are you expressing with all that?"

I smiled and dipped my needle again.

"What do you think?"

"Hm. Well, there's a nautical theme. It's all kinda piratey. Goes with the name of the studio too. I guess you either like adventure or you're looking for treasure."

I chuckled.

"Why can't it be both?"

"But I thought we were enlightened artists who were shunning material goods."

"There's more than one kind of treasure."

"I suppose the—ow! I suppose there is. What's yours?"

"Freedom."

It dropped out of my mouth before I thought about it. Freedom from money worries. Freedom from expectations. Freedom from guilt. And for that, I needed to be alone. It was the only way to be sure I was never the noose that weighed anybody down. Not again.

She was quiet for a long time, and I kicked myself. Probably wasn't the most tactful thing to say to a single mother. My habit of sticking my big foot straight in my mouth was one of the many reasons I shouldn't get involved with her. It was better all around, for her sake as well as mine.

CHAPTER ELEVEN

Olivia

"Come on, Liv! You've kept me in suspense all day. Let me see."

As luck would have it, my tattoo appointment coincided with Granny V's offer to take Abby for the night so I could have a 'grown-up playdate.' This translated to Alana and Jess coming over for wine and Netflix. Alana had pounced on me the moment they arrived.

"There's not much to see at the moment," I said, handing her a glass of red. "I'm still covered in saran wrap."

Alana turned to Jess triumphantly.

"What'd I tell you? I've told him about film dressings a hundred times and he's still usin' saran wrap. That boy is so stubborn!"

Jess never took her eyes from her Nintendo Switch, but she chuckled knowingly.

"That reminds me," I said, picking up my glass and eyeing Alana sternly. "I have a bone to pick with you."

"What?"

"If I'd known who owned Sailor Joey's, I never would have gone there!"

Alana blinked.

"I have no idea what you're talkin' about, nena."

"Remember my story about how I was accosted by a cranky Viking outside Sticky Treats?"

Alana's mouth slowly opened as comprehension dawned.

"No way! Joey is the salty snack?"

Damn! I was hoping that name wouldn't stick.

"Have you been talking to Erin?"

"No!" Alana took a shifty sip of her wine. "Granny V told me when we had brunch last week."

I groaned and slapped my palm against my forehead. The entire universe was conspiring to smoosh me and Joel together.

"According to her," Alana continued, "the two of you had crazy chemistry."

"She was wrong. I mean, yes, he's good-looking—"

Alana scoffed.

"I think the term you're looking for is smokin' hot."

"Fine! Yes, he's hot. But he's also—"

I paused and ran my hand over my tender midriff. I remembered how caring and sensitive he'd been. And how my eyes had welled up when I'd looked at the finished tattoo in the mirror.

"He's actually less of a jerk than I thought. But that's hardly grounds for calling in a wedding planner."

"Pfft!" Alana gestured dismissively. "No law against a little no-strings fun."

I shook my head and topped up my glass.

"I'm not jumping into bed with some random guy just because he's hot. It'd be irresponsible."

"Irresponsible." Alana said the word slowly, as though trying out the feel of it in her mouth. "I think you're mispronouncing the word 'fun,' sweetie."

"Are you auditioning to be the devil on my shoulder?"

"Someone needs to be."

Alana picked up her glass and sat back, draping an arm around Jess's shoulder. Jess snuggled into her automatically.

"Are you honestly telling me you don't want to?" she asked, carding her fingers through Jess's hair.

"Yes! Yes, that's exactly what I'm saying. I have no desire to sleep with Joel."

"Your words say no. Your blush says yes."

I choked on my wine. Jess had spoken up out of nowhere, as if she'd read my mind. It was easy to forget she was always listening, no matter how oblivious to the conversation she seemed. This, combined with the zero filter, created a combo that took some getting used to. Alana smirked and gave her a sidelong glance.

"Think she's holdin' out on us?"

Jess hit pause on her console and gave me an appraising look.

"I'd say she's two glasses of wine from spilling the tea."

"Two?"

"Conservative estimate."

"Excellent."

Alana reached forward and pointedly topped up my glass.

"You're incorrigible!"

"I know, but I also come bearing gifts."

Leaning down, she rummaged in her purse, bringing out a white oblong box.

"I suspected Joey might be stuck in his ways, so I brought you a box of film dressing. Fantastic stuff. It's designed for burns, but it's great for healin' tattoos. Cuts down on the itching and the peeling."

"Thanks," I said, picking up the box and examining it.

Alana smiled slyly.

"You're welcome. Now you have no excuse not to show us your new ink. Take off the saran wrap, and I'll show you how to put this stuff on."

I threw up my hands and rolled up my top. Alana was a diabolical genius. She could pull anything out of anyone—almost. I was happy to show her the tattoo, but there wasn't enough wine in the world to persuade me to talk about what happened afterward. I could hardly believe it myself. Weird as it sounded, that tattoo session was one of the most erotic things I had ever experienced. Every time he touched me, I felt like I was on fire. I was mortified. By the time we were done, my nipples were like bullets, and I was throbbing between my legs.

Somehow, I kept it together long enough to pick Abby up from gymnastics and drop her off with my grandmother. Granny V had even asked if I was coming down with something.

You look so flushed, dear.

As soon as I was home, I raced upstairs and flopped onto the bed. My first thought had been the vibrator in my top drawer, but I didn't reach for it immediately. For a long while, I lay there and stared at the ceiling, breathing hard. Joel's face floated into my mind like a sexy bad penny.

I cupped my breasts, shivering as I rubbed my thumbs over the tight, sensitive points of my nipples. Every brush sent a tingling jolt to my pussy. I teased myself until I couldn't bear it anymore, then I ran a hand down my belly and fumbled with the buttons on my jeans. Holding my breath, I slid my fingers under the waistband of my panties and stroked the swollen folds of my pussy. Fuck! I was drenched. I caressed my soaked lips until my fingers were slick, then, I slowly circled my clit, barely biting back a moan. The little bundle of nerves was achingly stiff and swollen. My eyes drifted closed, and my mind flashed back to Joel on his knees, applying that damn stencil. When I pictured his smoldering grey eyes staring up at me, my circles sped up. I felt that familiar delicious warmth, coiling like a spring in my belly. I came with a strangled yell, back arching off the bed, stomach muscles quivering.

I took a large gulp of wine and tried to think cold-shower thoughts. When had my brain become so X-rated?

The tattoo was covered in several layers of saran wrap. You could see the outline of the image, but the details were fuzzy. It was like looking at it through frosted glass. Alana squatted in front of me and helped me peel the surgical tape from the clear wrap. I bit my lip, trying not to think about the brush of Joel's fingers in the same spots.

"Wow," Alana breathed. "That's gorgeous! Granny V is gonna love it. Plus, Abby will lose her mind. Major 'cool mom' points there."

"I was terrified to show Joel the design," I said. "I thought he'd laugh at me."

"Why would he?"

Alana's brows knitted as she carefully smoothed the film dressing over the tattoo. It was strange stuff. Once it was applied, it was almost invisible.

"I don't know. Rabbits, children's books—it didn't seem like his thing. Turned out he was really sweet about it. And his design was incredible. He immediately understood what I was going for and he even put his finger on some stuff I didn't know was there."

"Told you."

Alana heaved herself to her feet and flopped back on the sofa.

"He's prickly, but he's professional. Plus, he's way more sensitive than he'd want you to believe."

"Seems like you know him quite well."

Alana pursed her lips thoughtfully.

"He's done most of my ink, so I've known him a long time. Wouldn't say I know him *well*. Not sure many people do."

"So, no idea why he's so abrasive?"

Alana shook her head.

"Always figured he was one of those guys who was just kinda grumpy. He's got a soft center, though. He had a rough time growin' up, so now he feels super strongly about helping troubled kids realize their potential."

"What sort of rough time?"

I tried to sound casual, but I shifted forward in my seat, eager for more. I wasn't sure why I was so curious. Joel and I barely knew each other. I'd probably never see him again. Yet my mind kept going back to him, like an itch I couldn't scratch. Now someone was feeding my addiction.

Alana tucked her legs underneath her and swirled the wine in her glass.

"He's never gone into it, and I haven't liked to ask. But—"

Her lips curved into a smirk.

"If you got to know him a little better, you could find out for yourself. You should call him and tell him how happy you are with his work."

"Do you have *any* shame at all?"

"Nope," Alana and Jess chorused.

I don't know how they did it; Jess still hadn't looked up from *Mario Kart.* My hand was slightly unsteady as I emptied the wine bottle into our glasses. Time to cut myself off. I picked up my phone and stared pensively at the screen. As soon as I'd seen Joel's design, I'd made it my wallpaper.

"I should at least leave him a review. He deserves it."

As a freelance web designer, I knew how important reviews were, and how rarely clients bothered to leave one. The website took some finding. If Alana hadn't assured me that he had one, I'd have given up. After convincing Google that I genuinely didn't mean Sailor Jerry's, I found it lurking on the third page of results. When I got it open, my eyes widened in horror.

"Holy HTML! Who is responsible for this abomination?"

Alana had been snuggled up to Jess, watching the Switch screen over her shoulder, but she looked up when I gasped.

"What is it?"

"Have you ever seen this website?" I asked, throwing her a link.

Alana made a face.

"Oof!"

Jess paused her game and peered at Alana's screen.

"I think I just threw up in my mouth," she said tersely.

I scrolled through the ugly, clunky webpage and shook my head.

"It looks like somebody imported this thing directly from Myspace. Doesn't look like they're even on any social media platforms. It's no wonder Sailor Joey's is a best-kept secret. Nobody can *find* them."

Alana emptied her glass and laid it on the table with a soft clink.

"I think you know what you have to do," she said, looking at me seriously.

"What?"

"You have to save him."

CHAPTER TWELVE

Joel

"Who wants dessert?"

The sight of Aunt Loretta emerging from the kitchen with a pie plate gave rise to a murmured chorus of approval. Dustin threw his arms in the air and stretched like a contented cat.

"Hit me with it," he said. "My body is ready."

Crystal raised an eyebrow.

"You just said you were stuffed."

Dustin clasped his hands behind his head and grinned.

"As a certified medical professional, I happen to know that dessert is processed in an entirely separate stomach. Mom's pies might even get a third stomach all their own."

Dustin was Crystal's older brother. Terminally good-natured and fatally credulous, he had learned a lot of lessons the hard way. When his girlfriend walked out and left him literally holding the baby, he learned that single fatherhood did not go well with long shifts as an EMT. I don't know what he would've done if his parents hadn't stepped up to help him raise Kylie.

Yellow custard quivered as Aunt Loretta's knife broke the surface of the pie. She extracted a perfect slice and passed a plate to Uncle Jeff.

"I always said, the way to a man's heart was a good old-fashioned cream pie."

Kylie snorted and Dustin's ears turned pink. Crystal groaned and put her face in her hands.

"Mom! I'm begging you, please stop saying that."

"What? It's true. Your father and I had it on our first date. Banana cream pie, al fresco."

At this point Crystal let her head fall on the table and Kylie dissolved into breathless giggles.

"Settle down, Kylie."

Dustin's stern father voice wasn't very effective at the best of times. On this occasion, it was undercut by the fact his lips were twitching. Aunt Loretta sighed and shook her head.

"I don't know what you're all sniggering at, and I'm sure I don't want to. I'm just relieved the little ones are tucked up in bed. Joel, as my children and my granddaughter have their minds in the gutter, would *you* like the next slice of pie?"

"Not for me, thanks," I said, waving the slice away.

She frowned.

"What's the matter with you tonight, Joey? You barely touched your chili and now you don't want dessert."

"Been meaning to ask about that," said Dustin. "You haven't insulted me all night and you usually inhale three servings of Mom's chili before you pause for breath."

He crossed his arms over his broad chest and narrowed his eyes.

"What gives?"

"Butt out, jughead."

"Eh. I'm not convinced your heart was in that."

"Don't tempt me, bro. I'm already in debt to the swear jar."

I punched him softly on the arm and tried to summon a chuckle. Family dinners on Dustin's rare nights off were traditional, but today my mind kept wandering. And it always wandered back to the same place.

I couldn't understand what had come over me. It wasn't as

if I'd never tattooed an attractive woman before. Name a body part and I've probably inked it. Zel and I talk about it a lot. Once you get used to working with a living canvas, you can flip a switch in your brain, so you don't get embarrassed—or worse, embarrass yourself. But with Olivia, suddenly my penis was running the show. All I could think about was how soft her skin was and how delicious she looked, lying on that bed. And the noises she made. My dick responded to every gasp and twitch like a salivating dog to a bell.

Minutes after she left, I was in the bathroom with my cock in my fist. Bracing one arm against the wall, I jerked myself frantically. I came embarrassingly fast, groaning as scalding jets of cum spurted over my fingers.

I'd tattooed breasts and butts without turning a hair. Yet, somehow, tattooing Olivia's stomach was enough to have me yanking it in the bathroom like a pathetic loser.

It wouldn't have been so bad if it had purely been about sex. I could've dismissed it as pent-up energy, stress, even an early midlife crisis. But it was more than that. Olivia touched something raw inside me. It made me feel as though I were being turned inside out. I wasn't sure if I loved it or hated it. Maybe both.

When she was with me, everything else fell away, even when we were ripping each other to shreds. Suddenly no one else existed. And then there was the time thing. Whatever skullduggery she was working on me made time evaporate. All that time I was working on her, I never even thought to wonder why Zel and Lily weren't back yet. (Turned out donuts had devolved into a field trip to the mall.)

It was a good thing I'd probably never see her again. Whatever fit of madness was on me now, it was obvious we didn't fit. She seemed like a smart, successful woman. On top of that, she had a kid to raise. What would she want with a guy like me? I was a grumpy, aging hipster with a failing business and more baggage than an airport carousel. Even if she was interested, she'd quickly realize I had nothing to offer. Or worse, she'd try to help me. I couldn't let that happen. People who stepped in to help me always ended up in a boatload of trouble. Aunt Loretta and Uncle Jeff were proof of that. Lately, my aunt had taken to trying to hide the mortgage bills, but I'd seen the red-stamped envelopes in the recycling. Then there was Mom, of course.

I pushed that thought firmly aside and tried to join in the chatter over dessert. I even forced myself to eat a slice of pie so my aunt would stop worrying.

We'd almost finished clearing the table and loading the dishwasher when my phone buzzed in my back pocket. Frowning, I fished it out and made a beeline for the back porch. The only person likely to call me was Zel, and he had a date tonight. I nearly dropped the phone when I saw Olivia's name on the screen. For an insane moment, I was convinced she'd heard me thinking about her. Maybe she was calling to tell me what a disgusting perv I was.

"Hello?"

Silence. Maybe she'd butt-dialed me. I was on the point of hanging up when I heard her voice.

"Hi. Um, sorry to disturb you so late, but I felt like I had to tell you that..."

She trailed off and I held my breath.

"Your website sucks."

I blinked. She'd fired the words out in a garbled rush and now I could hear her breathing at the other end of the line.

"Glad you got that off your chest."

"God! I'm sorry, that came out wrong. I just meant that I looked you up to give you a review and I...couldn't believe how terrible it was."

"Yeah," I said wryly. "That sounds much better."

"To be honest, it was a miracle I found you at all. You don't even come up on the first page of results. And as for your social media presence—"

"This going somewhere? Or did you just call to massage my ego?"

"I know this didn't come out right, but if you pull your head out of your ass for one second, you'll see that I'm trying to help you."

"Why?"

I slumped onto the porch seat and stretched my legs out. Weirdly, now we were snarling and sniping again, the tension in my chest had eased off. I was enjoying myself.

"Because apparently I do stupid things when I've had more than two glasses of wine."

"And how were you proposing to help me, exactly?"

"By building you a website that looks like it was designed this century by someone who knows what SEO stands for."

"You think I don't know what SEO stands for?"

"Do you?"

"Yes!"

Super enhanced...octopus? Special enchilada olives?

"But anyway," I said, swiftly changing the subject. "I'm not sure this is something we need right now. I only made that stupid site to get Zel off my back."

"You don't think your business needs a website?"

"No."

I'd always found advertising distasteful. If my work couldn't stand on its own merits, then I wasn't meant to succeed. I wasn't prepared to beg people to come to me. This conversation was starting to sound more and more like a sales pitch. I swatted irritably at a mosquito. If that was the only reason she'd called, I was ready to nope out. Let her find herself another cash cow.

"Ok, give me a chance to prove you wrong."

I raised an eyebrow. It wasn't the tone I was expecting. It was soft and coaxing.

"Why are you pushing so hard on this?"

"Because you do amazing work and it's sad that so few people know about you."

Dammit!

She was like some weird conversational ninja. I got my guard up, braced for an attack from the front, only for her to sneak up from behind and pull my emotional pants down.

"Thanks," I said lamely.

"And you never know. If you drummed up a little more business, you might be able to install a coffee machine."

My face relaxed into a smile.

"Careful. Magda will come for you if you take away her best-looking customer."

"You make a good point. Zel is pretty hot."

"Ouch! Hope you're prepared to fight my Aunt Loretta for him."

"It's ok. He's not really my type."

"Oh? What is your type?"

Anyone who claims you can't hear an awkward pause has never steered banter into the danger zone. Who was I kidding? Conversations with Olivia consisted entirely of danger zone. Riptides, eddies, and sharp rocks under the surface. Her brain ship obviously had the more competent captain as she seized the helm first.

"I don't think that's an appropriate question for a business meeting, Mr. Morris."

"You always open your business meetings by telling your clients they suck?"

"Yep! Tough love. Can't help noticing you just called yourself my client. Does that mean you're on board?"

The ninja strikes again.

"I don't know. I'll think about it, ok?"

"Ok," she said. "I didn't expect to get this far, so I'll put it in the win column."

"This was a win? What were you expecting to happen?"

"Thought you might accuse me of interfering. Or tell me to stick it up my ass and hang up on me."

My stomach twisted. I remembered storming off at the launch. I had the urge to apologize but couldn't get my mouth around the words.

"How much of an asshole do you think I am?" I asked, trying to sound outraged.

"Want me to answer that?"

"Maybe not. My ego's taken a beating as it is."

"Sorry about that."

"Eh. It's ok."

Another awkward pause. Ending the conversation shouldn't have been so difficult. I usually loved hanging up the phone.

"I'd better go. I've abandoned my guests for long enough."

"You have company?"

I was more interested than I had any right to be.

"Just Alana and Jess. Should I tell them you said, hi?"

"Yeah, cool. I'm actually at my aunt's place for dinner so—"

There was an abrupt beep and then silence.

Did she hang up on me mid-sentence? Was I that boring?

Fuck! Why the hell do you even care?

The mosquito whined past my ear, and I swung wildly. My hand exploded with pain as it thwacked against the arm of the bench. Mumbling a string of curses that would have emptied my entire bank account into the swear jar, I stalked back into the house, cradling my hand to my chest. The TV blared from the sitting room. They were watching *The Bachelorette*. Or, more accurately, the girls would be watching *The Bachelorette*, while Dustin and Uncle Jeff pretended they weren't into it.

It occurred to me that I should go home. The chances of me being good company were zero. I was about to go into the sitting room and say my goodbyes when I spotted a light under the dining-room door. Aunt Loretta was sitting alone at the table. Her laptop was open on a spreadsheet, and she had her head in her hands. Dread settled heavily in my chest.

"Hey," I said tentatively.

She looked up and gave me a tired smile.

"Hey, Joey. You been on the phone all this time?"

"Yeah, I guess I have. Are you ok?"

"Ugh!"

She leaned back in her chair and rubbed her temples.

"I'm fine, hon. I'm just going cross-eyed staring at this thing."

I peered over her shoulder and frowned at the figures.

"This doesn't look good."

She reached back and patted my hand.

"We'll be fine," she said breezily. "I'm sure there's more corners we can cut. I just have to find them."

Clasping my hands behind my neck, I grimaced at the ceiling.

"This is my fault."

Aunt Loretta twisted in her chair and looked at me severely.

"No, it is *not*! How many times have we been through this? Jeff and I don't regret a single cent we gave you. We've seen how you've poured your heart and soul into that place and we're proud of you."

She paused for a moment.

"Your mom would be proud too."

I shifted uncomfortably and looked away.

"Never made enough to pay you back though."

"You will. I know you, Joel. There's nothing you wouldn't do to get that place on its feet."

Nothing I wouldn't do.

When I fell into bed, I stared at the ceiling for a long while, unable to sleep. Maybe it was time to put my pride to one side and stop sabotaging every opportunity that came my way. I owed Aunt Loretta and Uncle Jeff that much. I'd blown a fantastic networking opportunity at the launch of Sticky Treats. Could I afford to throw this opportunity away because things felt...weird? Because I was scared of...what exactly?

This was stupid! I was a grown man, not some horny teenage boy. Whatever odd fixation I had with Olivia was bound to dissipate once I spent more time with her. Besides, she clearly wasn't interested. She was so eager to get away she'd hung up on me. Stretching out, I plucked my phone from the charging dock and squinted at the screen. I had a message.

Olivia: Sorry. Hung up on you with my face 😊

Joel: 'S ok. I was actually about to send you a message.

The three dots that indicated she was typing popped up immediately. I didn't even notice I was grinning until my facial muscles twinged.

CHAPTER THIRTEEN

Olivia

When I stepped through the door of Sailor Joey's, my stomach fluttered. I clutched my folder to my chest and sternly reminded myself that this was a business meeting. It didn't matter that I'd been fantasizing about him for two weeks straight. I was a grown woman with professional integrity. There was no excuse for acting like a teenager with a crush.

Like last time, it was a moment before anyone noticed I was there. Zel was painting and Lily was absorbed in her phone. When I looked at Zel's model, I felt silly that I'd been self-conscious about taking my top off. The woman was completely naked. Her upper torso was painted blue and Zel was meticulously painting her legs with iridescent fish scales. The effect was beautiful, but the woman looked bored. Zel's face was inches from her crotch, and she was scrolling through her phone like someone waiting for a bus. I envied her confidence.

Lily looked up first. She saw me and her face split into an evil grin.

"Joel," she called. "Your girlfriend's here."

Zel snorted. The model continued swiping as though nothing had happened. I stood awkwardly, trying to pretend my cheeks weren't roasting. Half a second later, a door flew open at the back of the studio and Joel stuck his head out. His hair was caught up in a black paisley bandana, making him look more like a pirate than ever.

A sexy pirate. Jack Sparrow can suck it.

I gave myself a mental slap and pushed aside any terrible puns involving my decks getting swabbed or my timbers getting shivered. Joel glared at Lily and then turned to me. He didn't smile or offer any form of greeting. He beckoned me with a jerk of his head and disappeared again. I wasn't sure whether the tension in my stomach was arousal or that feeling you get when you've been summoned to the principal's office. I followed him, wondering whether I was going to be put in detention or made to walk the plank.

Either could be fun.

There was a tiny alcove with a bathroom and a door leading to one other room. I edged through it and into a tiny, crowded office. Most of the space was taken up by a desk and a filing cabinet. The walls were painted black and covered with an assortment of sketches and paintings. My eyes leaped from one to the other. I felt disorientated by the mishmash of colors and images. The whole place smelled faintly of that smoky apple scent that I'd noticed on Joel before.

"There's a chair if you wanna sit."

He waved vaguely in the direction of the one remaining chair. I pulled it up to the desk and perched on the edge, gripping my folder for dear life.

"I brought you coffee."

The abrupt tone sounded more like he was accusing me of something rather than offering a drink. Reaching under the desk, he produced a takeout cupholder containing 4 cups of coffee and dumped them in front of me. My gaze flickered between him and the cups.

"Do I look that tired?"

His ears turned pink.

"I wasn't sure what kind of syrup you took. I knew it was some kind of nut, but I couldn't remember which one. And somehow—" He paused and a muscle ticked in his jaw. "Magda couldn't remember either. So, I got you all of them."

He crossed his arms and looked away. It was adorable. I bit my cheek to hold in my laugh.

"That's very thoughtful. Thank you."

I investigated the cups to hunt down the hazel and he made a big production of shuffling things around on the desks. Uncertainty radiated from him in waves. It was endearing.

At one point, his wrist brushed his mouse, and the computer screen beeped into life. I hadn't expected to be confronted with a close-up photo of my stomach, complete with its new sylvan tableau. When he caught me looking, Joel's blush darkened.

"It's some of my best work," he mumbled, shrugging defensively.

I swallowed and tucked a strand of hair behind my ear. He'd seen me half-naked. Why did a picture of my stomach on his computer make my mouth go dry? Averting my eyes, I fumbled to open the folder on my lap. Then I sat up straighter and tried to adopt my most official voice.

"Before we can really get started on a website design, I'll need to ask you some questions," I said. "I usually start by asking clients to sum up their business in a few sentences."

Joel shifted.

"Tattoos. We design them and put them on people."

"Ok. I guess that's technically more than one sentence. Can you be more specific?"

He crossed his arms tighter and twisted his neck. I heard a faint click.

"We insert pigment into the dermis layer of the skin to create an indelible image."

I took a long slow breath.

"Right. And who is your target audience?"

"People who want tattoos."

The more questions I asked, the more defensive he became.

"Can you explain the ethos behind your brand?"

"No."

I bit the tip of my tongue and drummed my nails against my folder.

"I hate to break this to you," I said. "But I don't think you'll be making the shortlist for the most helpful client of the year. Why do you hate this so much?"

"I don't hate it."

I raised an eyebrow.

"You're growing prickles. I can see them sprouting in real-time. Soon you'll be the grumpiest cactus ever to sail the seven seas."

He frowned.

"Don't cactuses belong in the desert?"

"Typically, yes, but we've already established your piratey credentials."

His mouth twitched reluctantly into a smile.

"I'd forgotten about that. Is that why you started rambling at me about parrots that one time?"

"No. That was an entirely different branch on the insanity tree. However, you're avoiding my question."

"Which was?"

"Why do you hate this so much?"

He sighed and slumped back in his chair, swiveling restlessly.

"I don't like to think of this place as a business. I know it is, but it means so much to me. It's hard to step back and think of it in terms of quarterly goals and spreadsheets and stuff. It's like that thing at school where the teacher asks everyone to stand up and say how they spent their summer vacation. You can have the best vacation ever, but once you get up and recite it to the class, it just sounds like homework."

"But that's the point," I said gently. "That's why you should pay attention to this stuff. I know it feels like we're pulling in two different directions here, but we want the same thing. You're doing something you love, and I want you to be able to keep doing it. You *did* do something amazing on vacation and we want everyone to sit up and listen. That's why I need you to—"

"Do my homework?"

"In a manner of speaking, yes."

He smiled ruefully and I felt myself flush again. Joel had an uncanny ability for making blood flow to places it absolutely *wasn't* needed. I took a gulp of coffee and unnecessarily consulted my list of questions.

"Ok," I said. "Let's approach this from a different angle. Sailor Joey's—how'd you come up with the name? I mean, your pirate pedigree is beyond question at this point, but I've never heard you go by Joey."

Joel spun through 180 degrees, presenting me with his back.

"It's what my Aunt Loretta called me when I was little."

"That's cute."

"Thanks. I hate it."

"Oops. Sorry."

He swiveled back around and gave me a strained smile.

"Hate's a strong word. But it always felt like a kid's name. Now, of course, half my customers call me Joey."

I finished the hazelnut coffee and began eyeing up the macadamia.

"It's what Alana called you when she recommended this place," I said. "It's why I was so surprised to see you. If you don't like it, why did you use it?"

Among the assorted items on the desk, there was a white unicorn with a pink mane. He picked it up and closed his fist around its soft, yielding body.

"It was kind of a present to my aunt. Wanted to show her

that however old I got, or whatever stupid stuff I did, her Joey was still in there. A guy who remembers where he came from, and who's...grateful."

His knuckles turned white. The unicorn gave a faint squeak and its little eyes popped out on stalks.

"I owe her a lot," he said. "Heck, it's thanks to her and Uncle Jeff that we have this place at all."

He stared out of the one window, and I waited for him to continue, inexplicably spellbound.

"Dad was never in the picture and my mom died when I was eight."

"I'm so sorry. How did—"

"Car accident," he said tightly. "She was on her way home from work, and she veered off the road. Cops think she must've fallen asleep at the wheel. After it happened, Aunt Loretta and Uncle Jeff took me in and raised me. Treated me like a son. They even re-mortgaged their house to help me buy this place."

He gave the long-suffering unicorn another squeeze and his throat bobbed convulsively. My hand reached out of its own accord, but I closed my fist and jerked it back.

"That's amazing," I said quietly. "They must really believe in you."

He winced.

"Probably their biggest mistake."

"Joel—"

"They poured their livelihood into helping me and we're about to go under," he said bitterly.

"It doesn't have to stay that way. It's why I'm here, remember?"

This time I did reach out. I stretched my hand out and closed it gently over his wrist. His skin was hot under my fingers, and I felt the thrum of his pulse. Barely suppressing a shiver, I drew back. He looked at his wrist thoughtfully and then placed his other hand over the place I'd touched.

"That's why you're here," he repeated.

Shaking his head, he leaped up abruptly.

"I-I think this was a mistake."

I blinked.

"What do you mean?"

He turned away, shoving his hands in his pockets.

"It's not like we're on a date here," he said stiffly. "And I'm not even sure I can afford your time, let alone your services."

Ok. Glad we got that cleared up.

The sharp sting to my feelings took me unawares. Blinking rapidly, I rearranged myself in my seat. This guy was giving me serious emotional whiplash. One minute he was pouring his heart out, the next minute he was freezing me out. What the hell was his problem?

And why do you care so much?

"If you *had* done your homework," I said coldly, "you'd know that my preliminary consultation is always free. As for my fee, we can talk about that when—"

"I'm not looking for charity."

"That's not what I—ugh!"

My irritation bubbled over. It was all or nothing with this man. I either wanted to hug him, jump him, or throttle him; there was nothing in between. There was only one point in the month I expected my emotions to be on this kind of crazy teeter-totter, and I doubted salted caramel brownies would help in this case. Not unless I was throwing a platter of them in Joel's stupid face.

"Why did I talk myself into this? You don't need a web designer; you need a proctologist."

"A proctologist?"

"Yeah, and when they find whatever crawled up your ass, maybe we can talk like adults."

"You're the one making butt cracks."

There was a heavy pause, and he pinched the bridge of his nose.

"Probably should've said butt jokes, but regardless, I didn't ask you to interfere."

"Well, excuse me for believing in you," I yelled, hating the crack in my voice. "W-when I opened your tattoo design, I cried. You captured what I wanted so perfectly. I wanted to help you because I want you to have the opportunity to make other people cry."

I registered the wetness on my cheeks and swiped at them furiously. Joel's face softened. All at once, he was the picture of contrition.

"Apparently I'm good at making you cry," he said. "Not sure that's a talent I want to hone."

He looked around the office helplessly and then darted to the desk and opened a drawer, pulling out a faded purple bandana.

"Here."

He crouched in front of my chair. We were so close that I could see my reflection in the stormy pools of his eyes. Something stuttered in my chest, and I held my breath, heart pounding in my ears. He started to lift the cloth to my face, but at the last moment, he pulled back and pressed it into my hand instead. I drew in a deep shuddering breath and dabbed at my eyes.

"I'm so sorry I got so defensive," he said. "You might've noticed I'm terrible at accepting help."

I made a sound halfway been a laugh and a sob and offered him the bandana back. He waved it away and stood up.

"Keep it."

"O-ok."

We were silent for a while. He perched on the edge of the desk and traced patterns on the floor with the toe of his boot. Meanwhile, I sat, staring at my hands in my lap and knotting the purple bandana around my fingers. I nearly jumped out of my skin when my phone buzzed. Tapping on the notification, I rolled my eyes. It was a group email blast from the head of the

PTA. Classic Marsha. Passive-aggressive bullshit with an obnoxiously cheerful candy coating. About as convincing as bunny ears on a cobra. I was on the point of deleting the e-mail when I was struck by a bolt of inspiration.

"Listen," I said, glancing around at the artwork on the walls. "If you're not comfortable accepting a discount, how about an exchange of services?"

CHAPTER FOURTEEN

Joel

"I got us a gig."

Zel paused with his burger halfway to his mouth. A glistening blob of ketchup dripped from the bun and landed on the plate.

"I don't know about you," he said. "But I haven't been in a band since high school. Since when do we have gigs?"

"A job then. Well, more of a favor."

Zel put his burger down and shook his head.

"Nuh-uh. The last time you gave me that look, I ended up in your sister's backyard wearing a rainbow wig and big floppy shoes."

"Sounds a lot like your regular wardrobe."

Today's ensemble consisted of a Hawaiian shirt covered in flamingos and bright pink shorts. It was like having lunch with a villager from *Animal Crossing*. He gave me a severe look and deftly swiped two of my chili-cheese fries.

"Can we not make light of my severe psychological scars, please?"

He went back for more fries, and I slapped his hand away.

"I can't believe you're still bitching about that. You were on for less than an hour, and you're usually great with kids."

"Say what you want, those rugrats were a tough crowd."

"To be fair, your balloon animals *did* suck."

"Words can be hurtful, Joel."

He wiped his fingers and threw the balled-up napkin at me. "Anyway, never again. I don't care how sick the clown is."

"This is actually different," I said, shooting for my best casual tone. "Although it does involve kids. It's an elementary school carnival. Their face painter pulled out at the last minute."

Zel picked up his strawberry milkshake and held my eye as he took a long pull on the straw.

"If I were to search for details on this particular school," he said, putting his glass down with exaggerated delicacy, "would I find that the lovely Miss Reid is a member of the PTA?"

I scowled and rubbed at the back of my neck.

"Yeah," I said. "She asked me—well, us—to step in."

"Uh-huh."

"What? Why are you grinning at me like that?"

Zel popped an onion ring in his mouth and shrugged.

"PTA events, kiddie face painting. It's not exactly your scene, is it?"

"Not usually. It is yours, though. I know it's below your paygrade, but you've done it plenty of times before. Cody and Kelvin would probably stage a full-blown riot if you came over without your paints."

"So, when you say we're doing a favor, you mean you volunteered *me* to do a favor."

"I'll help too. I'm not as good as you, but I have been to art school. I know my way around a sponge."

Zel raised his eyebrows.

"Wow. I've never seen you work this hard to impress a woman before."

"That's not what this is."

I drained the last of my coke and put the glass down with a

thump that made the ice cubes clink. The family at the next table glanced over nervously.

"Calm down, J-bear," Zel soothed. "I think this is a good thing."

"I've told you before about calling me J-bear."

"I've seen the way you look at her," he said, ignoring my interruption. "I know you're dead-set on ending your days as a lonely bitter old man, but the universe may have other plans. It's nice to know someone can still bring a blush to those scratchy, yet pinchable, cheeks. Maybe she can sand off some of your crusty edges."

Why does everyone keep saying I'm crusty?

"It's not like that. In case you haven't noticed, we're singularly gifted at pissing each other off."

"So are we," Zel said. "But you adore me."

"Sure I do."

"Everyone has a different love language. Yours is grumpiness."

"I am not trying to impress Olivia. This is a business deal. We're doing her a favor in exchange for a discount on the website. Remember the website? The whole reason she came to the studio in the first place."

Zel finished his milkshake with a rasping slurp.

"Is that why she left all flushed with your old bandana clutched to her bosom?"

I narrowed my eyes.

"Did you seriously just say bosom?"

I shook my head and pushed the remains of my hot dog away.

"Candice was right. You *do* read too many romance novels."

Zel leaned back and ruffled a hand through his candy-pink hair.

"Proof that we weren't meant to be."

I shook my head.

"I could come up with a whole bunch of better reasons than that. So, will you do the face painting?"

"Fine. You've convinced me. On a more serious note, your girl had better work some magic with this website. I've been going over the accounts and things are looking bleak. Another quarter like this and we'll have to let Lily go."

Lunch churned in my stomach. I knew all this; I'd had the same thoughts myself. But hearing it from someone else felt worse. This was another reason not to let things get complicated with Olivia. I couldn't afford to mess up. This had to stay professional.

I might have managed it if it hadn't been for the maple donut glaze.

Olivia had come in for a meeting. It wasn't the first time. She'd drop into the studio now and then to go over various aspects of the website design. Her dedication to the project was impressive. I hadn't expected her to come in person every time she wanted my feedback. Amazingly, in all that time, I managed not to put my foot in it.

Our informal meetings usually ended with one of us going to Magda's for coffee and lemon bars and then we'd just hang out for a while. I'm not exactly what you'd call sociable, but this was different. She was easy to talk to when we weren't ripping chunks out of each other. I'd been surprised when I'd opened up about Mom at our first meeting, and it turned out it wasn't a fluke. Soon we were chatting about anything and everything. I loved hearing her tell stories about her family and their crazy antics. She got this warm, tender expression on her face when she talked about them, and she had a sharp, witty turn of phrase that made me crack up. I actually enjoyed her company, and provided we stayed on either side of a desk, I had no problem controlling myself.

This time she'd brought some more samples of Granny V's artwork for me to look at. My mouth fell open when I got to the sketches of a familiar pirate girl.

"You're kidding," I said. "Your grandmother created ViVi Tempest?"

Like a lot of people my age, I'd loved the ViVi Tempest books as a kid. The adventures of the 10-year-old pirate captain and her wisecracking parrot, Bones, had captivated me. Aunt Loretta had read them to me and my cousins. It was probably the origin of my pirate obsession. If I was ever in the same room with Granny again, she was not leaving without giving me her autograph.

I squinted at the little redhead in the oversized tricorne and bunny slippers. Then I looked at Olivia. Suddenly it was unmistakable.

"Of course! The fluffy terror!"

"Excuse me?"

"The first time we met you reminded me of someone, but I couldn't figure it out. It's been driving me nuts."

"Oh God."

Olivia flushed and raised her hands to her face.

"Even in her pink fuzzy bunny slippers, Vivi still struck fear into the heart of every scurvy pirate who sailed the high seas. They called her the fluffy terror!"

Olivia smiled wearily.

"I *may* have been a part of the inspiration," she admitted. "I'm surprised you picked it up, though. I'm not much like that anymore."

I frowned. ViVi was characterized as a fearless firecracker, and so was Olivia. The woman took crap from no one. It was one of the things I liked about her.

"What're you—"

At that moment the office door opened and Zel stuck his head in. I suppressed the urge to punch it right off his shoulders.

"Hey, busy bees. Lily and I just got donuts. Wanna come out and join us?"

I really, really don't.

"That sounds great!"

Sounding a little too exuberant, Olivia gathered up her papers and followed Zel into the main studio. I sighed and joined them a couple of seconds later.

Olivia's donut taste fell slightly short of perfection. She went with the maple-glazed cruller. I could forgive her, though. It meant I was only fighting two people for my share of the jelly filled. We were talking and laughing, and everything was going fine until I noticed that Olivia had glaze on her cheek. Without thinking, I reached out and brushed it away with my thumb. Her eyes widened and she flushed. I tried to cover the gesture by playfully dabbing the glaze on the end of her nose, but at the last moment she moved her head and my thumb slid over her lip instead. I felt a warm, wet tickle as the tip of her tongue grazed over my skin. It was so brief I was half convinced I'd imagined it. I inhaled sharply. My heart pounded against my ribs and there was a familiar tightening in the crotch of my jeans. I swallowed hard. It was like having a golf ball stuck in my throat.

Out of the corner of my eye, I caught Zel smirking. He took a deliberate bite of his donut and a jet of Bavarian cream spurted out the other side.

Should've stuck with lemon bars.

CHAPTER FIFTEEN

Joel

I sat bolt upright in bed, sweaty and panting. It had happened again. I'd dreamed about Olivia. She was there every time I closed my eyes, and the dreams were getting crazier. This time we were having sex on a bed of giant donuts. Our naked bodies writhed on the endless expanse of pillowy dough until we were both covered in glaze. Olivia's skin was warm and sticky against mine and my senses were overwhelmed by the heady scent of sugar. Now and then, a knee or an elbow would break the surface of a donut, sending great arcs of thick cream spurting into the air. Finally, an almighty thrust caused the donut to collapse under our weight and we fell into a pocket of molten custard. I woke up just as we slipped beneath the surface of the warm viscous goo.

I pushed the sheets back and grimaced.

Shower time.

The powerful jet of water scourged the clinging tendrils of sleep from my body. It should have been pleasant, but I was too distracted to enjoy it.

This had to stop. It was getting embarrassing. My scalp tingled as I angrily lathered my hair, viciously working the menthol shampoo into the roots. If I couldn't talk sense into myself, maybe I could scrub it in.

I guess it was no surprise that my nocturnal fantasies had kicked up a notch. It had been less than 24 hours since I'd had Olivia's thumb in my mouth.

Stupid donut glaze.

For some reason, it always came back to donuts. I'd gone to get donuts the day I met Olivia and now they seemed determined to stick us together. All my resolutions to behave and keep my distance were undone by those sticky glazed temptresses with unnecessarily suggestive holes.

It wasn't too long ago that I'd hated this woman. Now that hate had turned into...something else. She still drove me nuts, but I was drawn to her like a moth to a flame. Obsessing over her, over-analyzing every word, every gesture, every tiny tongue tickle.

I turned off the water and grabbed a towel. Today was gym day and I was looking forward to it. Hitting the weights with Dustin usually cleared my head.

He was already warming up when I arrived. For me, working out was another form of anger management, but for Dustin, it was a passion. At least it was now. He'd always been a little heavy, even when he was a kid. Crystal and I used to tease him about it. It made me ashamed to think back on it, but kids can be assholes. As an adult, he wasn't huge, but he had a physique that inspired words like comfortable and cuddly. As far as anyone knew, he was perfectly happy that way, but after Kirsten left, something changed. A few weeks after she walked out, he started hitting the gym and he never looked back. He wasn't cuddly anymore; he was an imposing wall of muscle. On the outside, anyway. Inside he was soft as a Twinkie.

I'd never asked what prompted the change. Maybe it was a way to take his mind off things or get his confidence back, but

I suspected there was more to it. In 14 years, he'd never revealed why Kirsten left, or what she'd said beforehand.

I joined him and started stretching the kinks out of my muscles. Afterward, we hit the treadmill. Gradually, I cranked up the speed. I relished the feel of my chest opening and the pleasant burn in my muscles, but I couldn't stop my mind racing. I upped the incline, chasing the blissful blankness that came when I worked up a sweat.

On the treadmill to my left, I heard the regular thump of Dustin's feet and the harsh sound of his breathing. Now and then he gave me a sidelong glance. This went on for several kilometers until I hit the down button and slowed to a walk.

"Out with it."

"What?"

He'd slowed down too. Now he looked at me innocently.

"I can hear you not saying something. It's getting on my nerves."

"Ok."

He stepped off the treadmill and rubbed his face with a towel.

"I didn't think I'd notice, given that you've been such a colossal bag of dicks lately, but you're extra prickly today."

I stepped down and tightened my bun.

"It's nothing. I didn't sleep well."

We hit the free weights next. I was in the middle of a set of dumbbell curls when he dropped the bomb.

"Trouble with your new girlfriend?"

I nearly dropped the weight on my foot.

"What the hell are you talking about? What new girlfriend?"

"I was hoping you'd tell me," he said, switching his dumbbell to his other hand. "Seems like the sort of thing you'd want to share with your family."

"Why is everyone so obsessed with my love life? It's bad enough I have Crystal constantly setting me up on blind dates.

Now I have you dreaming up imaginary girlfriends for me. If you're that starved for your romance fix, I'm sure Zel would happily share his Kindle library."

"I didn't imagine it," he said. "Crystal ran into Zel and Lily at the mall. They both hinted that there was a new woman in your life. Usually, I'd have called bullshit, but the signs are all there. You're acting all moody and secretive. Reminded me of our junior year of high school when you were mooning over Vanessa Dawson."

"You're such an asshole."

I replaced the dumbbell and grabbed a kettlebell.

"If that's the best comeback you got, then I'm definitely on to something."

"You mean besides my last nerve?"

My triceps bulged as I stretched my arms up and lifted the kettlebell above my head.

"There is a woman in my life. But it's not what you think. It's a business relationship."

Dustin's eyes widened and his mouth fell open.

"Not like that! She's a web designer. We hired her to build a new website for Sailor Joey's. Apparently, our old one sucks."

"Not my area, bro," said Dustin cheerfully. "So, you're saying Zel was yanking Crystal's chain? Things between you and this woman are strictly professional?"

"Mostly."

I attached some weights to a barbell and lay down on the bench. Dustin automatically drifted over to spot me.

"There might have been a couple of points where things got a little weird, but..."

Grunting, I pushed the bar away from my chest.

"Sexy-weird or weird-weird?"

I gritted my teeth and forced the bar up one last time. My muscles stood out in glistening cords and my chest and arms burned. I replaced the bar with a clang and sat up, bathed in a pleasant fuzz of endorphins.

"I'm starting to feel like one of us needs to be holding a cosmo before this conversation can continue," I panted.

Dustin looked at me severely.

"Ok. One, *Sex and the City* is a seminal show; don't dis it. Two, don't come at me with the men don't talk about their feelings bull-crap. Mom raised both of us better than that."

"I guess you're right."

"Damn straight."

He sat down next to me and flipped the cap on a bottle of water.

"Now," he continued. "Sexy-weird or weird-weird?"

"Both, I guess."

"Sounds complicated."

"It really is."

I gave him the whole history. Everything from the meeting outside Sticky Treats to the incident with the donut glaze. He whistled.

"That's quite a story."

"Now I can't stop thinking about her."

"Is that such a problem? I mean, you're both single."

"It's not as simple as that."

"Why not?"

Because I'd drag her down and she deserves better.

I shrugged.

"Lots of reasons. Mostly, I don't think we'd be a good fit. She has responsibilities and a kid. Could get messy."

The plastic bottle cracked and buckled as Dustin took a huge gulp of water.

"People with kids can have relationships," he said gently. "At least, I hope so. I'd like to think I'm not doomed to die alone just because things didn't work out with Kirsten."

Me and my big fat mouth!

"I didn't mean it like that. I meant that she's a smart, successful woman with a lot on her plate and there's nothing I can bring to the table besides debt and a failing business."

"Maybe she's not as materialistic as you think."

"What I mean is, I don't want to go into anything feeling like a burden," I said impatiently. "Are you determined to twist everything I say?"

"No. But I know what you're like when you get like this. You decide everyone's thinking the worst about you, so you snap back first without giving them a chance."

"This isn't like that. I know I'm right here. I just need to find a way to stop obsessing over her."

Dustin was mercifully quiet for the rest of our workout. We'd showered and were on our way out to the parking lot before he struck again.

"I think you should sleep with her."

I'd just taken a sip of coconut water. I bent over gasping and coughing while Dustin gave me a helpful thump on the back.

"Have you not listened to a word I've said?" I choked, wiping my streaming eyes with the back of my hand.

"I have," he said cheerfully. "I'm not talking about a relationship. I'm talking about hot, meaningless animal sex. After all, you're both..."

I held up a warning finger.

"If you mention mammals or the Discovery Channel, we are ending this conversation now."

He grinned and raised both hands in surrender.

"Ok, ok, chill. Bloodhound Gang had a point, though. Sex can be a big deal, but it doesn't have to be. It can just be about two consenting adults having fun."

I narrowed my eyes suspiciously.

"I guess that's true. Assuming she's interested, of course. Where are you going with this?"

"You say you want to stop obsessing over her," he said. "This might be the way. Remember when we were kids and Mom would take away our Nintendo privileges? Have you ever wanted to play that Nintendo more than when you knew you couldn't? I don't know about you, but on days like that, Mario called to me like a little mustachioed siren."

"I worry about you sometimes."

"Listen, this totally makes sense. Maybe if you stop denying yourself and give in, your infatuation will fizzle out of its own accord."

"You think?"

"Yeah. You're a cranky asshole. I can count the number of people you stand to be around on one hand. If Olivia isn't the one for you, I'm sure she'll do something to piss you off before too long."

Could he be right? I'd spent a lot of time avoiding getting close to Olivia. Dustin's plan sounded like crazy talk.

Later that evening, I was on the couch with a beer, idly channel surfing when my phone buzzed. I felt that familiar thrum of excitement when I saw Olivia's name. She'd sent me an adorable picture of Abby on her way to a costume party. She was dressed as a pirate and Olivia had captioned the picture 'Vivi 2.0.'

When I caught myself with a big stupid grin on my face, I shook my head in frustration and flung my phone to the other side of the couch. Damn her! Why did she have to be so...perfect?

CHAPTER SIXTEEN

Olivia

I needed to keep my head.

Joel had his thumb in my mouth.

It was just a slip. It didn't mean anything. Above all, I needed to act normally. There was no reason to make things weird.

His actual thumb, in my actual mouth.

Ok. So, I found him attractive. What did that prove? That I was a heterosexual woman with functioning eyeballs? It didn't matter that my stomach performed crazy acrobatics whenever he looked at me. When it came down to it, he was just another client.

A client who tastes like salted caramel.

It was true that I enjoyed his company way more than I ever thought possible. I'd even started to look forward to our meetings. And that was a good thing. It's nice to get along with people you work with. It probably wasn't that unusual to message them outside of work hours now and then.

Or even constantly.

It wasn't that strange to send him the picture of Abby in the pirate costume. We'd just been talking about Vivi Tempest. I glanced at my purse, resting innocently on the front passenger seat. There was a slim gift-wrapped volume inside. After our last meeting, I asked Granny to sign one for him. I'd had to restrain her from writing a long, gushing message. I think she'd have done anything for him after I'd finally cracked and showed her the tattoo. She cried more than I had. Abby loved it too. Once she'd learned the history behind it, she'd demanded the bunny story every night at bedtime. The only thing she minded was that I'd gone to see Joel without her. Apparently, their brief meeting had made more of an impression than I'd thought. When I'd let slip that he'd be doing the face painting at her school carnival, her eyes lit up.

That was another reason to keep things professional. The last thing I'd want would be to let her get attached to someone, only to be let down when things inevitably went wrong. Ever since she was born, I'd tried to surround her with so much love that she'd never notice something was missing. So far it had worked. She was a well-adjusted kid, surrounded by people who adored her. Her life was happy and stable, and I refused to jeopardize that. Not for anything.

Jesus! All this from some frosting?

This argument had been chasing its tail around my brain since I'd pulled out of my driveway after lunch. Joel and I had scheduled a meeting to wrap up some final details before the launch of the website. I'd also drawn up a plan for dealing with their lack of social media presence. Lily was the lynchpin. I'd persuaded Joel he should take advantage of the fact that she was always glued to her phone rather than just complaining about it. The best way to navigate the digital world was to use a native guide.

I stopped for coffee on the way. I got as far as opening my mouth to give Magda my order before she plonked it on the counter, ready to go.

Damn that woman!

But it was impossible not to like her. And she had me over

a barrel. Coffee that good was worth the smirk and the suggestive wink.

I'd expected to find Joel alone. It was Lily's half-day and Zel had a booth at a fetish fayre. I wasn't sure if I was relieved or disappointed when I found him talking to a short older woman. The sensible skirt, floral blouse, and lack of any visible tattoos led me to think she wasn't a customer. It also seemed unlikely he'd let his customers brush imaginary lint from his shoulders.

He let you suck his thumb.

When the door opened, they both turned around. Joel flushed bright red, and the woman gave me a warm smile.

"Oh!" she said. "It looks like you have a customer. I should go."

"She's—"

"I'm not—"

We both rushed to answer at once, and the woman looked between us with polite confusion.

"Is this a friend of yours, Joey?"

Joel scowled and rubbed at the back of his neck.

"This is Olivia. She's been helping me build a website."

The woman's smile broadened, and she stepped towards me, hand outstretched.

"Hi, there! I'm Joey's Aunt Loretta. We've heard lots about you, of course. But it's nice to finally meet you."

"Really? Joel's talked about me?"

I shot a glance over her shoulder, but he refused to meet my eye.

"Not exactly. You know what he's like."

Loretta gave me a conspiratorial smile. I tried to smile back, but I felt uneasy. Joel looked uncomfortable and annoyed. He'd been perfectly friendly when I sent my last text. What had changed since last night? Loretta prattled on, oblivious.

"I just heard through the grapevine that Joel had been spending a lot of time with a young lady."

"When you say grapevine, you mean Crystal."

Joel was vigorously rearranging the various objects on the welcome desk. Now I knew something was wrong. He had a habit of moving things around when he was annoyed. I did the same thing. The kitchen cupboards were always at their most organized when I was dealing with a difficult client or experiencing a nasty bout of PMS. Loretta sighed.

"You know she means well."

"She needs to mind her own business."

"Crystal is my daughter," Loretta said helpfully. "Joel's cousin. Really, Joey! Haven't you told this poor girl anything about your family?"

"Why would I?"

It hurt. Despite the conversation I'd been having with myself in the car, the vehemence of the question hit me like a slap in the face. Loretta just smiled and shook her head.

"Don't listen to him," she said. "He's just in one of his moods. He's been going around for weeks with a face that would curdle milk."

"Oh."

The last few weeks. In other words, since he'd been working with me. A wave of humiliation washed over me, making my cheeks burn. I'd never felt like more of a fool. All this time I thought he'd been enjoying my company. Had I truly driven him crazy enough that his family had noticed something?

"I don't know what he's been like with you, Olivia," Loretta continued. "But I haven't seen him this cranky since he was a teenager. Just when you think he'd be all smiles and sunshine too."

I had trouble imagining Joel ever being 'all smiles and sunshine.' The shock and hurt twisted themselves into anger. Hotter, brighter, yet somehow less excruciating.

"I don't know," I said tightly. "People don't always say how they truly feel. Sometimes it can seem like someone's enjoying themselves when actually they'd chew their arm off to get away. It's tough when you run a business and you have so many tedious people making demands on your time."

Joel's dark eyebrows drew together, and he looked at me with a strange frown. Loretta chuckled.

"Joel's never been one to grin and bear things. Even when he should. You should come over sometime and I'll show you some of his school pageant photos. I've never seen a butternut squash look so furious."

Right now, he looked more like a furious beet. Or maybe an angry radish. He'd moved from shuffling papers to opening and closing drawers. Good, let him suffer. Memories of being forced on stage as a vegetable were obviously traumatic, but it was nothing compared to what I was feeling.

"After I'd spent all that time on the costume too," Loretta said. "Of course, I don't know what a butternut squash had to do with Thanksgiving. There were a lot of kids in his grade, and they wanted everybody to have a part, so they just kept adding vegetables."

It occurred to me that I should introduce Loretta to Granny V. They had the same circuitous approach to conversation. At a certain point, you just had to shrug and hang on for the ride.

"School pageants are their own special kind of torment," I said. "In the last few years, Abby's been a witch, a pirate, a polar bear cub, and a praying mantis with a passion for music."

That costume had been a real bitch. At the mention of Abby, Loretta's face lit up again.

"Oh, yes. Crystal mentioned you had a little girl. How old is she?"

I didn't know where Crystal had got her information, but I couldn't fault her research.

"Seven and a half."

"That'd put her in the same grade as Crystal's twins."

I braced myself. If she was anything like Granny V, the winding conversation train would turn into an unstoppable juggernaut once it moved into the territory of grandkids. I was so busy bracing myself to coo at photographs that she managed to blindside me.

"We're having a family BBQ on Labor Day weekend. You and your little girl should come along if you don't have plans."

Joel clasped the back of his neck with both hands and raised his eyes to the ceiling. I could hear him willing me to say no. Part of me wanted to say yes, just to spite him. But I was bigger than that. I turned back to Loretta and forced my face into a smile.

"That's a lovely offer, but I don't want to impose."

"Nonsense. We'd love to have you, wouldn't we, Joey?"

"Yeah," said Joel tonelessly. "Love to."

You bastard!

I frantically scrambled for another excuse, but Loretta was deaf to all protest.

"Good, it's all settled then," she said brightly. "Now, I must be getting along. I'll leave you two kids to your Google page or what have you."

Joel firmly ushered his aunt out while I silently fumed. He closed the door behind her with a bang that set all my nerves jangling.

"Great! Best timing ever," he snarled. "Now she's going to think we're dating."

"Yeah," I said bitterly. "Because that would suck, right?"

"And what's she supposed to think when you show up like that?"

Excuse me?

"We had a meeting!"

"I don't mean that. I mean you just breeze in all..."

He trailed off and made an incomprehensible motion with his arms.

"Am I supposed to have the slightest idea what that means?"

Joel clenched his fists and closed his eyes, grimacing like he was in pain.

"I don't know. Y-you just walk in and...and it feels like you belong here."

"Sorry to have overstayed my welcome," I said, fighting to keep my voice steady. "Best not drag this out any more than we have to."

I perched on the edge of the welcome desk, put down the cups, and rummaged feverishly in my purse. My throat constricted when I felt the crinkle of gift wrap.

God, I'm such an idiot!

Joel still stood by the door, motionless as a statue.

"Olivia," he muttered hoarsely. "I'm just trying to say that—"

"You don't have to say anything. A couple more meetings and we'll be out of each other's hair for good. It's what we both want, right? I brought you a coffee by the way. You should drink it before it gets cold."

He snorted mirthlessly and shook his head.

"Of course you brought me a coffee. Why wouldn't you? That's really fucking considerate of you! Is it too much to ask for you to make this easy for me?"

"Oh. I am so done with this."

I leaped up from the desk and swung my purse back onto my shoulder. Both cups of coffee went flying, their contents sloshing spectacularly across the desk. Joel swore and rushed to rescue the appointment book from the dark, fragrant tide. I noticed his sketchbook just in time and grabbed it automatically.

"Here," I shoved the book into his arms. Despite his size, I caught him off-balance, and he stumbled back. "Call me when you're done being an ass and we can reschedule this meeting."

"Come on, you're being ridiculous."

I blinked.

"Oh no! Don't you dare turn this around on me. I've had it with the mood swings and the mixed signals. I'm at least 10 years too old for that shit. It wasn't cute on Edward Cullen, and it does nothing for you."

"Edward Cullen?" he repeated. "Don't you think that's a little unfair?"

I shrugged.

"I don't think so. He's prettier than you, but you're both toxic jerks."

"Wait!"

I turned to leave, and his hand closed around my arm—not hard, but firm. I felt the heat of his grip through my sweater and my heart raced. I turned back, ready to tell him exactly how I felt about being manhandled, but the words died on my lips. His flinty grey eyes smoldered and there were two spots of color high on his cheeks. Time stopped. Tension crackled between us and every nerve in my body thrummed like a tightly drawn bowstring. We were both breathing hard. Then it happened. I don't know which of us moved first, but suddenly we were joined in a desperate tangle of limbs, our mouths crushing together. There was no finesse. Weeks of suppressed impulses and fevered fantasies broke out in a hot, pulsing deluge. I bit his lip and he grunted, fisting his hands in my hair. His tugging sent delicious prickles from my scalp to my toes, and I shivered against him. He ran his hands down my back, cupping my ass and pulling me against him. His mouth was hard and demanding and I parted my lips with a soft moan. Surrender never felt so amazing. I was drowning in him, and I didn't want to be saved. I wanted to caress every inch of him, feel his—

"Shit! Sorry. I can come back if—"

We broke apart hastily. A nervous young man with a Slipknot t-shirt and a face full of pimples hovered in the doorway. Mortified, I covered my face with my shaking hands.

"Olivia?"

Joel's voice sounded small and far away, barely audible over the roaring in my ears. I felt his hand on my shoulder, but I shrugged it off. Then I was running. I wasn't sure how or why. My body and brain had disconnected. Before I knew what I was doing I had shoved past the boy and out of the door. I kept going, not even sure where I was going. I just had to get away.

What the hell have I done?

CHAPTER SEVENTEEN

Olivia

"Regarding last-minute additions to our carnival fundraiser, I'm opening the floor to suggestions."

I sat up straighter and stifled a yawn. The meeting had been running for over an hour. At this point, any suggestions I had for Marsha involved serious breaches of the PTA code of conduct.

"How about something educational?"

When Dave-the-entomologist spoke up, I suppressed a grin. If his Facebook was anything to go by, Dave had added several new specimens to his massive tarantula collection, and he was always angling to bring them to school events. I had no issue with it, but looking at the expression on Marsha's face, he might have suggested an acid-chugging contest. Her sugary smile took on a frozen quality. She looked like she needed to pass gas.

"Thinking back to our Halloween festival and the unfortunate incident with the petting zoo, I don't think that poisonous animals—"

"Venomous."

"Pardon?"

"They're venomous animals," Dave said. "Poison is—"

"Getting back to the point."

Two spots of color rose on Marsha's cheeks and a muscle flickered below one eye.

"I don't want to be a downer here, but when it comes to the well-being of our children and the reputation of this school, we'd do well to remember our three watch words. What are they, people? Say them with me now."

"Age-appropriate, sensible, and safe," we droned.

At some point, I needed to quit the PTA and join a more reasonable cult.

"That's right," Marsha said. "When in doubt, we turn to A.S.S."

She didn't think that acronym through.

"On that note, Olivia?"

"Yes?"

I hated the heat creeping up my neck, hated that I sounded so flustered. If you ever wonder what happens to those mean girls in high school who giggle behind your back and make fun of your shoes—this is their final form. Petty dictators on local committees. If the universe were playing fair, she'd have been an uptight stick-in-the-mud in a twinset and pearls. It's easy to dismiss a walking cliché. Instead, she was a single mom, like me. A successful realtor who somehow had the time to raise her daughter, rule the PTA with an iron fist, and constantly look like she'd stepped off the front page of *Vogue.* I was willing to bet *she'd* never left the house wearing her morning coffee and a pair of ratty slippers. She either dabbled in black magic or she'd discovered the secret of time travel. If that wasn't bad enough, most of the kids loved her. She was a fun mom. A *cool* mom. The kind of mom who let her six-year-old carry a smartphone and thought bedtimes were old-fashioned. How could I compete with that?

"We're counting on you for the face-painting," she said. "Have the artists confirmed the booking?"

Define 'confirmed.'

I cleared my throat.

"We, uh, have an understanding."

That was one way of putting it. Definitely a better option than, "I'm not entirely sure. We kissed, I fled from his studio, and we haven't spoken in a week." I kept telling myself I should call him, or at least send him a message. But somehow, I always had something better to do, like baking cookies, folding laundry, or arranging my bookshelves alphabetically... and then rearranging them by color. Sometimes I even convinced myself I didn't need to call him. However awkward things were between us, we made a deal, and he wouldn't let me down. Would he?

Marsha gave a long-suffering sigh.

"I have to say, Olivia, this is all sounding a little bit nebulous for my taste. We're taking a big chance here."

Honey dripped from every word like venom from a cobra's fangs.

"Are we?" I asked innocently.

Marsha clasped her hands in front of her stomach and addressed me with exaggerated delicacy.

"Oh dear, I didn't want to bring this up in front of everyone. You and I both know we live in a colorful and diverse world. If it were up to me, I'd say live and let live but not everyone is as open minded as I am. Some of the other parents have raised concerns about exposing the children to the more unconventional members of your social circle."

You poisonous bitch.

I glanced around the room, but no one except Dave deigned to meet my eye. I knew what this was about. Marsha had wanted to give the commission to her niece, who was training to be a make-up artist. After a review of the portfolios, Joel and Zel had won the vote by a landslide. Marsha was still livid.

"Don't worry," I said tightly. "I think you'll find they're fully ass-compliant."

Someone snorted. The smile evaporated from Marsha's face, and she stared at me coldly.

"Let's hope you're right," she said smoothly. "Incidentally, the budget is stretched very tightly this year. It would be a shame if we needed to review the numbers for our trip to Montreal."

My mouth went dry. Surely, she'd never stoop so low. Abby's class was taking a two-day trip to Montreal in the fall, and she was incredibly excited. She'd traveled outside the U.S. before, but this was the first time she was doing it without me. The fact that they spoke a different language in Montreal made it feel even more like a voyage into the unknown. She'd be heartbroken if she couldn't go. I could only pray that my instincts about Joel were right. Despite her veiled threat, Marsha still had the gall to corner me before I left and remind me that she was waiting on my RSVP for Fiona's 7th birthday party.

As the day of the carnival drew nearer, my anxiety ramped up to a boiling froth. I barely got a wink of sleep the night before and I was functioning on autopilot. Before the morning was up, I managed to put salt in my coffee and accidentally email Abby's homework assignment to a difficult client. The anxiety of not knowing whether Joel would show up ate at me. The smug triumph on Marsha's face would be bad enough, but there was more than just my dignity on the line. I couldn't bear the thought of disappointing Abby. I was counting on Joel to come through, and that terrified me. After what happened with Abby's father, I swore I'd never rely on a man again. Being unceremoniously dumped while eight months pregnant is a pretty harsh lesson in self-reliance. But now (even if it was only briefly) my own and my daughter's happiness were in someone else's hands.

That was the maddening thing about Joel. He was far too good at taking my perfectly ordered life and upending it. When he was around, I lost all control over myself. Despite my resolutions, things between us had gotten complicated. We could deny our feelings all we liked, but we couldn't deny that kiss. Desperate, raw, hungry. Thinking about it still made me shiver.

If I was honest, I was terrified he wouldn't show up, but I was equally terrified of what might happen if he did.

I arrived late after a meeting with a client over-ran, and preparation for the carnival had already begun. The kids had been given a half-day from school so the adults could set up in peace. Abby would be showing up with Granny V and Russ later.

The bouncy castle stood half-inflated, like a melting dessert, and various stalls and displays peppered the football field. I scanned the area anxiously, but there was no sign of Joel or Zel. I bit my lip and tried to ignore the churning in my stomach.

An hour. Forty-five minutes. A half hour. Fifteen minutes. The opening of the carnival was rapidly approaching and still no Joel. Marsha caught my eye a couple of times and tapped pointedly at her watch. I managed to meet her raised eyebrow with a serene smile. It helped to imagine her head exploding.

Come on, Joel!

Finally, with less than 10 minutes to go, I spotted a familiar car. My heart leaped. I had never been happier to see anyone. Marsha had been moving towards me with a malevolent sense of purpose, and their arrival stopped her in her tracks. Joel was a handsome guy at the best of times, but now he seemed to glow, showing up in the nick of time and wiping the smirk off Marsha's face. We were entering knight in shining armor territory.

He came. He promised he'd show and he didn't let me down.

He didn't come over to greet me; I just got a stiff smile and a wave. This was something of a relief. I was so dangerously elated to see him that I didn't trust my mouth to listen to my brain.

I'd been put in charge of the lucky dip, and from where I was sitting, I had a clear view of the face-painting stall. They were certainly popular. From the moment they set up, they had a permanent line of kids. Lots of people who come to school events can be awkward with the children like they're dealing with an alien species, but Joel was so natural. I couldn't tell what he was saying to them, but there was a lot of giggling. At one point, I looked up to discover Joel sitting in the painting chair and Zel painting his face a violent shade of pink. This was clearly being done to indulge the crowd clustering around them. It was one of the cutest things I had ever seen.

All afternoon I could barely drag my eyes away from him. I sat in a dreamy reverie like a simpering schoolgirl. It was fortunate that manning the lucky dip didn't require laser focus. If they'd carried over our assignments from last year, I'd have been manning the shooting range. That could've gotten ugly. As it was, I almost missed a gangly freckled boy trying to slip his hand in the prize bucket without buying a ticket. After I'd finished chewing him out, I returned to my post and found Joel standing patiently at the front of the queue.

Suddenly my hands were sweaty and my tongue felt like wax.

Ok, Olivia, be cool.

"Hey! Hi, are you?"

Perfect.

He cleared his throat and tucked a stray hair behind his ear.

"I'm...uh. I'm fine. I guess. Can't complain."

The awkward silence swelled and condensed around us like damp fog.

"Wow," I chuckled ruefully. "We're so good at this."

"Yeah. Go us. Er, s-so how've you been?"

"Pretty good."

"Good."

He licked his lips nervously.

"Look, Olivia, about what happened—"

To my horror, my lips twitched, and a laugh bubbled into my throat. Despite my feelings, it was downright surreal to be having this conversation with the Pink Panther. In a faraway portion of my brain that hadn't been lost to hysteria, I made a mental note to book Zel for Abby's next birthday party. He was talented.

The giggle burst from my nose as a snort, and a hurt look flashed across Joel's face.

"I'm sorry," I said hastily. "It's not you, it's the face. You look kinda—"

"Ridiculous? Sorry about that. The kids insisted and Zel was more than happy to throw me under the bus. But hear me out for a minute. Close your eyes if you have to. What happened between us—it was intense, but I don't think it has to be a big deal. I mean, clearly, there was something brewing under the surface for both of us, but these things happen. We're both adults and I don't think we should over-analyze—"

Joel blushed. His monologue had been cut short by the sound of someone loudly clearing their throat. The stall had been quiet when he came over, but it wasn't quiet anymore. Neither of us had noticed the long, snaking queue building up behind him. I cupped my hands over my face.

Maybe the ground will open up and swallow me if I wish really hard.

Joel thrust his hands into his pockets and bit the inside of his cheek.

"Ok, so how does this thing work?" he asked gruffly.

"Um..."

I scrambled frantically for the missing pieces of my brain.

"You give me 50 cents and then you get to dip your hand in the bucket and pick out a prize."

He rummaged in his pocket and dropped the coins on the

table. One large, colorful hand disappeared into the bucket, and I heard the rustle of the packing peanuts.

"Huh. Look at that. Haven't had these in years."

His mouth quirked into a half-smile, and he held up a packet of Sweethearts.

Damn! Do they even make that candy anymore?

By the time the carnival wrapped up, I was exhausted. Granny V and Russ had volunteered to take Abby for the night, and I was thinking fond thoughts of the bathtub and my bed. I'd avoided looking at Joel since he'd walked away from my table with a roll of Sweethearts in his pocket and an unreadable expression on his face. I told myself I hadn't even been thinking about him. He and Zel were still packing up when I left to go to my car. I made sure to rummage for a vitally important, non-existent item in my purse when I walked past. Despite the prickling in the back of my neck and the somersaults in my stomach, I managed not to look back.

Flopping bonelessly into the driver's seat, I dumped my purse on the front seat and turned the keys in the ignition. My heart sank into my shoes. Instead of the thrum of the engine roaring into life, I was greeted by a series of loud, staccato clicks.

Fuck!

CHAPTER EIGHTEEN

Joel

"Toss me those pads."

Zel looked up from packing the paints away and threw me a packet of cotton pads.

"You could just go home and take a shower."

"I feel like an idiot."

I put lotion on the pad and scrubbed at my lurid pink cheeks.

"Lighten up, man. The kids loved it. If this is the scheduled time for you to turn back into a grumpkin, you should at least wait until we're off school grounds."

Without thinking, I raised my hand to flip him off. A blonde woman with a clipboard fixed us with a glare and I turned the gesture into a vague hand wave. It didn't matter anyway; Zel's attention was fixed on something over my shoulder.

"Your girlfriend's leaving."

I missed the makeup pad and squirted a blob of lotion into my lap. Cursing, I reached for some dry pads and dabbed hopefully at my crotch.

"She's not my girlfriend."

"Whatever she is, she's coming this way," Zel said urgently. "Say something!"

I kept my eyes fixed on my lap. It felt like my tongue was glued to the roof of my mouth. I couldn't see her, but I sensed her passing by and recognized the light floral scent of her shampoo. The hot blush spread from my neck to my ears. I wasn't sure whether I was relieved or annoyed that she hadn't acknowledged me. But who could blame her? I'd made a complete idiot of myself, and I'd embarrassed her too. What kind of moron approaches a woman for an intimate chat while made up as the Pink Panther?

"Really? Nothing?"

Zel shut the paint case with a snap and turned to me with a hand on his hip.

"You drove like a maniac to get here, but you barely said two words to the poor woman all afternoon."

"I'm here to work. And I wouldn't have needed to drive like a maniac if you'd been ready on time for once."

Zel shook his head with a resigned sigh.

"Mama told me the honeymoon period wouldn't last. If I'd known you'd be this much of a nag, I'd never have married you."

I rolled my eyes and wiped the final smear of pink paint from my nose.

"Seriously though," Zel said. "You've been acting weird all week and today you ran two red lights to get to a school carnival. You trying to claim you nearly killed us both in the name of punctuality?"

I closed my eyes and let out a slow breath. I had no answer for Zel. He was right. I was desperate to see Olivia, but at the same time, I didn't trust myself to be anywhere near her. Several times I'd been on the point of messaging her and canceling the booking, but the thought of letting her down triggered a sharp ache in my belly. It was why I'd yelled at Zel when he was late, and why I'd driven like a crazy person.

Despite all this, I hadn't been prepared for what would happen when I saw her. It was like being punched in the chest. I'd wanted to go and speak to her, but I couldn't manage anything more than a stiff wave.

You should sleep with her.

Dustin's words echoed in my mind. I wanted to. I wanted her so badly it hurt. And she wanted me too; kisses like that don't come from nowhere. It was one of the hottest things I'd ever experienced, but it had intensified my hunger rather than satisfying it. A tiny taste had taken a fascination and transformed it into a burning obsession. What would happen if we slept together? Would it loosen this permanent knot in my chest—or pull it tighter until neither of us could escape?

"Go catch up with her."

I blinked. Zel grabbed the back of my chair and began tipping it forwards.

"Hey," I yelled, digging my heels into the ground and scrabbling for purchase. "What the hell are you—"

"I'm doing you a favor. Now go."

I staggered to my feet and glared at him. He held up a finger, forestalling any protest.

"If you don't start walking, I'll tell Loretta about the time your special brownies got mixed in with the desserts for the 4th of July potluck."

On the upside, everyone really enjoyed the fireworks that year.

I clenched my fists and stormed off, fuming. I didn't have to look at Zel to know he was sporting a smug grin. Not that it mattered; she'd probably left already. That would be...a relief?

The parking lot was almost deserted. The families were long gone and most of the stalls had packed up too. I scanned the parking lot and saw Olivia's car. As I got closer, I saw her in the front seat. She was repeatedly gunning the engine and getting nothing but an ominous clicking sound.

Uh-oh.

I rested my hand on the roof and tapped gently on the

window. She rolled it down and squinted up at me. There were dark circles under her eyes, her cheeks were flushed, and her hair was in disarray. She looked—fuck! She still looked beautiful.

"Where's the pink panther?" she asked dully.

I shrugged.

"Cartoon maybe, or a fiberglass commercial. I don't know, he's a busy cat."

She narrowed her eyes.

"Has anyone ever told you you're lucky you're cute?"

"Not since I started growing facial hair. You having a little trouble here?"

She sat back in her seat and gestured helplessly.

"Can't get the darn thing started. I know it's not vapor lock and I changed the battery just last month."

"Hmmm."

I wandered to the front of the car and tugged the bonnet open. I don't know what I was hoping to achieve. I knew as much about cars as I did about brain surgery. I stared at the confusing tangle of metal innards and rubbed a hand over my chin.

"Yep!" I declared. "That, er...that definitely looks broken."

"Wow. Are you sure you're not a mechanic?"

I held my hands up sheepishly.

"You got me there. I've been told I'm a pretty passable chauffeur, though."

"What?"

"Zel should've finished packing up by now. We could give you a ride home if you like."

She looked at me for a long moment and chewed on her lip.

"O-ok," she said tentatively. "That'd be great if it's not too much trouble."

"No trouble at all."

I moved back to let her get out. When she grabbed her

purse and swung it over her shoulder a curtain of hair shifted, exposing the nape of her neck. I noticed that the label was poking out of the back of her shirt and my fingers itched to tuck it back in.

I thrust my hands into my pockets and encountered the small hard roll of Sweethearts. More for something to do than anything else, I took out the packet and opened it.

"Want one?" I asked, thrusting it at Olivia.

She gave me a withering look but held out her hand anyway. She held up the small, chalky disk and squinted at it.

If we were in a movie, it would say something cute.

"Apparently you need me to fax you."

Swing and a miss.

"I'm starting to suspect that candy might be expired."

Olivia smiled wryly.

"I wouldn't be surprised. I'm convinced someone at the PTA has a stash of unwanted Halloween candy and it just gets recycled for every event."

"Wow. Nasty."

"Believe me, you got lucky."

I raised a skeptical eyebrow.

"Seriously?"

"I was at that Lucky Dip table all afternoon. I've seen things. Many intrepid souls fell victim to the Necco wafers."

I snorted with laughter. How did she do that? It was the darndest thing. She could have me boiling mad within seconds, but at the same time, I couldn't recall laughing this much with anyone, not even Zel. We were still giggling when we made it back to the face-painting table. By this point, Zel had almost finished packing up.

"Hey, Zel. All packed up?"

"Pretty much."

He looked at Olivia and gave me a questioning glance.

"S-she had some car trouble," I said hastily. "We're giving her a ride home."

Zel raised his eyebrows, a grin slowly spreading across his face. I pushed a hand through my hair and shuffled awkwardly.

"So, um. Ready to go?"

Zel clutched his head theatrically.

"Silly me. I forgot to tell you. There's been a slight change of plans."

"What do you mean?"

"Something came up and I have to go."

I frowned suspiciously.

"What do you mean, you have to go?"

"I have an unexpected rendezvous at...a location within convenient walking distance."

"Zel," I growled.

He shrugged apologetically.

"Sorry. Gotta go. Can't keep my unspecified companion waiting."

With that, he bounced off, thumping me affectionately on the shoulder as he breezed past. I closed my eyes and clenched my jaw.

I'm going to kill him.

I looked at Olivia out of the corner of my eye. She looked like she was trying not to laugh.

The car ride home was quiet. Barring one embarrassing moment when I remembered I had no idea where she lived, we didn't talk much. I kept sneaking glances at her. For most of the journey, she sat back in her seat staring out of the window. I wondered what she was thinking. That was another strange thing about her. I usually had to know someone longer than a couple of months before I gave any thought to what was going on in their head.

Her neighborhood was just what I'd expected. A cozy suburban street filled with gleaming cars and perfectly manicured lawns. The kind of street where the sight of someone like me provoked raised eyebrows and twitched curtains. I glared at the surrounding houses, daring their neat facades to judge me. I didn't belong here. Olivia probably felt it too. Time to drop her off and be gone as quickly as possible.

"Would you like to come in for coffee?"

"Huh?"

I blinked at her stupidly. She blushed and bit her lip.

"I-I could show you the final design for the website. Also, I have something for you. I meant to give it to you last time we met but—"

I licked my dry lips.

"Sure," I croaked.

What could she have to give me? I stepped from the car as if in a dream. I felt curiosity, but there was something else too. Trepidation? Anticipation? Numbly, I followed her onto the porch and hovered behind her as she searched her purse for her keys. Unspoken tension crackled between us, and I was hyper-aware of everything. I wasn't just going through a door. I was crossing an invisible, more significant threshold. I couldn't shake the feeling that once I entered that house, there was no going back.

CHAPTER NINETEEN

Olivia

"Would you like to come in for coffee?"

I knew how it sounded as soon as the words were out of my mouth. But I couldn't take it back now. I wanted to give him the book. It was a great way of saying thank you, and constantly carrying it around in my purse was getting weird. I'd reach in for something else, my hand would find it and I'd remember that day, the taste of him, the feel of his lips. Then the blush set in. I'd had more than one person delicately ask if I was feeling well.

Having Joel in the house was strange. Abby and I had guests all the time, but this felt different. I never usually have the urge to run around straightening things up, or panic that I'd left my underwear in the dryer. The fact that Joel had already seen me in my underwear made no difference. This was a different kind of intimacy—like I'd just opened a door that had been closed for a long time.

Leaving Joel in the sitting room, I retreated to the kitchen and soothed myself with the familiar rituals of making coffee. As an afterthought, I grabbed the bottle of honey and put it on the tray.

I found Joel squatting by the couch, inspecting the tableau

of stuffed animals still there from Abby's last play session. As I watched, he picked up a sparkly purple dragon, fiddled with its wings, and turned it over to examine its tags.

"If you're going to do that to Mr. Sparkle Dragon, you should at least buy him dinner first."

Joel froze, squatting on the floor and looking at me wide-eyed. This 6-foot-4 man covered in tattoos suddenly looked like a kid who'd been caught with his hand in the cookie jar.

"Sorry. I-I was a little curious as to what was going on here."

He grinned sheepishly and gestured at the plushie summit.

"That's a maternity ward," I said, placing the tray on the coffee table. "Olaf's expecting."

"Isn't Olaf a dude?"

I shrugged and flopped onto the couch.

"I find it's best not to ask. Just go with the flow."

"Fair enough."

He replaced the dragon and joined me on the couch. There was a respectable distance between us, but we were still pretty close. He'd missed a smear of pink paint next to his ear.

"So, is Mr. Sparkle Dragon the baby daddy?"

I raised an eyebrow and looked at him severely.

"Don't be silly! He's the doula."

He chuckled and shook his head.

"That's an impressive imagination."

"She's very excited to be getting a baby cousin. Erin's about to hit the third trimester, so the hype train has officially left the station."

I pushed the plunger on the French press and carefully poured two cups.

"It's not quite a black-eyed bee, but we do have some honey."

I nudged the bear in his direction, and he gave me a shy smile. For a few moments, we sipped in silence while my stomach did flip-flops. Giving him the book was meant to be something casual, but I couldn't work up the nerve to do it, and the longer I left it, the more significant it felt. It was a vicious circle.

God! Why is this so hard?

"Thank you for today," I said awkwardly. "It...it meant a lot to the kids."

He hunched his shoulders in a twitchy shrug.

"Deal's a deal. You've done amazing work on the website. It'd be pretty shitty of me not to hold up my end."

"I know. But it still meant a lot. Here."

I took the gift-wrapped book out of my purse and thrust it at him. He didn't say anything for a long time. When he turned to the first page and found my grandmother's message, he blinked rapidly.

"Wow," he said eventually. "This is awesome."

"It's no big deal. I knew Granny had some copies lying around from an early print run. It was easy enough to get her to sign one for you. I'm just sorry she got so carried away."

He traced his fingers over Granny V's scrawl and his lips quirked into the cutest half-smile.

"Take it she liked the tattoo, then."

"How could you tell?" I asked dryly. "In fact, she wants you to do her next."

"I'd be honored."

I arched an eyebrow. I'd expected him to laugh, but he seemed sincere.

At some point, he might stop surprising me.

He flipped to the first chapter and his grin widened.

"It must've been great to grow up surrounded by these stories. It's so cool that she's based them on you."

I grimaced and wound my hands tighter around my cup.

"Yeah I, er—I hated ViVi."

"How come?"

I took a deep breath. Was I really about to get into this?

"I was an adventurous kid when I was little. Granny loves

to tell everyone about the time she lost me at the play park. I must've been about three. Nolan was fussing so she turned her back on me for a second, and when she turned around, I was gone."

I stared into my cup, swirling the dregs of my coffee like I was trying to read tea leaves. Joel sat back with his hands on his knees. He wasn't looking at me, but I could tell he was listening intently.

"She looked frantically around for a minute or two before she finally thought to look up. I was still toddling, but somehow, I'd found my way to the very top of the jungle gym."

Joel smiled softly.

"A teeny-tiny explorer, huh?"

"Always. Lots of kids cry on their first day of school, but not me. I couldn't wait to get in there. Desperate for my next adventure. I wasn't afraid of anything until—"

"Until what?"

I swallowed around the lump in my throat. It was so rare I tried to put words around this.

"When I was 9 my parents divorced. Dad moved to Dubai and Mom had a meltdown. Nolan and I went to live with Granny."

"Sounds rough," said Joel gently.

"I guess it was. Granny was amazing. Still is. But everything changed so much and so fast. Suddenly the world didn't feel safe to explore anymore. I withdrew into myself and stopped taking risks. It felt like Vivi was based on a version of me that didn't exist anymore. She made me feel guilty, like I wasn't living up to her image or something. I think Abby's father was the first impulsive decision I'd made in years, and look how that turned out. I gave up a prestigious internship just to be with him, only for him to abandon me when I was eight months pregnant." I swallowed hard, unprepared for the lump in my throat. "When he left me, I was a wreck. I'd always been good at holding it together, but I completely fell apart. Granny basically had to come and rescue me. Charles probably wouldn't even have known his daughter's name if Nolan hadn't tracked him down and sued him for child support. I hated leaning on them like that—hated feeling so helpless."

I shook my head and put down my mug. I wasn't used to revealing this much and I was fighting the desire to cram the words back into my mouth.

"That person your grandmother saw is still in there."

I froze in the act of putting my mug back on the tray and stared at him.

"She came marching into my studio with her head held high and demanded I design her a tattoo."

He squeezed my shoulder with one hand and gently prized the cup from my fingers with the other.

"Your grandmother's a smart lady. It's not hard to see what she saw in you."

My eyes burned and my vision swam. I swallowed and blinked rapidly.

"So," I said, forcing a light-hearted edge into my voice. "I'm sitting next to a huge Vivi fanboy who also happens to be covered in pirate tattoos. I think you know what I'm going to ask."

He rolled his eyes.

"Yes. Yes, I do."

"Can I see?"

He heaved a long-suffering sigh and pulled his vest over his head. My heart sped up. I'd never seen him shirtless before. My fantasies didn't do him justice. His torso was a vibrant sculpted tableau of images that made me think simultaneously of lazy tropical beaches and violent stormy seas. He was breathtaking. He knelt in front of the couch with his back to me and glanced over his shoulder.

"It's on my back. Can't miss it."

Much of his back was taken up by a banana tree. The trunk grew up one side of his torso and the leaves fanned over his shoulder. And there, perched in the canopy, with a banana in his beak, was a familiar scarlet macaw in a tiny tricorne hat.

"Bones!"

"Yep. He was there before the tree was. One of the earliest tattoos I got."

Unable to resist, I reached out and stroked my fingers over the parrot. Joel shivered and a rash of goosebumps flared up under the ink.

"Why do you like the books so much?" I asked, still idly stroking his skin.

"Pirates are cool."

The words were flippant, but there was something strained in his voice. His breathing had become suspiciously heavy.

"Nothing else to it?"

"Nope. Well, mostly. The thing about Vivi was that she was always moving. I liked that idea. Whatever happened, she could always pick up the anchor and go to the next island. I remember every book always ended with the ship sailing off into the sunset. It was like a clean slate. Nothing weighing her down."

What's weighing you down?

The question I'd been yearning to ask. I could feel it with everything he said, every step he took. An invisible force pressed down on his shoulders. I wanted to ask but I couldn't find the words. Instead, I put one hand on each of his shoulders and squeezed, working my fingers into the tense muscle. Joel let his head fall back and groaned.

Fuck!

That noise went straight to my pussy. My mouth was completely dry. It seemed as though every drop of moisture in my body was soaking into my panties. I squeezed harder, his skin hot under my hands.

"Shit!"

He let out a strangled curse and his hand shot back and grabbed my wrist.

"Don't," he said sharply.

"What's the matter? Did I hurt you?"

"Nope. Definitely not."

I peered over his shoulder. The thick outline of his cock strained against the fabric of his shorts.

"Oh!"

I gasped and let go of his shoulders. He knelt up and shuffled around to face me.

"I'm sorry," I whispered. "I shouldn't have—"

My hands flew to my face, but he caught them and held them in both of his. We were nose to nose. I wanted to say something, but I'd forgotten how to breathe, let alone speak.

"We shouldn't stay like this," he breathed.

"No," I said. "One of us should stand up now."

"Yep. Any minute now I'm gonna get up and walk away."

One hand slid up and cupped my face. He smoothed his thumb over my cheekbone, staring at me as though hypnotized. I held my breath, trembling. My awareness of my body had condensed to three throbbing points of arousal. The thumb that had been stroking my cheek whispered over my lips, leaving delicious tingles in its wake. On impulse, I opened my mouth and sucked at this thumb, rippling my tongue over the tip, grazing it with my teeth. Joel let out a low, throaty moan. I released his thumb with a wet pop and stared at him, breath coming fast, lips slightly parted.

"Fuck it!"

With a low, rumbling exclamation that was almost a growl, Joel seized me around the waist and pulled me off the couch and into his lap.

CHAPTER TWENTY

Olivia

It wasn't soft. It wasn't romantic. The kiss was hard, fevered, frantic. My head spun with it.

It had taken a moment to regain my equilibrium after he'd pulled me into his lap, but now I straddled him and threw my arms around his neck. Weeks of yearning, of resisting. I'd hit pause on the looping track in my brain telling me what a bad idea this was. There would be time for 'ifs,' 'buts,' and 'maybes' later. All I knew was that I wanted him. I was hungry for him.

He ran his nails down my back, making my nerves crackle and buzz. It wasn't enough. I needed to feel his hands on my bare skin and press my body against his. Breaking the kiss for a moment, I reached down clumsily and yanked my top over my head.

All things considered, I probably shouldn't have thrown it. I dimly registered a crash and a clatter as something fell from the mantelpiece. Whatever it was didn't matter as much as Joel's lips on my collarbone, nipping and suckling at the sensitive flesh. My head lolled to the side as he kissed up my neck, locating the secret ticklish spot behind my ear. I mewled and whimpered. He rumbled a growl in my neck as I buried my fingers in his hair and tugged at his honey blond tresses.

God! I'd forgotten how good it could feel. The feeling of skin on skin. I needed more.

I pulled him away from my neck and sat back on my heels. He gave me a questioning look and I smirked. I unhooked my bra in one swift movement and tossed it aside. Joel's eyes were immediately riveted on my breasts, pupils almost obscuring the grey irises. He licked his lips. My nipples were stiff, aching points and I longed to feel his mouth on me. I arched my back and took his head in my hands, guiding him to where I wanted him. He was more than happy to oblige.

I felt the warm pressure of his hands in the small of my back, coaxing me to kneel up further. Once he had me where he wanted me, he captured one sensitive bud in his mouth and flickered his tongue over the tip. My mouth fell open and a cracked keening sound emerged from the back of my throat. Joel chuckled. It vibrated against me, making me shiver. Then he turned his attention to my other breast, moving back and forth between them until my nipples could have cut glass.

I felt the rock-hard bulge in his shorts, and I pressed down against it shamelessly. My hips began a slow, circling grind. Joel bit his lip and groaned. After a few seconds of this, he grabbed my waist and held me still. I pouted, already missing the delicious friction against my hot, swollen pussy. Joel grinned, eyes sparkling with mischief.

"Lie back," he said breathlessly.

Shuffling from his lap, I lay back on the carpet. My heart pounded and my mind raced. They say your life flashes before your eyes when you're about to die. Something similar happens at moments when anticipation fizzes in your chest and pleasure coils in your belly like a tight spring. My mind fractured, flying off into a million directions at once. Among my many disconnected thoughts was that I didn't usually get to look at the living room ceiling like this.

Is that a crack?

"Still with me?"

Joel knelt between my legs, eyebrow raised. I nodded frantically. He reached for the button on my jeans and paused, silently asking a question. By way of an answer, I lifted my hips, making it easier for him to ease my pants down my legs. My panties went with them, and cool air kissed my drenched slit. My cheeks burned as Joel pushed my legs apart and devoured me with his eyes. He gave me a smoldering look and then eased himself down to lay on his front between my spread legs. I held my breath. I'd fantasized about him being in this position so many times that I couldn't quite believe it was happening. It was just as wonderful as I imagined, whilst also being different. It was impossible to describe.

He began by placing soft fluttering kisses up my inner thighs, inching torturously towards my center. I whimpered and quivered. My eyes drifted closed. This meant I wasn't expecting it when he blew on me, his breath cool on my slick lips. Shuddering, I bucked my hips, wordlessly begging for more.

The next thing I felt was his tongue, soft and flat as he licked a broad stripe from my entrance to my clit. Then he did it again, and again. I writhed and squirmed, as each pass of his tongue briefly grazed the sensitive bundle of nerves.

"Joel, please—" I gasped, hips rising from the floor, chasing the stimulation.

He clamped his hands on my thighs and held me down. Tears of frustration sprang to my eyes, and I fisted my hands in my hair. If he kept this up, I was going to explode. Fortunately, he didn't keep me poised on the edge for long. He drew my clit into his mouth and sucked, teasing it mercilessly with his tongue. My eyes flew open, and my mouth gaped in a silent scream. The hot pressure that had been building in my lower belly unfurled. I bit the back of my hand to smother the strangled scream as my walls clenched and pulsed around nothing.

Joel continued to lap gently at my pussy, coaxing me through a series of shuddering aftershocks. Eventually, I got too sensitive, and he eased himself up alongside me and pulled me into his arms. I buried my head in his chest while I waited for my heartbeat to return to normal, hoping he wouldn't be able to feel the wetness of my tears against his skin. It was nice just to lie in his arms. Soothing. Safe.

Once I started coming back to myself, I recalled the pressing issue between us. Specifically, the issue pressing against my stomach. Easing a hand between us, I slipped my fingers into the waistband of his shorts and squeezed him through his boxers. He moaned and pushed into my hand.

"Don't get too comfortable," I said. "I'm not done with you yet."

"I-I, um." He closed his eyes, struggling to focus on his words and not the steady strokes of my hand. "I don't have anything with me."

"Well, this is your lucky day."

I pulled my hand from his shorts and eased him onto his back.

"Why's that?" he asked, staring at me through half-lidded eyes.

I straddled his hips and ran my fingertips over the ridges of his abs. His breath hitched and his stomach muscles contracted.

"Because," I said. "There's only one thing that deals with my cramps every month."

"Huh?"

"I'm on the pill."

He smoothed his hands up my sides and gazed at me affectionately.

"Have I ever told you you're incredible?"

I blinked, pretending I hadn't felt that catch in my chest.

"No," I said lightly. "But if it's something you want to make a habit of, I won't complain."

He chuckled and tilted his pelvis, allowing me to pull his boxers over his hips. He was quiveringly erect and a small drop of pre-cum glistened on the tip. Just imaging the feel of it inside me made my pussy twitch. I drew in a shaky breath and licked my dry lips. How was I still so fucking turned on?

Taking him in my hand, I rubbed the head of his cock over my moist folds. It bumped repeatedly against my clit, reigniting my arousal to a simmering boil. Joel lay back and watched me in rapt fascination, his chest rising and falling with his rapid breathing. He gasped and his eyes rolled back as I eased him inside of me, reveling in the exquisite sting of the stretch. When he was fully sheathed, I leaned back and braced my hands on his thighs. The angle was perfect, pressing against the sweet spot inside me that made me feel like my bones were melting. I rode him hard until we were both glistening with sweat and my stomach and thighs quivered with the strain. When I started to flag, he sat up and placed his hands under my rib cage, supporting me. I wrapped my legs around his waist and clung to him as he pumped his hips, driving his cock into my molten, clutching depths. My second orgasm drove him over the edge. His hips stuttered and he came with a yell, biting down on my shoulder, spilling inside me in scalding spurts.

I pressed my face into the side of his neck, refusing to look at the plushie tableau staring at me in silent judgment.

CHAPTER TWENTY-ONE

Joel

"I never knew this floor could be so comfortable."

I chuckled and ran my fingers through Olivia's hair.

"Hate to have to tell you, but that's not the floor. It's me."

She was sprawled over my chest like a human blanket, with her head tucked under my chin. It was adorable.

"Still comfy," she said sleepily.

"Speak for yourself. I've got rug burns on my ass."

She flailed a limp hand and vaguely patted my chest.

"Poor baby."

"I know!"

"Guess you'll have to use your mouth to talk."

I snorted and dropped a kiss onto the top of her head. Even fucked out and semi-conscious, she still rode my ass. This woman was something else.

"There's gratitude. Still giving me a hard time after I rocked your world."

"Is that what you think you did?"

"Yep! Made you all boneless."

"'M not the only one."

"I didn't have any complaints," I said. "Although next time I think we should try and make it to a bed."

Her head snapped up and she squinted at me blearily.

"Next time? We haven't discussed 'next time.' You wanna do this again?"

I tilted my chin and steadily returned her gaze.

"Why not?"

I wasn't sure what was happening, but it felt good. Being with Olivia, lying with her in my arms was soothing. For the first time in weeks, the ball of tension in my chest had loosened and everything was peaceful and mellow. Maybe Dustin had been right. Just because there was no way for us to have a happily ever after didn't mean we couldn't have sex. It would be good for me, good for both of us. We just had to keep things in perspective and not let our feelings get out of control.

Olivia slithered from my chest and half reclined next to me, propping herself on one elbow. I suppressed a shiver, immediately missing her warmth. Sticking my arms behind my head, I gave her a sidelong look.

"I mean, I don't wanna toot my own horn or anything, but it felt like you enjoyed yourself."

"I did!" she said.

"Then what's the problem?"

She heaved a sigh and her gaze flicked to the plush assembly. Thankfully I'd managed to temporarily forget about them. I wasn't the kind of guy who liked an audience.

"There's not just me to consider," said Olivia softly. "Abby's the most important thing in the world to me and I want her to have some stability. I don't want a string of strange men shifting in and out of her life. Not that you're strange. And not that I think we're—"

She huffed out a breath and gestured helplessly. I shifted onto my side and took her hand, rubbing gentle circles over her knuckles with my thumb.

"I get it. Neither of us wants things to get complicated. But that doesn't mean we can't enjoy...whatever this is. Might be good for both of us. I hope I'm not out of line, but this is the most relaxed I've seen you since we met. You're always running around taking care of people, adhering to this crazy schedule. Everyone needs to blow off steam once in a while."

"I—"

She gnawed on her lip, still looking unconvinced. I reached out with my free hand and carefully pulled her plump, reddened lip from her teeth.

"Maybe it's finally safe to start having adventures again," I suggested.

Her eyes shimmered and she swallowed hard. I pulled back my hand, adamant that I was imagining the sharp ache in my chest. We could do this. We *could.* Olivia closed her eyes and took a deep breath. When her eyes opened, all trace of vulnerability had vanished, and she looked at me severely.

"Ok. But we need some ground rules."

I raised an eyebrow.

"Is that your business voice or your mom voice? Because either option makes me feel weird about being naked."

"Just shut up and listen."

She held up a finger.

"Rule 1: Never under the same roof as my daughter."

"Sounds fair."

"Rule 2: No romance. No flowers, no mixtapes, no candy in cutesy heart-shaped boxes."

I snorted.

"Don't think I've ever bought anyone flowers in my life. Not about to start now."

"Seriously? *Never?*"

I shrugged.

"Nope. Never seen what's so romantic about severed plant ovaries. Besides, they always make me think of hospitals and funerals."

She narrowed her eyes.

"Sounds like there's a story there."

I tapped her playfully on the nose.

"And it sounds like you're getting distracted. What's the next rule?"

"Ok. Rule 3: No dates."

"Define date."

She rolled her eyes.

"A pre-arranged meeting with romantic intentions."

I smirked and waggled my eyebrows suggestively.

"How about booty calls?"

"Hmm."

She pursed her lips and pretended to consider.

"Booty calls are fine."

"Good!" I said huskily, edging closer and trailing my fingers up her arm. "Can I instigate one now?"

"Ah!" She swatted my hand away. "I'm not done yet. Final and most important rule. No drama. As you said, let's keep this simple."

"Well—"

I raised a hand and stroked the backs of my fingers down her cheek. She leaned into the caress.

"I am a simple man with simple tastes."

Olivia nuzzled at my palm. I hissed sharply when she bit down without warning.

"I don't know how you taste...yet."

She fixed me with a look that made my recently sated cock stir and then she slowly slithered down my body. When her hot wet mouth reached its destination, my eyes rolled back.

Fuck me! This woman is going to kill me.

"This is so cool!"

For once, Lily wasn't fused to her phone. She was on Zel's laptop, admiring our new website on the larger screen.

"It's like we're a real business!"

"We *are* a real business," I said. "And your *real* boss wants an update on that Facebook page."

She gave me an ironic salute and continued to click through the various sections on the site.

"I gotta hand it to your girl," said Zel, leaning over the back of Lily's chair. "She did one hell of a job on this."

"She's still not my girl, but..." I paused and smiled fondly. "You're right—she did. I think this could turn things around for us."

Zel blinked.

"Ok, what's going on with you?" he asked. "You came in this morning with a surprise box of donuts, and now you're all sunny and optimistic. Is it time to start worrying about pod people?"

"What?"

I reached into the box and swiped a second jelly donut.

"Can't I be in a good mood without arousing suspicion?"

Without so much as exchanging a look, Lily and Zel replied in unison.

"No!"

I shook my head and bit into the donut. The jelly squirted out faster than expected, forcing me to catch a rogue blob with my free hand. Following universal laws of excellent timing, I was in the middle of licking jelly from my fingers when the door opened and a tiny, heavily pregnant brunette shuffled in awkwardly.

"Hi!" she said cheerfully. "I don't know if you remember me. I'm Erin from Sticky Treats."

I could feel Lily and Zel's eyes on my back, sense them holding their breath. Clearly, they were waiting for me to explode. It was true that I'd made my initial feelings about Sticky Treats very clear but...well...a lot had happened since then. I smiled and offered Erin my non-sticky hand.

"Of course I remember! What can I do for you, Erin?"

Zel appeared from the sidelines holding a chair.

"Thank you!"

Erin massaged her lower back and grimaced, before easing herself gratefully into the chair. As Zel retreated, he caught my eye and pointedly rubbed a finger over his chin. I clapped a hand to my face and tried to surreptitiously wipe off a lump of glaze.

"Can I get you anything?" I asked. "Water, maybe? There's plenty of donuts left."

"Actually," Erin said, folding her hands over her bump. "This visit is more about what I can offer you. I have a proposition for you."

CHAPTER TWENTY-TWO

Olivia

"And then the word spit-roast came out of his mouth, and I had to put my foot down."

Erin sighed and slid a plate across the counter. It contained two golden fruit buns, fused in the middle. I chuckled unsympathetically.

"That's what you get for employing a child."

Erin scowled and swiped a smear of flour from her forehead.

"He's not a child. He's 20. It should have been safe to ask him to come up with a few sexy coffee puns."

"And yet."

The coffee machine gurgled noisily into life while Erin busied herself preparing a cup.

"I know this might seem like hypocrisy coming from the woman who's perfected the art of the buttercream vagina," she said, raising her voice over the rasp of the machine. "But there's a fine line between risqué and crass."

"And Jayden has a habit of skipping merrily over it?"

"He'll improve."

She delicately placed a cappuccino in front of me.

"Does this look like a pussy to you?"

I tilted my head, squinting at the blurry brown shape in the foam.

"Sorry. I'm still getting mutated walnut."

"Dammit!"

Erin drummed her fingers on the counter.

"I'm supposed to be an artist. How hard can this be?"

"Maybe you're being too ambitious," I said. "Turn a heart upside down and it's a butt."

She gave me a withering look.

"Eat your toasty buns. I want to know if I got the spice mix right."

Grimacing, she stuck out her swollen belly and massaged her lower back.

"I should just hire a barista," she said eventually.

"You're doing enough business."

Most of the tables were full. The addition of a sit-down coffee shop had proved incredibly popular with the Sticky Treats clientele. It had also become a popular hangout for artists, students, and of course, couples on dates. Erin's eyes lit up.

"Ooh! That reminds me. I think I've found someone interested in renting the first floor."

"Cool. Who?"

"Your friend, Joel. I went to see him earlier this week."

At the mention of his name my cheeks burned. I hadn't seen Joel since the night of the carnival. Not physically, anyway. We'd texted a little...ok, a lot. Sometimes we'd just chat, but there'd been more than one occasion, late at night, when chatting had devolved into...other things. He'd been very eloquent on the subject of what he'd like to do to me. Honey, peaches, and whipped cream would never be innocent again. It felt good to be impulsive for once. It felt good to misbehave. And, so far, the sky hadn't fallen in. I gave myself a mental shake and cleared my throat.

"He was interested?" I asked, trying to keep my voice level.

"You sound surprised."

"A little bit, yeah."

"Why? This is a prime location and there's a natural overlap in our clientele."

"I know. It makes sense. It's just that...Joel's stubborn. And he's made his feelings about this place pretty clear."

"He came to the opening."

"You can thank Granny for that. I don't think he'd have shown up if she hadn't bullied him into it. Not that I know him very well. Or at all, really."

"Maybe something changed his mind," Erin said innocently.

I got as far as opening my mouth to retort when the email alert on my phone pinged. When I saw the sender, my heart sank.

Great! Just what I don't need.

It must have shown on my face. I jumped a mile when Erin touched my arm gently.

"What's wrong?"

I patted her hand vaguely and placed my phone face down on the counter.

"Nothing serious," I said. "Just the head of the PTA. She's being a little bit—"

"Demanding?"

"Difficult."

Erin frowned.

"Difficult, how?"

I sighed. I hadn't wanted to get into this. Erin would discover the joys of parenting politics soon enough. I didn't want to burden her now. Besides, I could handle Marsha on my own.

"She's invited Abby to her daughter's birthday party."

"That bitch," said Erin dryly.

"I haven't finished yet! It's a makeover party. They're going to a spa and getting their hair done and stuff. I know it sounds like I'm making a big deal over nothing, but they're seven. It just feels so—"

I shrugged.

"No, I agree with you." Erin pulled my plate away. I'd been steadily shredding my bun into tiny pieces. "The whole thing gives me creepy kiddie pageant vibes."

"Anyway," I continued. "I'm trying to find a way to put Marsha off without offending her."

"Can't you just tell her how you feel? How scary can she be?"

I raised an eyebrow.

"You underestimate the occult powers of the PTA. You'll learn soon enough. You're right, though. I'm setting a terrible example for Abby by not dealing with this. I need to grab the bitch by the horns."

I fumbled with my coffee cup, slopping brown liquid onto the saucer.

"Grab what by the what?"

"Joel!"

"Hey, Liv."

What was he doing here? Had there been too many horny thoughts? Had I summoned him? Heat rushed to my cheeks, and I swallowed. He was as gorgeous as ever, but now I knew what was under the clothes. My stomach somersaulted. His sudden appearance was jarring in a way that elated and terrified me. If I were being honest, I wasn't entirely sure how I felt about him working in the same building as my sister-in-law. Despite all my efforts not to get attached to him, there seemed to be invisible tendrils busily weaving him into the fabric of my life. What next? Would he start coaching Abby's gymnastics team? Join Granny V and Jayden for their biweekly Sundae Sunday? That image was so ridiculous that I had to swallow a hysterical burst of laughter.

"Who are we gossiping about?" he asked.

"No one important."

Erin opened her mouth to contradict me. I glared at her, and she closed it with a snap. Dragging Joel into my parenting problems brought us one dangerous step closer to the 'r' word. We were already playing fast and loose with the rules.

"I see."

Joel's jaw tightened and a shadow passed over his face. What had I done now?

"Is this a bad time?" he asked, turning to Erin. "You said if I dropped by, I could get a look at the space."

"No! That's great, of course."

Erin glanced nervously between Joel and the chattering group of sorority girls who must have come through the door shortly after him. A few of them were looking at him with open admiration and I felt something hot and unpleasant bubbling in my chest.

"Olivia, I hate to ask, but could you take Joel upstairs? Looks like we're about to get swamped."

"Sure."

I gulped and accepted the keys. There were several reasons going upstairs with Joel felt like a bad idea. But what could I say? "Sure, but would it tank your health code if we fucked like bunnies up there? Asking for a friend."

Joel silently followed me upstairs, my heart pounding in time with our footsteps. The room was large and airy, with high ceilings, hardwood floors, and lots of light. It smelled of dust and floor wax. Joel stood looking at it with his arms folded. The longer the silence stretched out, the more awkward it got.

"As you can see, it's a lovely space with—"

"You gonna cut the bullshit now we're alone?"

I blinked.

"What?"

His mouth twisted and he stuffed his hands into his pockets.

"You clammed up pretty fast when I walked in. Any reason you didn't want me to know who you were talking about?"

"No, of course not."

"Then who was it?" he asked, his raised voice echoing in the empty room. "Is there some other guy in your life?"

My eyebrows shot up. All my nervous energy and latent horniness took a sudden wrong turn, funneling themselves into a wave of irritation.

"I think you even asking that question breaks at least one of our ground rules," I snapped. "We're supposed to be keeping things simple, yet here you are, acting like a jealous—"

"I am not jealous! I'm just—"

"Pissed off?"

He closed his eyes and took a deep breath.

"Concerned," he said in a tone of forced calm. "Or is that against the rules too?"

All at once, I felt like an ass. Even if he had been jealous, who was I to call him out? Hadn't I just felt the same thing with the sorority girls? A tiny, annoying voice pointed out that this was probably why I'd flown off the handle. I had been jealous, and it had scared me. I sighed and rubbed my hands over my face.

"No. No, of course it's not. It's nothing serious. Just the head of the PTA being a bitch."

Joel recrossed his arms and stuck out his chin.

"Erin seemed to think it was serious."

"It's really not."

He hunched his shoulders and swallowed.

"Look, I know we're keeping things casual, but you can talk to me about non-sex stuff. I mean, we're friends, right?"

"Of course we are. I just didn't want to bore you."

"I'm never bored with you. You piss me off too much."

I chuckled and slipped my arms around his waist. After a second, he unfolded his arms and cuddled me to his chest. It was warm and safe and—

God, how does he always smell so amazing?

"I appreciate the offer," I murmured. "It was very sweet."

"Oh, I'm not sweet," he said, tilting my chin up and placing light, fluttering kisses along my jaw. "I'm a very bad man."

I groaned and tilted my head to the side. Joel bit lightly on my earlobe and my breath stuttered.

"Erin could come up at any minute."

"Exciting, isn't it?" he said, running his hands down my back and squeezing my butt.

Damn him! He was right. Already my mouth was dry and my pussy wet. The thought that we might be discovered made the hot throb between my legs even more intense.

"You were wrong," I moaned. "You're not bad, you're terrible."

He chuckled darkly, sliding a hand up between us and cupping my breast. Everything was pounding and pulsing and buzzing...

Wait. Buzzing!

"Shit! My phone."

"Ignore it."

"I can't," I said regretfully, pulling away and reaching into my back pocket. "My car's still in the shop and I've got someone else picking Abby up from school. I need to be available."

I quickly scanned the message and cursed. Joel's forehead creased with concern.

"What's the matter?"

I bit my lip and pushed my hand through my hair.

"It's Alana. Nolan's court case overran so she can't do the school run. I'd ask Granny V, but she and Russ have tantric yoga on Thursdays."

Joel raised an eyebrow.

"Don't ask," I advised. "I guess I'll just have to book a cab and go myself."

"Why bother with all that? I've got my car with me. I can take you."

I opened and closed my mouth, unable to think of a compelling counterargument.

Yep. Tiny, invisible tendrils.

CHAPTER TWENTY-THREE

Olivia

Joel: Are you sure you want to come?

Olivia: You don't usually need to ask me that question 😉

Joel: Hey! Behave yourself. You know what I'm talking about.

I did. In all the chaos, I'd forgotten about Labor Day BBQ. The invitation felt weird at the time, and it was even weirder now. On the other hand, I wanted to say yes. I enjoyed being with Joel and I was curious to meet his family. Plus, I didn't want to disappoint his aunt; she reminded me of Granny V.

Olivia: Of course I'm sure. Unless you don't want me to.

Joel: Why wouldn't I want you to?

There were plenty of reasons. Our resolve to keep things simple had already taken a beating. When we'd shown up at the school to pick up Abby, we'd attracted more than a few curious stares. Abby had been excited to see him. She'd practically launched herself at him. She then demanded he stay for dinner. The three of us sat around a table, eating mac n cheese, and discussing our day. It was cozy, natural, and alarmingly domestic. We were already sailing close to the wind; now we were steaming toward that section of the map represented by unchartered seas and a writhing mass of tentacles. 'Here be dating.'

The sensible thing would have been to mention these concerns.

Olivia: I don't know.

But I had abandoned sensible.

Joel: Good. That's settled, then. I'll pick you both up at 11 a.m. on Saturday.

Olivia: Awesome.

Joel: Now we need to discuss when I get to see you without us being surrounded by friends and relatives.

I felt the grin spread over my face.

Olivia: Someone has a one-track mind.

Joel: Oh, come on. That's not fair. I've had at least two other thoughts since the last time we saw each other.

Olivia: You're incorrigible.

Joel: Bet you miss me, though.

Too much.

Olivia: Yeah, I wish you were here...so I could slap you.

The image of a dog with suggestive cartoon eyebrows appeared on-screen. I had to put a hand over my mouth to suppress a shout of laughter. Abby was sleeping in the room above my head, and she'd been uncharacteristically restless lately.

Olivia: I'm going to ban you from using that GIF.

Joel: You can't blame a guy for being a little hooked. You've been good for me.

Olivia: I know what you mean.

Joel: So, what are you doing now?

Olivia: Working!

Joel: It's 9 p.m.

Olivia: I have to finish this project by next week.

Joel: You work too hard. I'll have to start coming up with more ways to get you to relax.

Olivia: That's it. I'm sending you for a cold shower.

The thought of the creative 'relaxation' techniques Joel might come up with sent heat to my cheeks and triggered a familiar throbbing between my legs. Maybe *I* should grab a cold shower before bed.

Olivia: Gtg. Early start tomorrow.

Joel: Sleep well, Vivi xxx

I looked at the message and shook my head. When had that started? And when had I become so cool with it? It had been my childhood pet name, thanks to two-year-old Nolan's inability to pronounce Olivia. I'd violently shrugged it off when Granny's books started doing well. Nobody had called me that in years. Somehow, when *he* did it, it was different.

When Joel picked us up on Saturday, Abby was ecstatic to see him. I wasn't sure when they'd developed their complicated handshake/high five routine, but it was cute.

As we got closer to his aunt and uncle's house, we both became very quiet. Clouds gathered on Joel's face and his knuckles were white on the steering wheel. Was he as nervous as I was?

The house was a pleasant ranch-style building on a suburban street. I could already smell the smoke from the grill and I could hear children shouting in the backyard. Abby's grip on my hand tightened. I looked down and tried to give her a reassuring smile, but it felt strained and unnatural. It wasn't like her to be shy. It wasn't like either of us.

"Everything alright?"

Joel placed a reassuring hand in the small of my back and murmured in my ear. The tension in my chest vanished and I shot him a warm smile.

"All good. We should go in."

The house was neat, but it had a cozy, lived-in feel. There was the sound of a TV from the living room, but Joel headed straight for the kitchen. His aunt was at the counter tossing a salad, and a pretty blonde woman sat at the table with a little girl on her lap. Everyone looked up when we entered, apart from the little girl, who was absorbed in coloring.

"Hi!" Loretta beamed, dropping her salad tongs and coming over to greet us. "So glad you could make it!"

"Thank you for inviting us. Joel said I shouldn't bother to bring anything, but we didn't want to show up empty-handed, so I brought cupcakes."

I held up the box almost sheepishly.

"Oh, you shouldn't have!"

When Loretta's eyes fell on Abby, her face lit up.

"Oh, and this must be your daughter. Isn't she the cutest thing?"

"This is Abby," I said, putting an arm around her. "I'm sorry, it seems she's feeling a little shy today."

"Oh, bless her heart! We'll just have to make her feel welcome, then, won't we? Would you like a juice box, honey?"

"No, thank you," Abby said, looking down at her shoes. I squeezed her shoulders harder; I couldn't work out what had gotten into her.

The young woman at the table spoke up for the first time. She adjusted the little girl on her knee and gave Abby a friendly smile and wink.

"My two boys are outside playing tetherball. Maybe Abby would like to join them for a game."

At this, Abby turned away and buried her face in my thigh. I'd just opened my mouth to offer an apology when Joel crouched in front of her and gave her a gentle poke in the ribs.

"Hey! Where's that brave little girl who marched right up to me and asked me if I was a boss battle, huh? Where'd she get to?"

He poked her again and I felt her giggle.

"Tell you what, why don't we both go outside? I'll introduce you to Cody and Kelvin and we can all have a game together. We can team up and show those boys how it's done."

Abby slowly released her death grip on my thigh and smiled tentatively.

"O-ok."

I was so grateful I could have kissed him, right there and then. Instead, I had to content myself with a mouthed 'thank you.'

"That's a lovely idea," Loretta said. "Dustin's already out there trying to get the grill going, and Kylie and your uncle are watching one of those awful car-chase movies."

Joel looked back at me when he got to the kitchen door.

"Will you be alright?" he asked.

"Of course she will!" Loretta said. "What do you think we're going to do to the girl?"

"I know what you're both like."

Loretta swatted at his retreating back with a dishtowel and shook her head.

"Crystal, grab that jug of iced tea from the refrigerator. I need to get off my feet for a minute."

Crystal gently slid the little girl from her lap and deposited her on the floor, with her coloring book and crayons. Without missing a beat, she stretched out on her stomach and continued saturating the barnyard scene with a violent shade of pink.

"Sit down, dear," Loretta said.

I perched on a chair and sipped awkwardly at a glass of sweet, iced tea. I could feel the curiosity radiating from them and I was dreading the inevitable interrogation.

"Nice to finally meet you," Crystal said. "Gotta be honest. We've been pretty damn curious."

"About me?"

"Sure. Joel really likes you."

"W-what makes you think that?"

"You're here. He hasn't brought a woman home in a long time."

I blushed hotly.

"We're just friends."

Crystal raised an eyebrow and topped up my glass.

"You're his first guest who wasn't Zel in over six years. I

don't think you're *just* anything. You're telling me you haven't noticed the way he looks at you?"

"I-I—"

"Crystal!" Loretta said. "Don't bombard the poor girl. She just got here."

She leaned over the table and patted my arm.

"You'll have to forgive us for being a little over-excited. You've been such a good influence on Joel, and well...it's just nice to see him happy. I don't know if you've noticed, but he can be a little prickly at times."

Crystal grinned mischievously.

"Prickly is Mom-speak for cantankerous, misanthropic a-hole."

"*Anyway,*" Loretta interrupted, glaring at her daughter. "Since you came along, he's been much more relaxed. It's like a weight has been lifted from his shoulders."

I didn't know what to say. I was torn between desperately wanting to believe it and wanting to run from the kitchen screaming. I knew on some level I'd been good for him. We'd been good for each other. But I didn't want to read anything into that. We were just having fun—relieving stress. I was still trying to frame my reply when Loretta continued. She lowered her voice and addressed me in a confidential tone.

"Honestly, before you came into his life, we'd been more than a little worried about him."

I frowned.

"Worried?"

At that moment a voice drifted in from the living room.

"Grandma! Grandpa needs his tank changed."

"Want me to go?" Crystal asked.

Loretta stood up and patted her hand.

"No, hon, I'll go. You stay here and chat with Olivia." She smiled at me apologetically. "You'll have to forgive me, dear. I'll be back in just a moment."

When she was gone, I shot a questioning glance at Crystal. "Why did your mom say you were worried about Joel?"

Crystal sighed and refilled her tea glass.

"He has this tendency to drive everyone around him away. He's been like that ever since he was a kid."

"Do you know why?"

Crystal chewed her lip and gave me an appraising look.

"How much has he told you about his mom?"

I shrugged.

"He told me she died in a car accident. But he didn't seem to want to talk about it and I didn't want to pry."

Crystal looked at me again and then glanced nervously at the backdoor.

"Dammit! He'd kill me if he found out I told you, but I want this to work, so I'm going to give you a leg up."

"Want what to work?"

"Just listen."

Part of me felt like I should stop her. This didn't feel fair. Surely if Joel wanted me to know something, he'd tell me. In the end, my curiosity overwhelmed my scruples and I let her continue.

"Did he tell you how the accident happened?"

I nodded

"He said she fell asleep at the wheel."

"But did he say why?"

"No."

Crystal scowled into her glass.

"Joel's dad was an asshole. He abandoned them both before Joel was even born."

I grimaced sympathetically. I knew exactly how that felt.

"From what my mom says about him, they were better off," she continued. "Problem was, it left my aunt with a kid to raise on her own. I'm guessing we both know how much fun that can be."

I nodded. I wouldn't trade Abby for anything, but I'd never claim being a single parent was easy.

"Was she a good mom?"

"Yeah. Yeah, she was. I don't remember her that well, but she'd have done anything for Joel. She and my mom had to go without a lot of things growing up. They both wanted better for their kids. She worked two jobs to keep them afloat. She'd clean houses during the day and then, three nights a week, she'd leave Joel with us and pick up the late shift at a local diner."

"That's...a lot."

I suddenly felt very lucky. I worked from home and had a lot of help from family. Even then, I still felt exhausted most of the time. I couldn't imagine what Joel's mother must have gone through. Crystal gripped her glass and shook her head bitterly.

"Mom said it was an accident waiting to happen. Then she took on an extra shift for one week. I'm guessing you can fill in the blanks."

"Poor Joel!"

I could picture it. A miniature version of him, standing in this kitchen asking why his mother hadn't come home from work. It hurt my heart.

"I remember when he came to us. He wasn't crying or scared. He was just really withdrawn—like, pulled in on himself."

I could *definitely* picture that.

"Mom and Dad tried to make him feel welcome. To us, he was part of the family. Thing is, I'm not sure he truly believed it. Always seemed like he felt he owed us something. It got even worse when—"

She trailed off, spinning her glass in her hands.

"What?"

"Ugh!" She put down the glass with a thump. "I guess I

might as well tell you everything. Not a word to Joel, remember?"

I mimed zipping my lip.

"Ok, when he was 15, Joel got caught tagging on school property. The principal wanted to call the police, but the school counselor persuaded him not to. He took Joel under his wing and convinced him to apply for a scholarship to art school."

"Natural talent?"

"He was always drawing. Don't think it had ever occurred to him he could do anything with it. Mom and Dad were really proud. They'd been worried about him since he came to us. But it seemed like he'd finally found his thing."

"So, what went wrong?"

"When he was done with art school he apprenticed at some tattoo studios, but then he and Zel got an opportunity to set up on their own. Man! He was so excited."

One of the kids shrieked. Crystal and I both glanced nervously at the backdoor. When the shriek dissolved into a peal of laughter, we both relaxed and she resumed.

"They didn't have all the money they needed for the deposit and Mom and Dad offered to help. There were no strings attached or anything. They just wanted him to succeed. They were excited for him. We all were."

"I'm guessing there's another but."

She raised the jug and gave me a questioning look. I held out my glass. This conversation wasn't easy, but Loretta made the best sweet, iced tea I'd ever tasted.

"They gave Joel the money for the deposit. What he didn't realize was that they'd remortgaged the house to do it."

My hand flew to my mouth. Crystal shrugged.

"They didn't see it as a big deal. Mom said she'd rather help one of us kids get set up than go off on some cruise somewhere. Unfortunately, Joel's business didn't take off right away and then Dad got sick. Suddenly Mom and Dad were struggling, and Joel felt horrible about it. He said he'd ruined their lives and they should've never taken him in."

"That's ridiculous," I gasped. "I can see how he'd feel bad, but he must know your parents don't feel that way."

Crystal shook her head.

"They try to tell him that all the time, but he's stubborn when he gets an idea in his head. It really affected him. Now, he's afraid to get close to anyone. He's convinced he's a burden or that he'll ruin their life somehow."

She pushed her hand through her hair and blew out a breath.

"Oh boy! He'd lose his shit if he knew I told you any of this."

"What can I do?" I asked.

I wasn't supposed to be getting involved but this was different. Joel was my...friend. If it was in my power to help him, I would. Crystal reached across the table and pressed my hand.

"Just don't let him push you away," she urged.

I won't.

Later, while I was going to the bathroom, I bumped into Joel in the hallway. On impulse, I seized him around the middle and hugged him fiercely, burying my face in his chest.

"Hey!" He chuckled. "What's all this?"

"Nothing. Nothing important."

CHAPTER TWENTY-FOUR

Joel

"Aw! That's so cute!" Zel said. "The little butts have our logo on."

"It's not just the butts. It's on the boobs too. And the—"

"Thank you, Lily," I cut in. "We get the picture."

That morning, a courier had arrived at the studio with a huge box bearing the Sticky Treats logo. Turned out Erin had sent us a gigantic selection of cupcakes as a welcome aboard gift. It had taken a while, but I could admit I'd been wrong about Erin. She was the sweetest person ever to send me a box of dicks...and asses...and boobs. To be fair, they were pretty impressive, and the tattooed logos were a nice touch.

"Erin's a genius! Did she really do all this with buttercream?"

Zel poked an experimental finger into one of the butts. I reached across and slapped his hand away.

"Don't stick your finger in like that. And if you say, 'that's what she said,' I'm putting you on a timeout."

Lily giggled and Zel flipped me off with a creamy finger. Half a beat later he looked at it speculatively and popped it in his mouth. His eyes immediately rolled back in his head.

"Mm! If we're going to be working above this place, I might have to squeeze in an extra Zumba class."

"When are we moving in?" Lily asked eagerly.

Zel shrugged and snagged the remainder of the cupcake he'd violated.

"According to the lawyers, everything should be signed, sealed, and taken care of within six weeks."

"Cool!"

"Yep! Buckle up, kid. We're headed for the major leagues."

"Woah!" I said, holding my hands up. "Let's not get over-excited. It's all still very much up in the air."

Zel rolled his eyes.

"Would you listen to yourself?" he said, rolling up the cupcake casing and flicking it at me. "For the first time in over a year, things are going right. Business is picking up, thanks to our shiny new website and the stellar work of our social media manager."

He paused to allow Lily to take an elaborate bow.

"And an entire floor in the building we got outbid for just got dropped in our laps."

"Yes," I said. "But—"

"Look, Joel." Zel placed a hand on each of my shoulders and looked at me earnestly. "I know you love to be miserable. This is going to be a difficult adjustment. But for once the universe has thrown us a bone. Try to enjoy it. You could start by smiling."

"Smiling?"

"Yes. It's where you turn the corners of your mouth up, like this."

He placed his thumbs on either side of my lips and forced them into a grimace. I jerked my face out of his grip and aimed a smack at his head. He nimbly dodged and raised an eyebrow.

"Unless..."

"Unless what?"

"Unless there's something else on your mind."

I tucked my hands into my armpits and glared. There was something on my mind. The same thing that had been on my mind for months. It wasn't that things were going badly. Quite the reverse. I loved being with her, I could talk to her about anything, and our physical connection was amazing. After we'd sleep together, I'd cuddle her to my chest and each time it got a little harder to let her go. Last weekend she'd come to a family BBQ and everyone loved her. It felt like she belonged there. I'd catch sight of her playing with the kids or chatting to Crystal and get this pang in my chest. All the obstacles between us were melting away. She'd finished the website and my business was picking up. There was a chance I could enter a relationship without having to feel like a charity case. I couldn't ruin her life if I didn't need anything from her. And then there was the building. When we'd first met, it had been a prickly bone of contention. Now it could be something that brought us together. Everything was perfect. And that was the problem. I was waiting for the other shoe to drop. The studio, Olivia, Sticky Treats. They were woven intricately together, and I was poised for the entire structure to crash down around my ears.

"I don't think we can eat all these," Zel said. "And my thighs say we definitely shouldn't."

I cocked my head and examined the contents of the box.

"Normally, I'd say I'll bring some home for the family, but that has the potential to be—"

"Hilarious?"

"Awkward."

Lily pursed her lips.

"You could smoosh the frosting a little. Then they'd just look like regular cupcakes."

"I actually have a funny story about that."

We'd been so absorbed in the cakes that Olivia had managed to sneak up behind us.

"Don't look so surprised," she chuckled, stretching up and kissing my cheek. "I *have* been here before."

"Yes, but I'm usually expecting you."

Heat radiated from the spot she'd kissed, engulfing my cheeks in a fiery blush. Olivia's smile faded slightly, and a note of uncertainty crept into her voice.

"Should I not have come?"

"No!" I said hastily. "I mean, no you *should* have, not no you shouldn't have. I'm just surprised is all. It's a nice surprise, though. Surprises are good. Love surprises."

Lily snorted and Zel shook his head.

"Olivia," he said, stepping between us. "It's lovely to see you again. Can I offer you a seat while we wait for Joel to yank his foot out of his mouth?"

He took her hand and kissed it gallantly. I was taken aback by the surge of possessiveness that washed over me when he touched her. I was torn between wanting to punch his lights out and wishing I'd thought to do something like that. It would have been nice to be smooth, just once.

Once Lily had gone to Magda's for coffee and Zel had tactfully reabsorbed himself in examining the cakes, I came up behind Olivia's chair and rested my hands on her shoulders.

"I really am pleased to see you," I murmured.

She smiled softly and leaned her head against my arm.

My heart stuttered. It was a tiny moment, but that was when it hit me with perfect clarity. Despite all my best efforts, I'd fallen in love.

So much for Dustin's plan.

I was elated. I was terrified. I wanted to run, but I also knew I couldn't have let go of her hand if you'd paid me. I wasn't sure what to do, or if I should do anything. Even if I had known, it wouldn't have made a difference. We were in a public place; my best friend was there. It was hardly the moment to ask if those 'clear ground rules' we'd set up were negotiable. I stood like a rabbit in pink, heart-shaped headlights and let the autopilot take over the conversation.

"Did you just stop by to say hi?"

"Nope." She nudged a paper bag at her feet. "You left a sweater at the house. I washed it and brought it over."

"Thanks."

Is she being thoughtful? Or does she not want any trace of me left in her house?

I gave myself a mental shake, not liking that I was suddenly so paranoid.

"What's all this?" she asked, gesturing at the box.

"Erin sent them. Sort of a welcome gift, I guess."

"That reminds me," Zel piped up. "I believe you promised us a funny story."

Olivia smiled slyly.

"If you ever meet my brother, ask him about the time he ordered 'kitty cupcakes' for my daughter's sixth birthday."

Zel's eyes widened until they were round as saucers.

"You're kidding."

"Sadly, not. It's basically how he and Erin first met. It taught him to be *very* specific when making orders over the phone."

"Wait a minute," I said. "I thought you said they met at the bachelor party when he thought she was the stripper."

"That was when they *first* met. This one sealed the deal."

"He's a lucky man," Zel said. "Not many people get a third chance after making an ass of themselves twice."

Olivia smiled enigmatically.

"He redeemed himself," she said dreamily. "Some people are like that. They'll grow on you if you give them half the chance." She gave my arm a firm squeeze and my heart jumped into my throat. At that moment, Lily returned with the coffee. She was very upset that she'd missed the story, so Olivia told them both in more detail. Soon she had us all howling with laughter.

"Here," Zel choked, pushing the box at Olivia and wiping his eyes. "You haven't had one yet."

"You're right."

Olivia got up and inspected the box. When she was sure that neither Lily nor Zel was looking, she caught my eye and winked. I swallowed hard at the evil glint in her eye. The evil minx selected one of the cakes that sported a tumescent pink hard-on. She licked shamelessly around the head of the cock. The glistening tip of her tongue left a wet ripple on the surface of the buttercream. My mouth watered as my own cock rose rapidly to attention. A wave of reckless daring washed over me. My brain had taken a backseat. My heart and my loins were running the show.

"Can we dip into the office for a minute?" I asked, amazed at the steadiness in my voice. "I have some questions about that invoice you sent me."

Olivia's eyes narrowed and then widened as she quickly caught on.

"Sure," she said, abandoning her half-eaten cake, its wilted erection still oozing Bavarian cream.

Ignoring Zel's curious look, I seized her by the hand and pulled her towards the back rooms.

She was going to pay for that.

CHAPTER TWENTY-FIVE

Olivia

As soon as the office door closed, Joel grabbed me and pulled me to him. My head spun delightfully as he kissed me. He seized a fistful of hair at the nape of my neck and tugged gently, knowing it would drive me wild. I whimpered needily and my knees threatened to buckle as he nipped at my jaw and nibbled at my ear lobe.

He was fierce, possessive, almost feral. I felt his swelling bulge press against my stomach and pushed back against it. I was already soaked for him. This was what I'd been hoping for when I teased him. This was why I'd come. The sweater had just provided a convenient excuse. I cupped his steely erection through his shorts and squeezed, desperate to convince myself that hard flesh and greedy kisses were all I had come for.

As I teased his rigid length, Joel reached around and smacked my ass. I clutched at his shoulders, muffling my delighted squeak in his chest. Grabbing my hair again, he carefully tilted my head back and stared at me. He was breathing hard, and his pupils swallowed his grey irises until I was staring into two black pools.

"You're a naughty girl, you know that?"

The husky rasp sent a jolt of heat straight to my pussy. I

was breathing as hard as he was, and my cheeks burned.

"Maybe I am. What are you going to do about it?"

He pulled me into another hungry kiss.

"I think the question is, what are *you* going to do about this."

He grabbed my wrist and held my hand against his crotch. I raised an eyebrow.

"Zel and Lily are right next door."

"Then I guess we'll have to be quiet."

He let out a throaty chuckle and tweaked my nipple through my shirt.

"Now who's misbehaving?"

He rolled my nipple gently between thumb and forefinger, smirking like a contented cat.

"Think you can keep me in line?"

You bet I can, mister!

I seized the hand tormenting my breast and pulled it to my lips. Eyeing him steadily, I sucked his forefinger into my mouth and rippled my tongue over the tip. His cheeks darkened and he groaned. I released the finger from my mouth with a wet pop and smiled sweetly.

"Go sit in that chair," I ordered.

"Mm. Yes, ma'am."

Once he was seated, he reached up to kiss me. I caught his hands and placed them firmly on the arms of the chair.

"If your hands leave that chair," I said, "I'll stop."

He nodded eagerly, watching spellbound as I straightened up and stretched languorously. I trailed my hands up my stomach and cupped my breasts, shivering as I ran my thumbs over my nipples. Joel gulped. His knuckles were white on the arms of the chair.

It felt good to be in control. It felt safer. I needed to remind myself what Joel and I were about. I needed to focus on moments like this—hunger, excitement, and pure need. Not family BBQs, cozy chats over coffee, or tender hugs and kisses that reminded me of what I longed for but could never have.

It was getting harder every time I saw him. Whenever I saw him play with Abby, smelled his smoky apple scent on my pillow, or found one of his sweaters in my laundry. I knew I should end it, but I couldn't bear to. I was already in too deep.

I dropped to my knees and slowly unfastened his shorts. His erection strained against the grey fabric of his boxer briefs and there was already a dark spot where the pre-cum had soaked through. My mouth watered. Taking hold of the waistband, I pulled it away from his belly and eased them over his hips. He moaned with relief as his cock sprang free.

Gazing up at him, I opened my mouth and let my hot, moist breath ghost over the head. Joel breathed in sharply through his nose and gripped the chair tighter. I swirled my tongue slowly around the sensitive head, catching a salty pearlescent drop of pre-cum on my tongue. I kept this up for a while, probing and teasing the head with my tongue. Joel bit the inside of his cheek and the plastic on the chair gave an ominous creak.

"Gonna drive me crazy if you keep that up."

"Don't worry," I said. "I'll let you come, but you gotta ask nicely first."

His eyes flashed and his cock twitched under my lips.

"God, you're evil."

"You love it."

I took the head into my mouth and bobbed up and down, taking a little more into my mouth each time. Before long, his hips bucked, trying to thrust faster, deeper. I pulled off and held up an admonitory finger.

"Ah-ah. Stay still."

He growled and planted his butt more firmly on the chair. I slid my mouth over him again. When I fluttered my tongue over the vein on the underside of the shaft, he let out a high-pitched frantic noise I'd never heard from him before. I hummed my satisfaction and reached down to gently cup his balls.

I kept him on the edge. Every time I heard that hitch in his breathing that told me he was close, I'd pull back.

"Olivia, please. Come on. You gotta let me come."

Seeing Joel like this, writhing and desperate, made my stomach clench and my pussy ache. Knowing I could drive him wild like this felt amazing. I took him into my mouth one final time and pulled him over the edge. He came with a strangled yell, his cock pulsing and jumping as he spent in my mouth. When I looked up, I was amazed to see a tear spilling from the corner of each eye.

I buried my face in his thigh and waited for my heart to slow down. When he'd come, he'd almost taken me with him. After a minute or so, his hand fell limply on my head. I nuzzled into his palm as he stroked his fingers through my tousled curls. I was so content I could've stayed there forever.

Which is exactly why you can't.

"I think your coffee break probably ended quite some time ago," I said regretfully.

"They can do without me for a few minutes more. I'm pretty sure I've melted."

"But what if a customer comes in?"

"Then they'll have to wait. I'm not safe around sharp objects right now. Come 'ere."

He hauled me into his lap and kissed me. It was soft, languid, and almost unbearably tender. I melted against him with a sigh, momentarily surrendering to the comforting warmth of his arms.

The inevitable knock on the door came like a bucket of cold water. I leaped from Joel's lap, and he slumped back in the chair with an annoyed grunt.

"This better be important."

"You tell me," came Lily's muffled retort. "Some weird lady just showed up. Said she's looking for Olivia."

CHAPTER TWENTY-SIX

Olivia

We came back to find Marsha examining the studio artwork and Zel fidgeting uncomfortably. Marsha had this way of looking around a room—like she was mentally valuing the place. She did it with people too. One appraising glance was all it took to determine how much of her time you were worth. Did you get her business card, her home number, or a condescending smirk?

She looked up when we entered, and her face shifted seamlessly into her sunniest smile.

"Hey, girlfriend!"

I tried to return her smile and my cheeks ached in protest. I hated everything about her, from her bouncy blonde hair to that stupid waggly finger wave. What the hell was she doing here?

"Hey, Marsha. This is a nice surprise."

I grimaced through her air kisses, cursing my burning cheeks. I was an adult. Where I chose to spend my time was none of her business. So why did I feel like she'd just busted me?

"Oof. You are one tough lady to track down. Anyone would think you were avoiding me."

"Why would I be avoiding you?"

My attempt at an incredulous chuckle came out as nervous bark. Marsha smiled thinly and my insides shriveled.

"When you weren't at Pilates, I thought I'd swing by your place. But then I saw you'd checked in here on Facebook."

Fuck!

After a lot of cajoling, Sailor Joey's finally had a social media presence, and I'd been doing everything I could to help raise their profile. No good deed goes unpunished.

"Checking in on Facebook? Do people still do that?"

Zel's whisper was barely audible. Lily's reply, on the other hand, cut through the air (and my soul) like a razor.

"Mostly just old people."

"I'm 35!" I hissed.

"Yeah, my point."

"Lily!" Zel gasped. "That is so rude! Don't listen to her, Olivia. You don't look a day over 24. Although good for you with the trying to stay limber. If Pilates isn't working out for you, you should try Zum—"

"Can we help you?"

I sensed Joel's warm, solid presence behind me, and I instantly felt better. Marsha looked up and blinked as though noticing him for the first time. I could practically hear the elastic twang as her smile snapped into place.

"Sorry to barge in," she said airily, "but I need to borrow Olivia here for a teensy momentito. Then you can get back to...whatever this is."

Her unspoken question hung in the air as she looked curiously between us.

"It's a work thing."

I'd said it too fast. I avoided looking at Joel. Hopefully, he didn't think I was ashamed of him. Dammit! This was none of Marsha's business. Why was I incapable of standing up to her?

"What's so urgent?" I asked.

She rolled her eyes.

"What do you think, silly? Fiona's big day is less than a month away. We need to get this hype train rolling to partay town."

That's funny, the ticket says we're going to cringe-ville.

"Of course!" I clapped a hand to my forehead. "I'm sorry, Marsha. Things have been so crazy I just forgot."

"Well," said Marsha. "No pressure, girlfriend, but I do need to confirm the spa booking. Abby is going to be joining us, right?"

My skin prickled. It felt like I was standing in the spotlight. I'd rehearsed this conversation fifty times but I never imagined I'd have an audience. It was tempting to manufacture a social engagement at the last minute but then I'd be just as two-faced as Marsha. Besides, Abby might let something slip to Fiona, and it wouldn't be fair to make her complicit in my lie. It was time to put on my big girl panties and stand up for what I believed in.

"I'm sorry, Marsha, but I'm not sure I'm comfortable with letting Abby go to a makeover party."

"I'm not sure what you mean, hon."

Marsha's simpering grin flickered for a fraction of a second. I swallowed hard.

"I don't think it's age appropriate. It won't be too long before our little girls will be saturated with media telling them that their appearance is the most valuable thing about them. I'd like to protect Abby from that message for as long as possible."

"Uh oh. Looks like the party train is about to be derailed to no-fun town."

Marsha jabbed me playfully in the ribs and I fought the urge to slap her. Once again I had been crowned queen of the no-fun zone, and I was getting sick of it. All I was trying to do was raise my daughter responsibly. Somehow, that made me the bad guy. I was doomed to be the uptight foil for the 'cool moms' and irresponsible uncles. And then when I did cut loose for once, the universe punished me for it. As soon as I threw caution to the wind and grabbed a quickie in Joel's office, the universe sent Marsha, like a karmic bolt from the blue.

"It's nothing to get your panties in a bunch about, honey. It's just a little pampering at the spa, a session with hair and makeup, and then out for mocktails."

"I'd rather let kids be kids."

Marsha gave me a withering look.

"And what would be your idea of a party? Cake and ice cream at the petting zoo? It's not the 1950s. Today's children expect more."

She stepped closer and placed a hand on my arm.

"I know it can be tough raising a kid on your own. Sometimes I forget that other people don't have the inner reservoir of strength that I do. But is it fair to let Abby suffer the consequences of your emotional baggage? How will she ever learn to cut loose when she sees her mom being so uptight?"

I opened my mouth to retort and nothing came out. As usual, Marsha had homed in on my insecurities with pinpoint accuracy. My well-rehearsed arguments crumbled and I stood mouth agape.

"You're out of line, lady."

Joel stepped up next to me and my resolve immediately revived. My stomach leaped as his arm brushed my shoulder. Marsha's triumphant sneer evaporated.

"Getting a man to fight your battles for you? I thought you were supposed to be a feminist."

"I'm not fighting her battles for her," Joel said. "I'm fighting this battle *with* her. Not that she needs me to. Olivia's an amazing mom and I won't let anyone stand in my studio and say different."

A lump rose in my throat. I hadn't expected Joel to back me up. I wasn't used to anyone backing me up. Yet, here he was, standing at my side. It was weird. Letting him fight my corner didn't make me feel weak. I felt twice as strong.

Is this what it's supposed to be like when you...

"Well, you can please yourself, I'm sure. Far be it for me to tell anyone how to raise their child. I suppose I'll see you at the next PTA meeting if you can cram us into your schedule. I imagine virtue signaling and saving the world with body positivity is rather rough on your time."

She slammed the door hard on her way out. A framed painting of a dragon jumped from the wall and Lily rushed to retrieve it. I didn't hear everything she muttered but I was sure I heard the word 'mominatrix.'

"Are you alright?"

Joel squeezed my shoulder. I started to tell him I was fine. I suspect it would have been a lot more convincing if I hadn't burst into tears. I had no idea what was wrong with me. I rarely cried. I certainly didn't cry over little things like this. What was happening to me? Joel guided me to a chair and sent Lily to get me a glass of water.

"It's ok," I said between sobs. "I'm fine."

I felt extremely foolish. Joel squatted next to me and laid a hand on my shoulder.

"I'll be the judge of that," he said softly. "You look stressed and exhausted. Let someone take care of *you* for once."

"Lily can reschedule your appointments for this afternoon," Zel said. "You should take her home."

I made a token effort to protest but, in the end, I let Joel wrap an arm around me and walk me to his car. I was still feeling shaky, and it was nice to lean on him for a little while. When we got to my house, I expected him to just walk me to the door. Instead, he came inside with me and pulled me down onto the couch. I collapsed against his chest and let him hold me. It was wonderful. Everything from his smell to the rhythmic thump of his heart acted as a soothing balm to my frayed nerves. I told myself sternly that I couldn't fall asleep. I had projects to finish, dry-cleaning to pick up and a daughter to collect from school.

"Thank you for sticking up for me."

"Thank you for letting me."

I opened my mouth to tactfully point out that it was getting late, but something entirely different came out.

"Will you stay with me a few minutes longer?"

"I'm not going anywhere, Vivi."

He leaned down and kissed me softly on the mouth. I melted against him with a sigh, boneless and pliant. I don't know how we got to the bedroom, but that's where we ended up. We could have floated there on a cloud for all I cared.

Sex with Joel was usually hard, passionate, and frantic. This time it felt different. It was gentle, caring, and unhurried. More relaxed, yet somehow more intense. When the exquisite tension collected in my belly, I squeezed my eyes shut and bit my forearm to muffle my cries.

"Don't."

Joel caught my arms and held them by my head.

"Look at me."

He stilled his hips and stared down at me, eyes wild. I stared back at him, unable to breathe, utterly captivated by the weight of the moment.

"Don't hold back," he ordered. "I wanna hear you."

He held my gaze and thrust into me hard and fast, hitting that sweet spot inside me that made me tingle all over. I came with a hoarse scream, grinding my clit against his pelvis as tears streamed down my cheeks. He followed seconds later, hips stuttering, face buried in my neck. We lay there for a long time, not moving, breathing hard. I'd half fallen asleep when I heard him speak.

"Liv?"

"Hmm, what?"

"I want to break the rules."

CHAPTER TWENTY-SEVEN

Joel

"I want to break the rules."

She didn't say anything for a long time. I was glad I still had my face buried in her chest. It was the most terrifying confession I had ever made. All the years of telling myself I was better on my own. And of feeling like a disaster who brought nothing but bad luck to the people who loved me—it all made what I was about to ask seem impossible. I felt her breath catch. I held my breath too. The whole world was on pause. Eventually, I couldn't take the tension anymore.

"Aren't you going to say anything?"

I still hadn't lifted my head from her boobs. I soothed myself with the sound of her heartbeat. The familiar smell of her body wash mingled deliciously with fresh sweat and arousal.

"Yes," she said softly. "But I think it's still your turn."

Groaning, I lifted myself from her breasts and rolled over. I lay beside her and propped myself up on my elbow. Her tattoo stood out vividly against the pale skin of her belly. I traced it lovingly, stroking my fingertips over the red-hued bunny. She quivered slightly, immediately coming out in goosebumps.

I knew what the tattoo meant to her, but I wondered if

she knew what it meant to me. The thought that she'd trusted me with a secret part of herself tugged at something just behind my breastbone. I took pictures of my work as a matter of course but the pictures didn't usually end up as the wallpaper on my phone and the background on my computer.

Is that cute or creepy?

I licked my lips and continued to pet the russet bunny.

"I-I want the two of us to go out to the same place at the same time and spend time together."

Olivia smiled mischievously.

"Time together with our clothes on, you mean?"

"Initially."

I moved my caress a little lower. She bit her lip.

"That sounds a lot like a date."

"I guess it is. I know we agreed to keep things simple, but I'm not sure I can do it anymore. When you and Abby came to that barbeque and I saw you with all my family, it felt—"

"Weird?"

I shook my head emphatically.

"No! That was it. It should've been weird, but it wasn't. You just slipped in. I don't know what I feel exactly, but I can't keep pretending I don't feel *something*. And it's not just with my family. You've slipped into my whole life. You're everywhere. You come to my work, there are little reminders of you all over my house, and even if you're not physically there, I can't stop thinking about you."

A worried line appeared between her eyebrows.

"Are you saying I don't give you enough space?"

"I wish."

"Huh?"

I lay back on the pillows and threw my arm over my eyes.

"That'd be a simple feeling to unpack. The way things are now—you're there and I *want* you there. If you're not there, it feels like something's missing."

I screwed my eyes shut as the heat of my blush warmed my arm.

"I thought sleeping with you would cure me of this...obsession, but—"

The mattress shifted and I felt her roll over to look at me. I kept my arm resolutely over my face.

"So," she said slowly. "What you're saying is, you were sleeping with me because you wanted to get rid of me?"

"I know how stupid that sounds. It's like when I was a kid. I had this Nintendo and...ugh!"

I growled in frustration and rolled onto my stomach.

"This made a lot more sense when Dustin explained it."

"Maybe you should call him over here to help you out."

I gave her a sidelong glance. Her lips twitched.

"Don't be ridiculous," I said seriously. "He's working tonight."

There was a pause before she burst out laughing and shook her head.

"I must be insane."

I raised hopeful eyebrows.

"Does that mean what I think it means?"

By this point, she'd composed herself again. She pressed her lips together and frowned.

"Maybe? Despite the strange detour you took to explain it, I knew what you meant. Those things you're feeling, I'm feeling them too."

I half sat up, my heart in my throat.

"Really?"

She nodded.

"But there were reasons we didn't want to do this. Good reasons."

"Maybe there were," I said, reaching for her hand. "But the more I think about you and what we could have, the less important those reasons seem. Especially after today. I was so fucking angry I wanted to take that woman's head off."

"I noticed," she said with a small smile. "But what if we're wrong? What if this whole thing is just raging hormones?"

I shrugged.

"We're both grown adults, right? If this doesn't work out, we can agree to shake hands and walk away amicably."

She looked at me skeptically.

"That easy, huh?"

"I know this is scary," I said earnestly. "A big part of me is wondering if I've gone insane too. But let's give it a chance. Let me take you out this weekend."

"Joel, I have a kid, remember? I've said this before. Abby comes first. I can't just offload her any time I want to go off and have fun. In fact, we need to wrap this up in the next 30 minutes because I have to be at the school to pick her up."

"I know. You think I don't get it, but I do."

I sat up properly and took her other hand.

"Look, new plan. Instead of me taking you out somewhere, why don't the three of us do something together?"

She looked at our joined hands and sighed.

"It's a big step," she said doubtfully. "Introducing someone new into Abby's life... It's—it's not something I'm willing to do lightly. I don't want her to get upset, or confused or—"

"I understand that, but you have nothing to worry about," I promised. "I love spending time with Abby. We get on great. I would never do anything to hurt her, Olivia. I swear."

I watched her as she deliberated. I knew what I was proposing was a big step—possibly even several big steps. To be honest, I didn't know if I was ready either, but for once I was going with my gut.

"I guess I have been promising her a trip to the zoo soon. I finally started reading her the Vivi Tempest books. Granny V was delighted."

"What did she think?"

"Oh, she loved them, but now she's obsessed with parrots."

"Not tattoos anymore?"

"Both actually. Now she wants a parrot tattoo." She narrowed her eyes playfully. "You're a bad influence."

"I try. So, it's agreed then. We'll all go to the zoo."

"Fine! I surrender."

"Good, otherwise I'm showing up at your place with a parrot."

"Don't you dare!"

I chuckled and pulled her against me, nipping playfully at her lower lip.

"Sorry, Vivi. That's what happens when you take up with a pirate."

"Chaos?"

"Always."

She snuggled back into me, and I closed my eyes. I wondered if I should be freaked out that I wasn't freaking out.

A family outing.

Even thinking it sounded strange.

CHAPTER TWENTY-EIGHT

Joel

"Wow. Are you breaking up with your wardrobe?"

Zel had walked into my bedroom to find me staring at a jumbled pile consisting of every garment I owned. It was a sea of black. Band t-shirts, leather jackets, jeans with chains. Nothing remotely...wholesome.

"No. I'm taking Olivia and Abby to the zoo tomorrow and I wanted to find something that looked normal."

Zel picked up a Smashing Pumpkins hoodie and inspected it critically.

"I see. And why would you want to do that?"

I rubbed at the back of my neck and shrugged.

"I guess I didn't want to embarrass her by sticking out too much."

Zel looked at me with good-natured exasperation.

"Joel. You are 6 foot 4 inches of tattooed masculine beauty. I don—"

I held up a warning hand.

"Lines like that are the reason you don't get to give speeches at my birthday parties anymore."

"The point is, you're always going to stick out...and Olivia clearly digs that," he added hastily.

I frowned.

"You think so?"

"Of course! Don't you think if she'd wanted normal, she could've had it? I'm sure there are plenty of lonely single daddies ready to park their car in her—"

"Hey!"

"*Driveway,* I was going to say. Jeez, why do you have to make everything dirty?"

"Because I *know* that's what you do."

I threw a pair of balled-up socks at him, and they bounced off his head. Zel just gave a long-suffering sigh and began refolding my shirts.

"I think we need to listen to Mr. Cobain on this one," he said.

"Huh?"

"Come as you *are.* Just come as Joel. Joel the terrible host. We should take a break from trashing your bedroom and grab a beer. I *know* you have some chilling in the fridge."

The evening was warm, so we settled on the deck with our drinks. The beer was so cold that condensation had settled on the bottle in sparkling drops. Zel sipped appreciatively and shot me a sidelong glance.

"You're really nervous about this, aren't you?"

I picked moodily at the label on my bottle.

"I'm not nervous. I'm just rusty."

"Can't argue with that."

"I just don't want to mess things up before they've even begun."

Truthfully, I was more than just nervous. I was terrified.

This was the first time I'd asked someone on a date in over five years. And it wasn't just a date. I wasn't only trying to show Olivia that I'd be worth a damn as a boyfriend, I was also hoping to prove that I was a safe person to bring into her daughter's life. I wasn't sure whether I truly believed those things myself yet, so the thought of convincing someone else was intimidating. I couldn't even say what had changed. I'd just had a moment of perfect clarity after an enormous outburst of passion. I wanted Olivia desperately, but there was a small, scared corner of my primal lizard brain that wanted to retreat to my familiar dark cave and brood.

I hadn't been this jittery since my art school interview. I had a keen sense of wanting to get everything right. And that didn't just go for how I looked. What about lunch? Should I bring a picnic basket? Would that suggest I'd gone the extra mile or that I was too cheap to spring for lunch? What's more, if I didn't show up with a picnic basket, would she think that I'd assumed she'd bring one? Like, 'me caveman, woman feed me.' Or if I did show up with one, would it seem like I was saying 'well, clearly, I didn't trust *you* to make any preparations.' These hypothetical picnic baskets and their unforeseen consequences mounted in my head until I called Aunt Loretta in a panic. Now I had a cherry pie and enough sandwiches to feed a small army chilling in the fridge.

It turned out the basket had been the right call. When Olivia saw it, she gave me a smile that made me feel like my chest was going to explode.

That smile set the tone for the rest of the day. It all went so...smoothly. When we stepped out of the car, I awkwardly held out my hand to Olivia. When she took it, the volcanic blush spread to the top of my head. I felt like an awkward high school kid again. We'd had sex plenty of times, but the simple act of holding Olivia's hand in public was almost a bigger deal. Abby looked at us for a second with an unreadable expression and then calmly took her mother's other hand.

We made an odd trio. Olivia wore jeans and the same soft, pink sweater she'd worn the day I met her, and Abby had a yellow sundress with dinosaurs stomping all over it. Then there was me. My black cargo shorts were covered in straps and unnecessary buckles, and I wore a black vest with a ghostly pirate ship on it. Between that and the tattoos, I felt like a Venus flytrap sprouting from a patch of daisies. I tried my best to be in the moment and not think about whether people might be staring, or what they might be thinking.

I learned several bizarre life lessons that day. One was that it was faintly embarrassing to be schooled on animal trivia by a 7-year-old. Then there was the fact that, the smaller the monkey, the more it looked like it would cheerfully kill you the first chance it got.

After we were done with the simians and lion country, we headed to the reptile house. Abby was fearless with the snakes and the iguanas. Even the Komodo dragons didn't faze her. As far as she was concerned, they were miniature dinosaurs and that was 'so cool.' She needed a little coaxing when it came to the acrylic enclosure with the 6-inch red-knee tarantula. When it moved, her little hand jumped into mine and stayed there. I held it carefully, suddenly conscious of how huge and clumsy my own hand was.

When we stepped back out into the bright sunlight, Olivia spotted Abby's grip on my hand and flashed me that smile again. Her hand slipped into my back pocket, and we walked off like that. There was no other word for it—we looked like a family. A weird family but still a family.

As expected, Abby was seriously excited about the parrots. When we got to the aviary with the scarlet macaw, she bounced on the spot and squeaked.

"It's Bones!"

"Kinda," I said. "It's the same kind of parrot."

"Do you think he can talk?"

"I don't know. Why don't you ask him?"

Her little face screwed up in thought for a moment.

"You ask him," she ordered, poking me in the belly.

I glanced at Olivia. She smiled and raised her eyebrows expectantly. Feeling slightly stupid, I cleared my throat and addressed the bird.

"Hey, Mr. Parrot. Got a little girl down here who'd like a chat."

The parrot cocked his head and eyed me beadily.

"Guess it can't."

"I don't know," said Olivia, eyes twinkling. "You weren't very polite."

I rolled my eyes.

"Ok." I took a deep breath and gave the parrot a beseeching look. "Pretty please?"

Olivia giggled behind her hand. The parrot ruffled its feathers and squawked indignantly.

"Aww!" Abby pouted.

"Well," Olivia said, "Bones doesn't always talk when he meets new people, does he? Sometimes he tricks them."

Abby eyed the parrot suspiciously.

"Do you think he's tricking us?"

I scratched my chin thoughtfully and pretended to scrutinize the recalcitrant macaw.

"It's possible. Parrots are a lot like people."

"Except with wings," Abby interrupted.

"Yes, but—"

"And beaks."

"True," I said patiently. "But what I meant was that they're smart, like people, so they might need time to decide they like someone. Maybe he'd trust us if he got to know us a little better."

"Like you and Mommy."

Ok. That, I hadn't been prepared for. This kid was dangerously smart. Not hard to see where that came from. I looked at Olivia. She bit her lip and looked away. Her cheeks were flaming with that vivid pink that made her eyes sparkle. I had a weird feeling behind my breastbone. Happy and overwhelmed at the same time. Once again, I was caught between the impulse to run and hide and the urge to hold on to her and not let go.

"Hey," I said, changing the subject. "If this was Bones, you know what might work?"

"What?"

"If we offered him a banana. They're his favorite, right?"

Abby chewed that one over for a second.

"Mommy said you shouldn't try to make people like you by giving them things."

"Is that so?"

"Yes," Abby said emphatically. "Presents don't equal love."

I had an uncomfortable memory of the time I'd suggested to Olivia that she might like a man with a bigger bank balance. My debt to my aunt and uncle had so firmly tied money to my self-worth that I'd forgotten I could be appreciated for anything else. I felt like an ass for assuming Olivia would be that shallow. Even when I was protecting her, I was still hurting her. Assuming I knew what she needed better than she did. Once again, I was getting schooled by a kid. I wanted to take Olivia in my arms and tell her I was sorry. Instead, I ruffled Abby's hair awkwardly. I hoped the present thing wasn't set in stone, though. I'd snuck to the gift shop after lunch and bought that plushie parrot she'd had her eye on. It was tucked under the front seat of my car in a gift bag.

Once we'd seen all the animals, we took Abby to the play area. Olivia had to leave to go to the bathroom, and she left me in charge. I stood watching Abby as she clambered over the jungle gym. When she got to the top, she grinned down at me and waved. I waved back as my chest swelled with a strange feeling of pride.

"That's a very pretty little girl you have there."

"Oh, she's not mine."

The words were out of my mouth before I'd thought them through. The speaker was a tired-looking woman with a double stroller. She looked slightly taken aback at my vehement denial. I put my hands in my pockets and grimaced awkwardly. My heart sank when I spotted Abby watching us from her perch.

"What I mean is, I'm her mom's—I'm here with her mom."

Something hot and uncomfortable squirmed in the pit of my stomach. I'd agonized over this. It wasn't like I minded being taken for Abby's father, it was more that I didn't want her or Olivia to feel like I was trying to muscle in and replace her dad. It was the right thing to do. The sensitive thing.

So why did I feel like an ass?

CHAPTER TWENTY-NINE

Olivia

"Did you have a nice time?"

"I guess."

I frowned. Abby huddled listlessly on the sofa, absent-mindedly clutching her new stuffed parrot. Usually, after a day out, she was bubbling with energy and eager to relive the highlights. I'd expected to find her at her desk, feverishly drawing parrot pictures. She'd been quiet on the car ride home and a little subdued when we said goodbye to Joel, but I'd put that down to simple tiredness.

For once, I was buzzing with energy and she wasn't. I couldn't understand it; it seemed like the day had gone so well. Wonderfully in fact. It was thrilling to be out in public with Joel, holding his hand, feeling his arm around my waist. And he was so good with Abby. Seeing the two of them banter made my heart happy. I'd almost melted when he pulled the parrot from under the car seat.

This didn't add up. Time for a test.

"Hey!" I suggested. "It's been a long day. Why don't we go grab dinner at Chuck E. Cheese?"

Abby shrugged.

Yep! Red flags ahoy! Damn, now I'm *thinking like a pirate.*

Chuck E. Cheese was the ultimate treat/premium tier bribe. Like most parents, I considered the brash, colorful eatery to be the ninth circle of hell. Sighing, I sat down next to her.

"What's wrong, sweetheart?"

"Nothing."

I scooted closer and put an arm around her.

"Abby, look at me."

She'd been absorbed in twisting one of the parrot's bright yellow legs. Now she looked up at me.

"We don't have many rules in this house," I said gently. "But what's the big one?"

She clutched the parrot close and mumbled into his wings.

"What was that?" I asked, maneuvering the plush away from her mouth.

"Don't lie about our feelings," she said miserably.

"Mmhmm. If something's bothering you, I need to know about it. I won't be mad, I promise."

For a long time, she didn't answer. She chewed her lip and flapped the parrot's wings in and out.

"I wanted to...ask something," she said eventually.

"You know you can."

That was the other big rule. It's always ok to ask questions. Admittedly, I sometimes regretted it. There was the time we'd been waiting at the doctor's office and she'd loudly asked why men had nipples. But embarrassing incidents aside, moments like this were the reason the rule was in place.

"Why don't I have a daddy?"

I hadn't been expecting that. Thanks to an abundance of amazing people in Abby's life, it often seemed like she didn't notice her father's absence. Or had I just missed it?

"You do have a daddy, sweetie. He lives in New York."

"I mean a *real* daddy. One who wants to—"

She took a stuttering breath and gripped the parrot harder. "One who wants to see me."

My heart broke. I knew this conversation might come up at some point. It would've been nice to have come prepped with some easy answers.

"It's not that he doesn't want to see you," I said. "But he's very busy, and New York's a ver—"

I cut myself off abruptly. I was doing what I promised myself I'd never do. I refused to do my child the disrespect of glossing over a difficult truth with a palliative lie. My arm tightened around Abby's shoulder, and I pulled her closer.

"I know it sucks, baby. I wished he tried harder too. It's difficult to explain it all properly without going into some grown-up issues that might be a little hard for you to understand. What you do need to understand is that these are *his* poor decisions. They don't reflect on you in any way. You're a wonderful little girl and I'm just sorry your daddy can't see how lucky he is to have you. You'd make any father proud, baby."

She dropped the parrot and cuddled into my chest. I couldn't hear any sobbing, but my top did feel suspiciously wet. If long-distance teleportation were a thing, a certain asshole would be getting the slap of his life right now.

"Besides," I said, "families come in all different shapes and sizes. Think about Alana and Jess and Jonathan and Ranjit. You might not have a daddy who lives with you, but you've got me and Granny V. and Russ and Erin and Uncle Nolan—"

She gripped the front of my shirt tighter.

"He'll have his own baby soon," she said. "He won't need me to be his baby girl anymore."

Uh-oh.

Another pothole I hadn't seen coming. I was really dropping the ball lately. She'd seemed so hyped about Erin being pregnant.

"It's true that this baby will change things, but it won't change the way your uncle feels about you. He loves you very much. And change isn't always a bad thing. Change can be exciting. Aren't you looking forward to being a big cousin?"

"I suppose so."

I took a deep breath. I hadn't planned to broach this subject for a while, but the conversation was naturally trending in that direction. Why not grab the bull by the horns?"

"And..." I said. "That's not the only thing that might change."

She raised her head from my chest and frowned.

"What do you mean?"

"Well, babies coming along isn't the only way a family can grow. Sometimes we make new friends and they become family too. We were spending time with a new friend today."

"Who?"

"Joel, silly. Who else?"

Her face fell and she chewed on her lip again. Uneasiness stirred in the pit of my stomach.

"You like Joel, don't you?" I asked.

She nodded.

"Good," I said, trying a little too hard to sound cheerful. "I was hoping you'd say that, because I thought it might be nice if we spent a bit more time with him."

She put her head on one side.

"Time doing what?"

"Lots of things. We could go to a movie, or he could come over for dinner one night, or—"

"If you and Joel get married and make a baby, what will happen to me?"

I gaped at her.

"Woah! Slow down. Sweetie, I think we might be jumping the gun a little here. Joel and I aren't ready for anything like that yet. And even if we were, nothing would happen to you. Do you think I could go off and make a new family without you? We're a package deal, kiddo. You're the most important thing in the world to me. That won't change."

Her face crumpled and she launched herself at me once more. I stroked her hair and made soft soothing noises. I hated to think how long she'd been holding on to this.

"But if you did get married to Joel, you'd belong to him."

"Well, we'd belong to each other."

"A-and if you had a baby, the baby would belong to him too."

"The baby would belong to all of us, sweetheart. It would be your brother or sister."

"But *I* wouldn't belong to him," she said. "Not for real."

I swallowed the ache in my throat.

"He might not feel that way. Lots of people call Granny V 'Granny' even though she's not their granny. People can decide to belong to each other, and that could be the case for you and Joel too."

She shook her head convulsively.

"He doesn't want me," she said vehemently. "A lady at the zoo said I was a pretty and Joel said I wasn't his."

At that point, she dissolved into floods of tears. I managed to calm her down enough to get some hot chocolate into her and put her to bed. But it felt like she had cried herself out rather than actually feeling better.

I sat on the couch with a glass of wine and stared unblinking at a random spot on the rug. The same rug Joel and I had made love on in a fit of ill-judged passion. All this time, I'd been so wrapped up in him that I'd missed the fact that my little girl was miserable. I had done the unthinkable and put my needs before hers. I had failed as a mother.

Like an idiot, I'd decided it was safe to let my guard down and let someone into my life. I'd convinced myself that taking this shot with Joel was the best thing for me and Abby, but I was kidding myself. By dangling Joel in front of her, I'd drawn attention to an absence she'd never had reason to notice before. And what if I managed to convince her to trust him with her little heart and then things didn't work out? No, I couldn't risk it. There was only one solution. I had to put my own feelings aside and do what was best for my child. I had to break things off with Joel.

CHAPTER THIRTY

Joel

I stepped back from the blanket and admired my handiwork. I'd been surprised when Olivia messaged so soon after our date to say she wanted to meet for lunch. Surprised, but pleased. It had only been two days, but it already felt like forever since I'd kissed her. I'd suggested we meet at this spot in the park so I could surprise her with a romantic picnic.

There was Cobb salad, lemonade chilling in the ice bucket, and leftover cherry pie from the zoo trip. I'd also brought a couple of candles and scattered some wildflowers. I'd wanted to go all out—champagne, fancy food, roses everywhere. But I couldn't. Not yet. The studio was doing better, but it would still be a while before we were on our feet. Things were looking up, though. On Sunday I'd been able to present Aunt Loretta and Uncle Jeff with a check. It was the first time in a long while and it felt amazing. They'd tried to refuse, but I'd insisted. My aunt tried to hide it, but I saw the flash of relief in her eyes. Until I'd paid them back, I just wouldn't have money to splash around.

And that was ok. What I'd prepared wasn't expensive, but it could still be special. Even the leftover cherry pie felt like a cute reminder of our last date. Our *first* date. At first, I'd been upset that I couldn't spoil Olivia the way I wanted to, but then Abby's little voice echoed in my mind.

"Things don't equal love."

"Wow."

I'd been absorbed in making minute adjustments to my romantic tableau and I hadn't heard Olivia approach. She looked pale, and she returned my welcoming smile with less than full enthusiasm, but I put that down to tiredness. She did have a full-time career and a kid to look after. I wanted her to know I understood that. I couldn't be second-guessing things every time her energy levels dipped.

"Hey, Vivi."

I stood up, threw an arm around her shoulder, and dropped a kiss on her head. Was I imagining things, or did she feel a little stiff?

Cool it, Joel. We're not second-guessing things, remember?

"What's all this?" she asked, gesturing at the blanket.

"A surprise. I believe it's a common element in a romantic gesture. I know; I looked it up."

No smile. Not even an eye roll. Unease grew in the pit of my stomach.

"What's the occasion?"

"You are."

I dropped my arm from her shoulders and thrust my hands into my pockets.

"Actually, *we* are," I amended. "I'm not good at the mushy stuff or talking about my feelings. But I wanted you to know that I had an amazing time on Saturday, and I wanted to do something to show you how much it meant to me—how much you mean to me. Happy second date-aversary."

"Y-you...you..."

She looked at me with suspiciously bright eyes and the unease grew.

"You went to so much trouble," she said eventually.

"Of course I did. Sit down."

I felt like I was having to shout over the pounding of my heart. We sat down and I poured her a glass of lemonade. She took a sip and grimaced as if it tasted bitter.

"Joel, we need to talk."

My whole body went icy cold. Every form of media in existence conditions people to dread that phrase before they've even contemplated their first relationship.

"About what?"

My voice came out as a tight croak.

She took a deep breath and sat up straighter, like she was preparing to speak at a press conference.

"Before I say anything, it's important you know that this isn't about you."

There it was. The boulder that had been teetering above my head dropped into my stomach. Acknowledging it hurt too much, so I decided to do the sensible thing. I'd bury it with hot, heaping shovels of toxic anger instead. I snorted bitterly.

"Let me guess, your next line is, 'it's not you, it's me?'"

"Joel, I—"

"Well, at least you're doing it right. You came prepared. Did you read a handbook? *How to End a Relationship One Cliché at a Time.*"

"I don't think you're being very fair."

"*I'm* not being fair? Well, guess what? Life's not fair. I should've remembered that. Do I even get a reason?"

My voice was getting gradually louder, but once the tirade had started, I couldn't stop. I'd just started to believe it was safe to open up, that maybe I was good enough. That I could make someone's life better, that I could take care of a family, maybe even that I deserved to be happy. I realized that Olivia was still talking, still scrambling to explain herself. I wasn't interested. I knew what this was about.

"Of course you get a reason. It's—well, actually, it's Abby. I don't think she's ready for another presence in her life. It would be too disruptive, especially with Erin and Nolan's baby on the way."

I barked with incredulous laughter.

"You're putting your brother's baby on the list of reasons to dump me? Well, at least that one's original, I guess."

Olivia closed her eyes and pressed her fingers to her forehead.

"I have to put Abby first," she said quietly. "I'm sorry. I know this is hard for you. It's hard for me too but—"

"Bullshit!" I shouted. "Abby and I were getting along great. You know I'd never hurt her. Single parents have relationships, Olivia. When are you going to stop using your daughter as a reason not to take chances?"

Her face hardened instantly.

"Joel," she said coldly. "You're making a scene."

Woohoo. Cliché bingo continues.

"And that's what this is about, isn't it? You're ashamed of me. I don't fit in with your cozy, middle-class bubble. What was it, huh? One too many sidelong looks when we were out? People wondering what that nice, suburban mom is doing with that shady, inked-up rocker boy. Maybe it made you ask yourself that question too."

"You're being ridiculous."

"Just admit it," I yelled. "Your open-minded, inclusive lip service makes great soundbites for the kid, but not much when it comes to actually applying it to your own life. When it comes down to it, I'm not good enough for you, your family, or your snotty PTA friends. Fine to be your dirty little secret, but not your boyfriend. Story of my life; Joel's not good enough."

She grabbed her bag and stood up, knocking over the lemonade.

"You know," she said furiously. "When we started this, you said we could walk away like mature adults if this didn't work out. And now you're acting like a spoiled child. Maybe you were right. Maybe you're not good enough. Maybe you never were."

She stalked off, nearly clobbering me around the head with her purse as she swung it over her shoulder. For a long time, I just sat there, staring at our untouched food while the lemonade stain spread across the cloth. My eyes burned and a horrible ache built up in my chest until I couldn't stand it anymore. I roared angrily, swiping my arm across the cloth, sending the bowls and plates flying. The candle tipped over, but the cloth was so wet from the lemonade that it didn't matter. I watched unblinking as the flame died with nothing but a tiny hiss and a wisp of black smoke.

CHAPTER THIRTY-ONE

Olivia

"O-M-F-G!"

We'd been sitting silently in the living room when Granny V suddenly exclaimed loudly. Nolan snorted into his beer. I looked up from my laptop and blinked.

"Do you even know what that stands for, Granny?"

She looked up from her phone and raised an eyebrow.

"I'm 80 years old, dear. I don't think I'd have lasted this long if a four-letter word could finish me off. Honestly, the way you and your brother insist on treating me like I came down with the last shower is enough to make me LMFAO."

"You can stop now."

"No," she declared. "Shan't. Jayden spent all of Sunday teaching me these."

She picked up a leatherbound notebook from the coffee table and thumbed through it.

"I've even made little drawings of the appropriate emoticons. I know how you all like to make fun of me when I get those wrong."

Nolan leaned back on the couch and put an arm around Erin. I couldn't help smiling when I noticed him resting a protective hand on her enormous bump.

"Does this mean the end of the era of the rainbow poop?" he asked.

"They always made me smile," Erin put in.

"Thank you, Erin," Granny said, glaring at Nolan. "I'm glad someone here has a sense of humor."

I rolled my eyes.

"So, are you going to tell us what prompted your initial acronym?"

Granny stared at her phone and bit her lip.

"First, I need to get one of you to read this and make sure it says what I think it says."

Nolan gestured for the phone. As he read, his eyes widened.

"It's from a film studio. They say they're interested in buying the rights to Vivi Tempest. They want to make an animated movie."

Erin and I gasped. Unfortunately, mine was accompanied by a wince. As soon as Vivi was mentioned, all I could think about was Joel. The feel of his skin as I stroked the parrot tattoo. The excitement on his face when I gave him the signed book. It was bizarre that a character that had haunted me since I was little—a character that my grandmother had created nearly 30 years ago—was now irreversibly associated with a man I had only known for a few months. It was a symptom of a larger problem. There didn't seem to be a single part of my life that wasn't somehow tied to Joel. I never wanted to see him again, but there were reminders of him everywhere. Of course, the biggest one was printed indelibly on my skin. As metaphors go, it didn't get much more fucking romantic. It had become a habit to dress very quickly and avoid mirrors. I'd briefly thought about having the tattoo removed, but I couldn't do it. It meant too much. The problem was, it represented what I didn't want to admit—that Joel had touched my past, present, and my future in a way that no one else had, and I was forced to carry the memory of him everywhere. It was bad enough when I could avoid him. I didn't know what I was going to do when Sailor Joey's moved to the first floor of Sticky Treats.

I glanced up and found Erin looking at me with a concerned frown. Aside from Alana, she had been the only person who'd suspected anything about what was going on with Joel. Over the past couple of weeks, it had been hard to stop myself from asking her if she'd seen him. I didn't need to know. I didn't want to know.

"Honestly, Granny, I'm not misreading this," Nolan insisted. "I can pass it to Erin if you like, and she can confirm it, but reading documents is literally 90% of my job."

Granny V's hand flew to her chest. She looked extremely flushed.

"It just doesn't make any sense," she said. "All this fuss for a little character I drew years ago. Do kids still read Vivi?"

"I'm slightly disturbed that you're asking me this," Nolan laughed. "Do you even glance at your royalty statements?"

"I can't be bothered with all that. That's what I hired Gus for."

Gus was Granny V's uncommonly good-natured and long-suffering accountant.

"Well," said Nolan patiently. "In the absence of Gus, I think this confirms they do—or at least that their parents do. This is a successful studio. They know what they're doing."

"I don't know how much of a litmus test she is, but Abby loves them," I added.

Part of me had hoped her enthusiasm would wane, but the opposite had happened. She hadn't mentioned Joel since that day after we'd gone to the zoo, but she insisted I read the Vivi books every night. Not only that, but she and that stuffed parrot had become inseparable. After three years, Olaf had been knocked from his lofty perch.

"Well," Granny said, "I'm all atwitter about this. What should I do?"

"Nothing yet," Nolan advised. "They won't expect a reply straight away. Give it time to percolate. And we'll have to make sure we can engage someone to look over any contract they send you."

"Can't you do it?"

"That's flattering, but it's not my area," he said gently. "I know some people, though. I'll see what I can do."

"I'd best send a message to my sugar bear." Granny tapped feverishly at her phone. "He should be nearly finished with his golf by now."

"How about it, Liv?" Nolan said. "You're going to be famous. Well, your pirate alter-ego, anyway."

I tried to enter into the spirit of celebration but I could only manage a pained smile. I'd just been starting to identify with the character again. Erin looked between me and Nolan, and then me and Granny V.

"Hey, Granny," she said brightly. "I think this calls for a round of celebratory hot chocolate. Want to help roll me to the kitchen so I can make some?"

"Yes. Yes, of course, dear."

Erin heaved herself from the couch and headed for the kitchen. Granny V floated distractedly after her, still staring at her phone. Nolan dropped into the seat next to me and I poised myself for a grilling. Had Erin said something? I was sure I hadn't been that obvious.

"Great news, huh?" Nolan ventured.

"Yeah. Great."

"So why do you look like your puppy just died?"

I closed my eyes and rubbed a hand over my forehead.

"I'm fine. I'm just tired."

"No, you're not. You're miserable. You've been miserable for the past two weeks."

"I'm not miserable."

Nolan sighed.

"Don't insult my intelligence. I'm your brother."

I put my laptop aside and folded my arms, refusing to meet his eye.

"I know I haven't always been what I should be," he said. "You've had to spend way too much of your life taking care of me and picking up after me. But things are different now. We're both adults. We can be there for each other. If something's bothering you, I want to know about it. Admittedly I'm not good with emotional stuff. I'm more useful if the thing bothering you is something I can punch or sue, but—"

"You have been there for me," I said hoarsely.

My vision blurred and a lump formed in my throat.

"When Charles left, you—"

"I know," he said. "I stepped in. I did what any brother should do. I remember it as the first and only time in our lives that you leaned on me. And for some reason, you've never forgiven yourself for that."

"I screwed up."

The lump expanded and tears streamed down my cheeks.

"I gave everything up for a guy who let me down."

"You made one mistake. Does that mean you never get to have any fun again?"

I put a hand over my face in a vain attempt to contain my sobs. Nolan pulled me against him in a one-armed hug.

"You're a good person and an excellent mother. You deserve to be happy, and if something—or someone—makes you happy, then you should think about letting it—or them—in."

I wiped my eyes and sniffed, before giving him a sidelong glance.

"This is becoming incredibly specific," I said suspiciously. "Has someone said something to you?"

"Nope."

He withdrew his arm from my shoulder and raised both hands in surrender.

"Entirely general. Pinkie promise."

"Well, ok. I'll believe you. You're aware I get to break your finger if you're lying to me."

"Seems harsh."

"Sorry."

I shrugged.

"I don't make the rules of the pinkie promise."

"Fair enough. I'd better go check on the kitchen crew. Between a pregnant Erin and a distracted Granny, I don't wanna think about what could happen."

He squeezed my hand and got up. When he got to the door, he looked back.

"By the way, I never had a chance to mention it, but I love your new tattoo."

"Thanks," I said, surprised at the change in direction.

"Yeah. It's not something I would have expected you to go for, but I think it might be perfect for you. Maybe it can remind you to give yourself a break once in a while."

Pinkie promise, huh?

The only break I needed was a clean break from Joel. Nolan meant well, but he didn't understand. He wasn't a parent yet. I'd made the right decision for Abby, and that was the important thing. All I had to do now was stick to it.

CHAPTER THIRTY-TWO

Joel

"Look, I don't quite know how to say this, so I'm just gonna come out and say it. I know this is going to sound sudden, especially when things were going so great between us. But, when it comes down to it, I think it's important to be honest. I don't think I can do this. I was flattered when you came to me, but I think deep down we both know there's someone out there who's a better fit for you. It's not you, it's me. I'm ju— Dammit! Why is this so hard?"

I closed my eyes and let my head fall forwards onto the steering wheel. Unfortunately, I also triggered the horn. I nearly gave *myself* a heart attack, never mind the little old lady walking past with her dog. She turned and glared. Still, what was one more person giving me the stink eye? Her, the parking attendant who'd circled the block at least three times since I'd been sitting here, Zel was mad at me because I hadn't been to work all week, Crystal was on my case about missing the last two family dinners, and Dustin was pissed because I'd missed our last two workouts. Then there was Olivia. I couldn't even let myself think about her. It was too much. Letting yourself fall in love for the first time since college and then getting the boot after one date was a hard pill to swallow. I'd always said I was better off on my own. I should've listened to myself. Maybe it really was time to condemn myself to a pirate's life. Sail off into the sunset somewhere no one would have to worry about me and I couldn't mess things up for anyone. I just had one last boat to burn.

I'd been sitting outside Sticky Treats for almost an hour, rehearsing what I'd say to Erin. It felt weird. A year ago I'd have done anything to get this place. Now I was about to willingly pass it up. After everything that had happened, I couldn't rent the upper floor. The chance of randomly bumping into Olivia was too high. Zel and Lily would be pissed, but they'd get over it. I was giving serious thought to selling Sailor Joey's. It was time to grow up and stop chasing dreams. Selling my half would go a long way to getting Aunt Loretta and Uncle Jeff their money back, and I could work to pay the rest off. Shouldn't be too hard to find a studio that needed someone for flash, especially if I relocated to a bigger city.

It all made sense, but I still felt like crap about it. But then, I felt like crap about everything lately. Couldn't turn around without bumping into someone I'd let down.

Time to disappoint someone else.

Sticky Treats was bustling, as usual. I couldn't see Erin, but Jayden was behind the counter. When he saw me, his face lit up. He'd been a fan of mine since the prairie oyster.

"Joel, hey!"

He tucked a wayward lock of green hair under his bandana and stuck out a fist. I bumped it half-heartedly.

"Hey, man. Erin around?"

"She's in the kitchen. She'll be out in a minute."

He reached along the counter and pulled a tray of cake pops towards him. They were long, twisty, flowing spindles on sticks. At first, I thought I was looking at coral, or purple seaweed. Then I noticed the suckers.

"We're expanding our cake pop range. Can I interest you in a hentacle?"

"A what?"

Jayden shook his head and tutted.

"Seriously? I thought you were a man of culture."

"Clearly not."

He sighed patiently.

"It's basically a mash-up of hentai and tentacle. You see, it's a common trope in erotic Japanese art to have these prehensile tentacles that—"

"Joel! This is a nice surprise."

"Erin. Hey!"

I was so relieved at the distraction that I almost forgot why I was here. Erin glanced between me and the cake pops and narrowed her eyes at her assistant.

"Jayden, I've told you at least 50 times. Stop harassing the customers with your tentacles."

"*Hentacles.*"

"Tentacles or hentacles, I don't care. As long as they're 'consentacles.' Don't shove them under people's noses."

Jayden scowled mutinously and withdrew the tray. Erin turned back to me with a weary smile.

"Sorry about that. What can I do for you?"

I tried to return her smile, but all I could summon was a grimace. Guilt squirmed hot in my stomach.

"I—uh. I wanted to talk to you about something."

She gave me a long, penetrating look. I pushed a hand through my hair and looked away.

"Alright," she said eventually. "Are you ok to step upstairs with me for a minute? I've got a couple of things I need to do."

I shuffled behind her, hands in my pockets. She was so big by now that every step looked like it threatened to tip her over. We had to stop halfway up the stairs so she could rest. She stuck out her belly and rubbed at her lower back, groaning.

"Oof. Gravity is really not my friend right now."

"You should start charging that kid rent."

She smiled wryly.

"Thank you for not seizing on this opportunity to tell me I'm 'glowing.'"

"I know better," I said. "Tried it with Crystal when she was pregnant with her twins. Got a 35-minute lecture on hormone fluctuations and morning sickness. Gotta admit it doesn't sound like much fun."

"This part definitely isn't."

Eventually, we made it up the stairs. After we'd paused so Erin could catch her breath, she unlocked the door to the second-floor studio. The room was exactly as I remembered it when I'd come here with... Must've been a similar time of day too. Even the light was the same.

Could've done without getting stabbed in the chest today.

Erin stood next to me. After a while I looked at her, confused.

"What do you need to do?"

"Nothing," she said casually. "I just thought you should take another really good look at the place before you did anything stupid."

Damn! Rumbled.

"Look, I—"

She held up her hand.

"I don't know what happened between you and Olivia. Honestly, I hope you work it out. But it shouldn't affect your decision here."

I crossed my arms and glanced around the high, airy room. It was an amazing space. I bit my lip.

"I'm just worried it might get...awkward, y'know? If we bump into each other."

She winced sympathetically.

"Things end that badly between you two?"

My jaw tightened.

"You could say that."

"Thought so. She's been pretty miserable."

"She has?"

On the one hand, I was glad that she hadn't just brushed our relationship off. At the same time, the thought of her in pain was...uncomfortable. It made all my muscles feel tight, like I was still poised to leap into action.

"Any chance you could work things out?"

I shrugged.

"I honestly don't know."

"Well, you don't know unless you try."

Erin fanned a hand in front of her flushed face and moved toward the windows. She had to stand on tiptoes to reach the catch and I stepped forward to help.

"Sometimes," she said. "You just gotta— Fuck!"

She stopped mid-stretch and clutched her stomach.

"What is it?"

I rushed to her side, panic fluttering in my chest.

"I think," she gasped. "I think that was a contraction."

Uh-oh.

CHAPTER THIRTY-THREE

Joel

"I think that was a contraction."

"Right! Shit! Uh—"

I looked around the room frantically.

"Don't move! Unless you should move."

Erin leaned forward with both hands braced on the window ledge. I watched her take slow, deliberate breaths and unconsciously tried to match them.

"Joel," she said tensely.

"Yeah?"

"It's probably going to be about 20 hours. You don't have to stand there like you're ready to catch a football."

"Right. Sorry."

I straightened up sheepishly and stuffed my hands into my pockets.

"Want me to get someone? Should I go get Jayden?"

"No! No. He'd just panic."

Yeah, not everyone can be calm and rational like me.

"Anyway, he's better off downstairs. I'd feel better knowing someone's holding down the fort."

"Ok."

I looked around the empty room again and bit the tip of my thumb.

"Do I start ripping up towels, or...?"

"Just—"

She took a deep shuddering breath.

"I left my phone in the kitchen. Could you go get it for me? I need to call Nolan and tell him to get over here with the overnight bag and the birthing tape."

"Sure!"

Relieved to be given a task, I shot down the stairs, nearly tripping in my haste. I'd only been inside the Sticky Treats kitchen once. Back then, all the equipment had been packed into boxes. It could've been anywhere. Now it actually looked like the gleaming chrome nerve center of an erotic bakery. For one thing, there were several finished projects on the central island.

Looking around, I could see a tray of marzipan penises with identical silver piercings, a 12-inch chocolate sculpture of a busty mermaid, and a big blue cake shaped like a... Hmm. Ok. So there was that.

Someone likes their alien ladies.

Pretty impressive how they got the folds to glisten like that. No phone though. Panic rising, I scanned all the surfaces. Nothing. Aunt Loretta's voice echoed in my mind asking me if I were having a man look, so I started moving things. I even opened cupboards and drawers and looked in there. There's an unfortunate thing about tall, bulky people in crowded spaces. We rarely realize how much space we take up.

I'd crouched down to check the shelf below the central counter. When I straightened up, my shoulder caught the mermaid right in the butt. It happened in slow motion. There was a sickening crack as the mermaid detached from her rock and slowly toppled over.

"Shit!"

Moving with speed and agility only possible with massive

amounts of adrenaline, I surged forward and caught it mid-tumble. Now I was stretched awkwardly over the table, holding a surprisingly heavy sculpture around the waist, and my grip was slipping.

"What the fuck, dude? Unhand that mermaid."

I was so shocked that I obeyed Jayden's instruction. We both watched in horror as the mermaid fell face down on the blue cake. It landed with a wet *thud*, spattering the table with iridescent white cream. Jayden's mouth opened and closed like that of a goldfish as he stared blankly at the carnage.

"This isn't what it looks like."

It was all I could think of to say. Jayden looked at me incredulously.

"Do you even know what this looks like? Does the term 'bukkake' mean anything to you?"

"Yes!" I said quickly. "Yes, it does. Please don't start explaining things again. Erin's gone into labor. She sent me down here to get her phone."

"So you decided to destroy the kitchen instead?"

"No. I can't find the phone. I was looking, but then I knocked over the—"

He held out both his hands.

"Ok, ok, I get it. Did you try calling it?"

"Didn't think of that."

Jayden blinked rapidly.

"How could you not think of that?!" he exploded. "What kind of crazy boomer are you?"

"I panicked, ok? I'll call it now."

I dialed the number. After a short pause, the tell-tale vibration sounded. We both looked around for the source. Turned out I'd been close when I checked the shelf. It was coming from underneath the central counter. I got down on my belly and peered underneath. There it was, surrounded by a pale blue glow.

"It's under there," I said. "But I can't reach it."

I got up on my knees and considered Jayden.

"You've got skinny arms. You try."

"Hey! Watch it, roid-rage. I'm a baker. I happen to be toned AF."

"Whatever. Just get down there."

As I'd predicted, Jayden's arm just fit into the narrow space. After some grunting and scrabbling, he managed to pull it out. Straightening up, I looked guiltily at the mess on the table. At least the mermaid looked like she was having a good time.

"Is there anything I can do or should I just...?"

Jayden rolled his eyes and jerked his head at the door.

"Just get that to Erin. Customers are waiting outside, and I need to try and rescue the mermaid from the alien cream pie."

I probably won't ever hear that sentence again.

I knew something was wrong before I got halfway up the stairs. Erin's pained moans floated clearly through the closed door. I quickened my pace, taking the remaining stairs two at a time. I found her slumped on the floor under the window ledge, a puddle forming underneath her. Her cheeks were flushed and sweat glistened on her forehead.

"Something's not right," she gasped, face contorting with pain.

"What do you mean?"

I rushed over and crouched anxiously by her side.

"All the classes...said...it should start with...mild...contractions every 20 minutes."

"This is mild?"

"Do they look mild to you?!"

"Nope. Sorry, you're right. Here, I brought your phone."

She managed to unlock it but before she could dial, she hunched over, howling with pain. My stomach churned. I felt helpless, clueless, and utterly fucking useless.

Just like always.

"C-call, Nolan," Erin grunted. "T-tell him my...water broke, and my contractions are...five minutes apart. He'll know what to do."

I blinked and fumbled with the phone. My fingers felt huge and clumsy. A familiar female voice answered on the second ring.

"Nolan Reid's phone."

My brain stalled.

"Her contractions have broken."

A long pause.

"This isn't Erin, is it?"

I started shaking my head before remembering that Alana couldn't see me.

"No, it's Joel. But—"

"Joel?" she repeated. "What are you doing on Erin's phone?"

"It doesn't matter. Just—"

"Is Olivia with you? Because—"

"Baby!" I shouted desperately.

"What?"

"Baby! Coming now! Erin's having a baby."

There was another contraction proceeded by a bellowing wail.

"So I hear," Alana said. "So, when you say now, do you mean now-now?"

"I *mean* that her water broke, and her contractions are five—"

"Three," Erin corrected.

"Three minutes apart."

"Shit!"

"Yeah, that's pretty much what I said."

"No, I mean, shit, Nolan's court case overran. We're still there and they're all in session right now."

My heart threatened to hammer itself out of my chest and sweat broke out on my forehead.

"Well, he can't be held up," I said, trying to keep the panicked wobble out of my voice. "Go in there and get him."

"I can't just interrupt a court proceeding. I'll have to wait for the next recess."

"Isn't there anything you can do?"

She paused. I could practically hear the gears in her head turning.

"I could pull the fire alarm, I guess."

I gave it more consideration than I should have.

"Probably shouldn't do that," I said reluctantly.

"Prolly not. Look, I'll get our boy over there as soon as possible. In the meantime, call Granny V. She'll have a backup plan."

"Right."

"Or—"

"Or what?"

"Or you could grow a pair and call Olivia."

"Look, I don't think this is the right time for this conversation. And whatever's she's told you, I wasn't the one who called things off."

"Ay. Seriously, I'm gonna bang both your heads together."

"Bite me."

She chuckled.

"No can do. Jess pouts if she doesn't get to watch. Good luck, nene."

I breathed a sigh of relief when I found Granny V listed on Erin's phone as 'Granny V.' I didn't know her first name. I was less relieved when her phone went straight to voicemail. I found Olivia's name and my thumb hovered over the call button. The handset nearly slipped from my grip when Erin gave an agonized scream. I ran back to her side and gave her my hand to squeeze.

Big mistake.

I kept my sounds to a restrained whimper, but I swear I felt bones crunch.

"Erin," I gasped. "Nolan's held up in court and I can't get hold of Granny V. I could call Olivia."

I was ashamed of my relief when Erin bit her lip and shook her head.

"No. If Alana's in court and..." Her face screwed up and she gave my hand another bone-crushing squeeze. "...and Granny's not picking up, they'll be no one to collect Ab-Abby from... school. Joel, I hate to ask, but w-would you drive me to the hospital."

I was dangerously underqualified for this mission, but there was only one answer I could give.

"Of course I will."

CHAPTER THIRTY-FOUR

Olivia

"Have you seen my glasses, Olivia?"

"They're on the chain around your neck."

I hadn't even needed to look up from my laptop. Granny V had asked me the same question three times in the last hour. I would have been worried about her if I hadn't known how stressed she was. She'd received an email offering a last-minute spot on a panel at a children's science fiction and fantasy convention. Once Alana, Jess, and I had explained what that meant, she'd been extremely excited—and then terrified.

"I swear, I don't know if I'm coming or going today," she lamented. "Every time I think I'm all packed for the weekend, I remember something else. I'm just glad I was able to reschedule my bunions for this afternoon."

"Sit down," I ordered. "I'll make us some tea."

I stood up and winced. The griping belly pain that had been plaguing me all morning suddenly struck. An unpleasant stab just below my belly button. Granny instantly stopped twittering about bunions and hurried to my side.

"What's the matter, dear?"

"Nothing," I groaned. "Just a little cramp."

"Ah!"

She rubbed my shoulder sympathetically.

"It's one of the few compensations for getting old. No more monthly check-ins at the Red Roof Inn."

I shook my head and groped my way to the stove.

"I wish you wouldn't use euphemisms like that. Last time I ended up in a very long and confusing conversation with Abby about who Aunt Flo is and why she doesn't visit you anymore. Anyway, this isn't that. It must be something I ate."

Granny eyed me beadily.

"You're not taking care of yourself. You've been picking at your food all week, and I can tell you're not sleeping."

I watched the steam rise as I poured the water into the mugs. What could I say? I had no answers for her.

"Look," she said. "Are you sure you won't come with us this weekend? The convention center is near a lovely lake. Russ was thinking we could hire a boat, maybe even do a little water skiing. It'd be good for you to get a breath of fresh air after...everything."

I had no idea how much she knew. She had never mentioned Joel by name, but she'd guessed something was wrong. Whether Erin or Nolan had aided her guessing was another matter. I was grateful she didn't press for details. I wasn't ready to talk about things yet.

"I'll be fine. A quiet weekend might be just what we need. Abby's been a little distracted. I thought I'd stream a couple of her favorite movies, maybe bake some cookies."

I went to put Granny's mug in front of her and she laid her hand on my forearm.

"You just promise to call if you need us. And I won't be getting out of your hair today until you promise you'll take a nap before you have to pick Abby up from school."

Maybe that wasn't such a bad idea. I felt terrible.

I ended up sleeping for longer than I had intended. I don't know what would've happened if I hadn't been yanked roughly from sleep by my phone ringing.

"Olivia! It's happening."

"Nolan?"

I ran a hand over my face as my sleepy brain tried to process my brother's panicked voice.

"It's happening. It's happening now!"

Sometimes I wished that Alana handled his personal calls as well as his work ones.

"What's happening?"

"Baby! Erin— Hospital."

When we were kids, I'd regularly wake up to the sound of my little brother yelling in my ear. I expected it to stop when we were adults. But he just acquired things like smartphones so he could do it from anywhere. I rubbed my eyes vigorously, still struggling to keep up.

"But she's not due for four weeks."

"Tell the baby that!"

"So, you're at the hospital now?"

"No. I'm stuck in traffic."

"What?! Is Erin in the car with you?"

I had horrible visions of my niece or nephew being born on the freeway.

"No, she's not. That's part of the problem. I got held up in court. According to the hospital, a friend drove her in. I'm going to miss the birth of my child over a contentious claim on a box of cereal!"

"Nolan, listen to me. Calm down."

I swung my legs over the side of the bed and groped for my clothes. I'd hoped the stomach pain would go away while I slept. It hadn't. I got a less than gentle reminder of its existence when I bent over. But there wasn't time for that now. My brother needed me.

"I have to pick up Abby from school in—" I checked my watch. *Shit!* "—35 minutes. But we can go straight to the hospital from there."

"The way things are looking now, you'll probably beat me there."

"I hope not. Look, Nolan, try not to panic, ok? Erin's exactly where she needs to be."

"You're right."

"Congratulations, Daddy."

"Hey, sis."

"Yeah?"

"I love you."

"I love you too."

"Give Abby a kiss from me."

It turned out I needed all of those 35 minutes. The pains got more frequent, and I kept having to stop for a breather. I scoured the house for over-the-counter remedies and found nothing. I'd have to settle for picking something up at the hospital pharmacy. I made it to the school gate with barely a minute to spare. I spotted Marsha shepherding her daughter into their station wagon. She ostentatiously blanked me. I decided I should piss her off more often.

It took some time for Abby to clamber into the front seat. She was hampered by her book bag in one hand and her parrot wedged under the other arm.

"Hey, sunshine. How was school?"

She shrugged.

"It was ok."

"Just ok?"

She nodded, squeezing on the parrot's beak with one hand and stroking his wing with the other.

"Surprise quiz?"

"Dodgeball."

"Oof. Ok, well, I have some news that might help."

She perked up a little.

"Really?"

"Yeah. Auntie Erin went to the hospital this afternoon. She thinks it's time for the baby to be born."

Abby looked up from her parrot apprehensively.

"Now?"

"Yep."

"Today, now?"

"Probably."

"But—"

She gave the wing a twist and her knuckles went white.

"But you said the baby wouldn't be here until next month."

I wasn't surprised at the reaction. Ever since our talk, she became incredibly subdued every time the subject came up. I'd assured her everything would be fine. I'd even had Nolan talk to her. All the same, her plushie maternity ward had mysteriously vanished. It had been replaced by a bizarre courtroom setup. The parrot presided Judge Judy style from his lofty perch on the coffee table. She seemed to rotate which plush was on trial, but the outcome was always the same. The perpetrator would be sentenced to 'go away forever.'

"The due date was next month," I said. "But due dates are only a guess. Babies tend to come along whenever they feel like it."

I poked her gently in the arm.

"You were late."

"I was?"

"Yeah. Guess you were comfy in there. Even back then I couldn't get you out of bed."

I'd hoped this might provoke a laugh, but her face remained frozen in its worried little frown.

"Will the baby be there when we get there?"

"Probably not. It usually takes a while. It's going to be hard work for Auntie Erin, and it might be scary for her too. I think she and Uncle Nolan might appreciate it if we get on over there and see how they're doing."

"Ok."

She bit her lip and nodded. I stroked a hand over her hair and started the car.

I nearly doubled over when we got to the hospital. I *needed* to find that indigestion remedy. Fortunately, I was able to get myself under control before Abby noticed. She clutched my hand tightly as we made our way to the busy reception and then took the elevator to the maternity ward. We spotted Nolan and Alana immediately. They were standing outside Erin's room talking to...

No way!

"Joel?!"

CHAPTER THIRTY-FIVE

Joel

"I really can't thank you enough."

As we stepped outside the hospital room, Nolan shook my hand for the third time. I forced a smile and bit back a wince. That hand had taken a beating today.

"It was nothing, honestly. I just did what anyone else would do."

Nolan and Alana had just arrived, and Erin was being prepped for an epidural. I was taking advantage of the quiet moment to slip away—or so I thought.

"Look, are you sure you don't want to stick around? According to the nurses, it probably won't be long now."

Hell, no. Bad idea.

I shook my head and clapped Nolan on the shoulder.

"Thanks, man. I'm flattered, but it's not my place. I don't want to intrude."

"You wouldn't be. You're kind of Erin's hero at this point. And I know you've met my grandmother at least once. That's more than long enough for her to have decided that you're family."

Maybe I could've been.

"Plus, there's—"

"Joel?"

Dammit!

I'd hoped to slip out before Olivia arrived. But there she was, standing in the middle of the corridor, holding Abby's hand. A flash of color caught my eye. Abby was clutching the parrot I'd bought her at the zoo. I swallowed and raised my hand in a feeble wave. I knew seeing her would hurt, but I hadn't expected it to hurt this much. For a second, I couldn't do anything. I just stood there with my hand in the air like an idiot.

Nolan opened his mouth to say something, then Erin called out to him. He looked between us apologetically and ducked inside. Without missing a beat, Alana stepped forward and held out her hand to Abby.

"Hey, *mija*. I saw a machine down the hall. Why don't we go get you a soda?"

"But I'm not thirsty."

Abby turned big solemn eyes on all three of us and adjusted the grip on the parrot. She knew something was up.

"Trust me," Alana said. "You're parched. I think you might be hungry too. How about a candy bar?"

That was evil. No matter how curious they are, there's only so much temptation any kid could stand. Abby's eyes rounded.

"Before dinner?"

Alana's eyes flicked upwards, and Olivia gave the tiniest nod.

"Sure," she said, taking Abby's free hand. "And you can choose anything you want."

As the two of them ambled down the corridor, I tried to decide whether I was pissed at Alana, or I owed her a large drink. Olivia didn't look sure either. For a few seconds, we didn't say anything. She hunched her shoulders and rubbed her hand up the sleeve of her sweater like she was cold. I put my hands in my pockets and examined my laces.

"How've you been?"

"Fantastic," I snapped. "You?"

"Fine."

She didn't look fine. She'd lost weight. Under the stark hospital lights, her skin looked almost grey and there were purple shadows under her eyes. Her face had an odd shine to it as well, like she was clammy. It was on the tip of my tongue to ask if she was sick. I had to angrily remind myself it was none of my business anymore.

"Well, good talk," I said. "I guess I'd better—"

"Wait! What happened? How did you...end up here?"

At least she didn't say "What are you doing here?" I shrugged.

"I'd stopped by Sticky Treats to tell Erin... Well, to talk some business. Then everything kicked off. Your brother was held up in court and, for some reason, your grandmother wasn't picking up."

"Bunions," she said.

"What?"

Olivia screwed her eyes shut and grimaced. I bit my tongue again. There was a chance I was imagining it anyway. Might've just been the effect of talking to me.

"She had an appointment with the podiatrist, but it doesn't matter. Did anyone manage to get hold of her?"

"Alana got through."

The conversation was starting to feel numb and dreamlike. I wished it was a dream.

"You could've called *me,*" Olivia said reproachfully. "I know we've had our differences but—"

"I offered. Erin wouldn't let me. Said there'd be nobody to pick up Abby from school. Anyway, there was no one else around, so I drove her in."

"That was really nice of you."

I laughed bitterly. The polite formality scraped over my raw nerves like a belt sander.

"Yeah. Guess I can be trusted to do some things right after all."

She took a deep breath and pinched the bridge of her nose.

"My sister-in-law is in labor. Can we not make this about us?"

"My mistake," I said acidly. "It's clearly not the time to bring up something so trivial."

"You're being an idiot."

Her hands flew to her hips and my belly tightened. Damn! I wondered how long it would be before that gesture stopped doing things to me. It made me want to kiss her, even after she'd just called me an idiot. I needed to get out of here before I did something stupid.

"You know what? I'm just gonna go. I don't belong here."

I waited a fraction of a second too long. Maybe secretly hoping she'd stop me. For a moment it looked like she was going to. But then she crossed her arms and looked away. I turned on my heel and stalked off. When I got to the corner, I snuck a glance over my shoulder. She was slightly hunched over, both hands pressed to her stomach. For a moment I almost went back.

Back in my car, I checked my phone before I drove off. Two missed calls and a message from Zel. I scowled and shoved the handset back into my pocket. It was family dinner night too. Crystal would flip out on me if I missed another one. Couldn't be helped. Zel, my business, my family. All those things could wait until tomorrow. Tonight, I just wanted to forget.

The whiskey had been a gift from a client. It still had a glittery gold bow around the neck. It had been lurking in the back of my kitchen cupboard for months. I'd been considering regifting it. I hadn't done any serious drinking since my art school days. Now, though, the idea of blissful alcohol-soaked oblivion was incredibly appealing.

I choked on the first glass, throat burning, eyes watering.

The second and third went down easier. Then I stopped bothering with the glass.

I'd had the foresight to relocate to the sofa, being as my vision went double and my legs went numb. I lay in an undignified half-sprawl, watching the room sway back and forth. I couldn't feel my face anymore. I couldn't feel anything anymore. Little snatches of Olivia kept bobbing to the surface of my brain. Her eyes, her hair, her laugh. At one point I was convinced I could smell her.

I never made it to my bed. My dreams were strange, psychedelic. I was on a ship on the ocean. That explained the bobbing up and down. A beautiful red-haired pirate woman poked me towards the edge of the plank. I should have known better. Captain Olivia's crew weren't taking applications right now, and there was no way she could accept a pathetic drunken stowaway. I tried to turn around but that stupid parrot kept flying in my face. Now it was pecking at my forehead. Driving into my skull like a drill...or a hangover.

The bright dawn light filtered through the window and poked me awake like a cat demanding its breakfast. I forced my gummy eyes open and groaned. I was lying face down on the couch in a pool of my own drool. My head pounded and my mouth tasted like morning breath on steroids.

There was one thing I was thankful for—that my house had a downstairs toilet. I wouldn't have made it otherwise.

When I got back from the bathroom, I forced myself to drink a glass of water, closed the blinds, and flopped face down on the sofa again.

What the fuck?

Summer strawberries? Now I knew why I'd smelled Olivia last night. A soft pink sweater wedged down the side of the couch cushion. She must've left it last time she was here. How had it stayed here all this time? I picked up the sweater and raised to it my face. That horrible lump returned to my throat and my eyes burned.

Fuck!

I scrunched the sweater into a ball and hurled it across the room. I needed to forget how I felt about Olivia and move on. But how was I supposed to do this when she'd scattered herself all over my life like some sort of cursed pixie dust?

I jumped up, instantly regretting it when pain lanced through the top of my skull. Clutching my head and moving more gingerly, I staggered to the basement to hunt down a cardboard box. I had to do this. Hangover or no hangover, it was time to purge every trace of Olivia from my house once and for all.

CHAPTER THIRTY-SIX

Olivia

"Mommy?"

Abby?

"Mommy, wake up!"

Yep. That was definitely Abby. I couldn't remember the last time she'd gotten up before me. I forced my eyes open, and she swam into focus. Not only was she up, but she was standing by my bed, fully dressed. How long had I slept in?

"Uncle Nolan's on the phone."

Nolan. The baby. I sat up and cried out sharply. The cramping pains just below my belly button were still there and they were getting vicious. Abby frowned and chewed her lip.

"What's wrong, Mommy?"

"Nothing, baby. I just sat up too fast. Did you bring the phone up for me?"

She nodded and held it out. Her big green eyes watched me anxiously. I smoothed a reassuring hand over her curls and held the phone to my ear. Nolan had insisted that Abby and I go home at around 3 a.m. Abby had been asleep in my lap, and I'd been about ready to throw up. I put it down to exhaustion and the unexpected meeting with Joel.

Of all the people to...

No. That wasn't fair. He'd really come through. It had just been gut-wrenching to see him when things were still so raw.

Bad choice of words.

I bit my cheek as another spasm hit.

"It's a boy!"

"Wha—?"

My brother's excited voice was much too loud.

"The baby."

"You have a little boy?"

My brain was processing information at half speed. Eventually, my comprehension and my emotions caught up. Erin had had the baby. My brother had a son. I had a nephew. Despite the pain in my stomach, my face split into a grin.

"Yep," Nolan confirmed. "As of 5:27 a.m. Erin made me wait a couple of hours before calling you."

Best sister-in-law ever!

"Congratulations. Does he have a name yet?"

"Yeah...about that."

Nolan cleared his throat.

"What?"

There was a long pause. Abby climbed onto the bed and curled up in a ball, laying her head on my knee. The shifting of the mattress prompted another spasm of pain and I inhaled sharply.

"We named him Felix," Nolan said eventually. "But given what happened yesterday, Erin wanted to give him the middle name Joel. We both thought we should ask you first."

Something twisted inside me that had nothing to do with whatever was going on in my abdomen. I swallowed hard and rubbed at my eyes with the heel of my palm.

"It's fine."

"Are you sure?"

"Yes!"

Absolutely not.

But I had to be ok with this. Things had gone badly

between me and Joel. But that was just the way things panned out sometimes. I needed to start behaving like a sensible 35-year-old woman, not a silly teenager sobbing her way through her first breakup. Maybe this was the best way to move on. A new start and a new Joel. In time, I'd come to associate the name with my nephew, not some random guy I'd had a fling with for a few months.

"So," I said briskly. "When do you want to be bombarded with visitors?"

There was a hissing as Nolan sucked air through his teeth.

"I'd love to say today, but maybe tomorrow? Erin's pretty beat and Granny and Russ are coming back this afternoon."

"Good! I mean, that's fine. That's understandable."

"Hey, Liv? Are you ok? You don't sound so good. You looked pretty out of it at the hospital yesterday too. I meant to say something, but—"

"I'm fine. I just didn't get a lot of sleep."

"Are you sure? Granny's pretty set on canceling her weekend trip. If you're sick, I can send her over."

"No! No. She has a shiny new grandbaby to gush over. I don't want to drag her away."

"I just thought you might need help with—"

"I said I'm fine!"

Sure, I felt like death. But it was only a stomach bug. My family had more than enough going on. I wasn't going to make them take care of me. I could look after myself. I was the strong one. It was what I did. I took care of them, not the other way around. Granny V was right; I hadn't been taking care of myself. It was my own fault I was sick. I wouldn't let my family suffer the consequences of my poor decisions—not again.

Should probably try not to yell at them, though.

Abby had twisted in my lap. She looked up at me with an anxious frown and I squeezed her shoulder.

"Jesus. I'm sorry, Nolan. I didn't mean to bite your head off."

"It's ok. After 33 years of it, I think I've got a neck callus."

"You suck."

"Hey, I'm a father now," he teased. "I have to start working those bad joke muscles."

"I think they were over-developed already."

"Maybe. Hey, sis."

"Yeah?"

"I'm a dad. Isn't that amazing?"

Amazing indeed.

My attempts to go about my day like a functional human being were less impressive. I managed to prepare breakfast with a lot of grimacing and leaning on the counter. I'd hoped to distract Abby by letting her have Pop-Tarts, but my kiddo was far more observant than I'd given her credit for. She solemnly chewed on her pastries after remarking that my face was a funny color. The next time I passed a mirror, I saw she was right. I was pale as a bowl of old oatmeal and sweat glistened on my forehead.

I suspected it wasn't a coincidence when Abby declared she didn't feel like baking and maybe we should just watch movies instead. I didn't know whether to cry or kiss her.

So we nestled under blankets to watch *Encanto.* Or, more accurately, Abby watched it. I stared at the feverishly swirling colors and tried not to whimper at every stab of pain. It was getting worse. Every time I moved, it was like a knife slicing through my belly. Icy fingers of panic crept into my chest. My insistence to myself that this was a stomach bug rang hollower with each spasm. What if I passed out? Who would take care of Abby? Would she know whom to call? Would anybody pick up?

"Mommy?"

Abby's tiny, scared little voice sounded distorted, like I was hearing it underwater. Closing my eyes, I forced myself to breathe slowly. I could do this. One step at a time. The sofa shifted. I opened my eyes to find Olaf's smiling face looming closer. Abby had fetched her faded *Frozen* washcloth and she was using it to dab at my forehead. It was damp and cool, and it felt amazing. A lump rose in my throat and my eyes stung. This was where my stupid pride had gotten me. I'd insisted I could do it all myself and now my 7-year-old was taking care of me. What kind of a mother was I?

The doorbell rang and we both jumped. I yelped as a particularly violent twinge had me afraid I was going to puke all over the sofa.

"Should I get it?" Abby asked.

"No."

I put a hand on her arm.

"We don't know who it is. I'll go."

Steeling myself, I stood up shakily. The room lurched alarmingly around me as I shuffled towards the door. Nothing prepared me for what was on the other side. Joel stood on my doorstep holding a cardboard box. The sun streamed in behind him, surrounding him with a halo of light. Was this a dream? Had I nodded off on the sofa?

"J-Joel?"

"Fuck, Liv! You're white as a ghost. What's going on?"

His words and his mouth were weirdly out of sync. My knees buckled and I gripped the doorframe. Joel dropped the box and lurched forward to catch me. My head fell on his chest, and I breathed in his familiar smell. He was solid and warm. Somehow, I knew that if I just held on to him, everything would be all right. I didn't have to be strong anymore. He cradled me with one arm and pressed his other hand to my head.

"You're burning up."

"I-I don't f-feel so..."

Trying to talk was a mistake. The nausea I'd been fighting all morning surged over me. I *almost* turned my head in time.

"I'm sorry," I whimpered, tears cascading down my cheeks.

"Hey," he soothed. "Don't worry about that. Let's just get you inside."

"B-but you're..."

"Eh. I never liked this shirt much anyway."

He scooped me up in his arms and my head lolled onto his chest.

"Where's Abby? Is she ok?"

A new urgency crept into his voice, and I felt him looking around.

He remembered to ask about Abby. He really cares about her.

Everything was jumbled and confused. One minute I was in Joel's arms, and the next minute I was on the couch again. I heard Joel and Abby talking quietly. I had to tell him to call someone. Someone had to take care of her. There were instructions, lists, and emergency plans. I opened my mouth and tried to issue instructions, but my tongue felt strange.

"A-ab... Joel?"

He was there again. Low soothing voice, cool hand on my brow.

"Right here. Don't you worry, Vivi. I'm not going anywhere."

CHAPTER THIRTY-SEVEN

Joel

I'd had it all planned out, everything I was going to say. I'd rehearsed it on the way over. Then she'd opened the door and it had all vanished. All that anger and burning resentment just went *poof*! Olivia was pale, sweaty, and doubled over with pain. It was terrifying. I barely noticed when she puked on me. All that mattered was taking care of my girl—my girls. Was Abby even here? How had Olivia been coping by herself? These questions chased each other around my brain as I maneuvered her to the couch. I'd almost got her settled when a little voice piped up behind me.

"What's wrong with Mommy?"

Abby was looking at me with big, scared eyes and clutching her parrot like a lifeline. I moved to squat in front of her and put my hands on her shoulders. She felt so tiny and fragile, it seemed like one wrong move would crush her. But now wasn't the time to second-guess myself. Olivia needed me to step up.

"Hey, kiddo. Mommy's gonna be fine. She's just a little sick. It's ok, though. We're gonna look after her."

I sounded a lot more confident than I felt. I doodled on people for a living. I was seriously out of my depth with this. But Abby was looking at me, desperate for reassurance.

"I put a washcloth on her head," she said, chewing on her lip. "But I don't think it worked."

Probably better than I'd have done, to be honest.

We needed someone who knew what they were doing. That's when I remembered that it was Dustin's day off.

"That's good," I praised. "You did good. I think we might need a little extra help, though. I'm going to message my cousin, Dustin. He's an EMT. You know what that means?"

She nodded solemnly and rested her cheek on the parrot's head.

"Means he drives an ambulance."

"That's right. So he'll know what we need to do with Mommy. It's gonna be ok, kiddo. I promise."

She dropped the parrot and flung herself at me, throwing her skinny arms around my neck. I blinked in surprise then returned the hug, holding her very gingerly in case I hurt her.

"Joel?"

"Yeah?"

"You smell funny."

I chuckled softly.

"Harsh but fair. We should probably find me another shirt at some point."

"Ooh. I know!"

She pulled away from me and barreled up the stairs. I had no idea what she was up to but for now, I was pleased she was distracted. Olivia let out a heart-rending moan as soon as Abby's feet hit the stairs. I wondered if she'd been waiting for her daughter to be out of earshot. I typed a quick message to Dustin, describing Olivia's symptoms. I'd just hit send when she called out feebly.

"J-Joel?"

"I'm right here, Vivi. I'm not going anywhere."

She clutched my hand and my chest tightened. Just then, Abby came thundering back downstairs and proudly presented me with a black t-shirt.

"Mommy keeps this under her pillow," she said. "I don't know why she hides it, though. She said you're never too old for stuffies."

"She's right."

So that's where my Alestorm t-shirt had disappeared to. My phone buzzed and I cleared my throat rapidly.

Dustin: Where's the pain? Right side or left side?

Shit! I have no idea.

I squeezed Olivia's fingers and ran the back of my hand over her cheek. Her skin was hot and moist.

"Where does it hurt, Liv?"

"No...don'—"

"Abby," I said urgently. "Did Mommy tell you where her tummy hurts?"

Abby raised both hands to her mouth and shook her head. I licked my lips and tried to swallow past the solid lump of panic in my throat.

"Do you think you could guess?"

She frowned and a tip of a pink tongue poked out of the corner of her mouth.

"When she said ouch, she went like this."

She screwed up her face in an exaggerated grimace and clutched the right side of her belly.

"Good girl."

Joel: Right side.

Dustin: Fever? Vomiting?

I glanced down at my stained shirt.

Joel: Yep.

Dustin: Sounds like appendicitis. It's ambulance time, bro.

It wasn't good news. It was scary news. But at least I knew what to do now.

Joel: Gotcha. Thanks.

Dustin: Here for you if you need anything.

Olivia retched violently. I barely had time to grab a wastepaper bin. Over the sound of Olivia vomiting, I heard Abby whimper. Her eyes were big, anxious saucers. I looked around desperately and spotted the discarded washcloth.

"Hey, Abby. Little job for you. Go get this wet again so we can put it on Mommy's forehead."

I did my best to keep her distracted until the ambulance arrived. By the time they pulled up, I was running out of errands. We watched helplessly as the EMTs loaded Olivia onto a stretcher. When I moved to follow them out of the door, one of them barred my way.

"Are you family or next of kin?"

"No, but—"

"Then I'm sorry, but I can't let you into the ambulance with us."

"This is—"

I started to raise my voice then I felt something clutch at my shorts. Abby was looking up at me, eyes full of tears. She needed me to make this ok.

"This is ridiculous," I said, forcing myself to sound calm. "She needs someone with her."

The EMT sighed sympathetically and shook his head.

"I'm sorry, sir, but rules are rules. The best thing you can do right now is take care of the little girl."

I'd never felt more useless than when I stood by the roadside, watching that ambulance drive away.

Come on, Joel. They need you. Olivia's spent her whole life being strong for other people. She needs you to be strong now.

I put a gentle arm around Abby's shoulders and steered her back into the house. She huddled on the couch, clutching her parrot, while I made frantic attempts to contact people. When neither Granny V nor Nolan picked up, I raised my eyes to the ceiling and cursed whatever Gods happened to be listening. They were possibly all at the hospital cooing over the new baby. Then I went back to the couch and sat next to Abby.

"I couldn't get hold of your granny or your uncle, so it looks like you're stuck with me for a while. How do juice and pecan pie sound?"

I felt like Abby needed to get out of here, and there was nothing for a kid at my place. Taking her to sit in a hospital waiting room didn't seem like the best idea either, so there was only one place I could think of.

Aunt Loretta's mouth fell open when she answered the door. I couldn't blame her. It's not every day your nephew goes off the grid for two weeks and then shows up on your doorstep with someone else's kid in tow.

"Joel! This is a surprise. And Abby too. How are you doing, honey?"

Abby clutched my hand harder.

"My mommy's sick," she said mournfully.

"Oh no! That's too bad. Well, come on in, the both of you."

I ushered Abby inside and gave my aunt an apologetic look.

"I wanted to get her out of the house, and I figured she could do with a drink and something to eat."

Aunt Loretta didn't miss a beat, bless her.

"Come with me, sweetie. Let's see if we can find you something."

When Abby was settled with pie, apple juice, and coloring pencils, I filled my aunt in on what had happened. She didn't comment. She just went to the fridge and poured me a glass of iced tea. I leaned against the counter and sipped silently for a minute or two.

"I'm sorry I haven't been by in a while," I said eventually.

"That's ok."

Loretta picked up a basin of peas and began shelling them into a pan.

"You ready to talk about it yet?"

I frowned.

"Talk about what?"

"Whatever it was that went sour between you and Olivia."

"How'd you—"

She looked up from the peas and gave me an exasperated smile.

"I've been your aunt for 35 years, Joey. You think I can't see through one of your sulks?"

The tea was slightly too sweet for my taste. I took a large gulp and shrugged.

"I thought everything was going great. And then she broke things off out of the blue."

"Did she say why?"

"She said it was Abby."

I mouthed the name so sensitive little ears could remain happily oblivious.

"Said she couldn't risk hurting her by bringing someone else into her life who might leave. She has this weird conviction that everything in her life will go south if she lets someone in."

Loretta scowled at a blackened pea pod and threw it on the trash pile.

"Now, *that* sounds familiar."

"What do you mean?"

"I had the same conversation with your mother years ago."

I raised my eyebrows. This was a story about Mom I hadn't heard.

"Mhmm. There was a short-order cook at that diner she worked at. The two of them really hit it off. But after what happened with your dad, Connie wouldn't chance it. Said she'd built a life for the two of you and she wasn't going to risk disrupting that. She was determined to do it all by herself. And she passed a good part of that stubborn streak on to you."

I experienced a weird stab of guilt. I hated the idea of being an obstacle to my mother's happiness. As if reading my mind, Loretta looked at me and raised an eyebrow.

"I see what you're thinking," she scolded. "I didn't tell you this story to give you another stick to beat yourself with. The truth of it was that she was just scared."

"Scared of what?"

"Scared of getting her heart bruised again, of course."

"You think Olivia's scared too?"

"Would that be so surprising?"

No. No, it wouldn't.

I remembered what Olivia had told me about her ex—how he had abandoned her when she was pregnant with Abby. Of course she'd be afraid to open her heart again. And I'd gone off on her like an asshole, tried to make it all about me.

Loretta scooped up the empty pods and dumped them in the trash.

"I'm going to take a wild stab and guess that you weren't the sensitive and mature adult that you should've been when she broke things off."

She knew me way too well.

"Nope. I fucked up big time."

The expletive slipped out of my mouth before I could catch it. That was when I knew for sure that this was an important conversation. Loretta didn't even call me on it.

"You won't be the first," she said, wiping her hands on a dishtowel. "We all say things we're not proud of when we're hurting. The important thing is, what're you going to do about it now?"

"Do?"

"You want her back, don't you?"

"Yes."

There was no point in lying to my aunt or to myself. I was in love with Olivia. I wanted her more than I'd ever wanted anything. She opened my eyes to something beyond my miserable lonely existence. Now I'd had a tantalizing glimpse, I couldn't go back to the way things were. I just wasn't sure how I'd go about it. Loretta kissed my cheek as she walked past me to get to the refrigerator.

"Then you just have to show her there's nothing to be afraid of."

Easy as that, huh?

I'd been so used to the idea of my solitary bachelor existence—a pirate sailing the seven seas alone. Convincing Olivia I was a safe bet as a family man seemed like a tall order when I'd only just got done talking myself around. Until very recently, I'd been convinced I was no good for anyone. While my aunt took my uncle a glass of iced tea, I went to the table to check on Abby. I found her engrossed in her drawing.

"Hey, kiddo. What're you up to?"

"Making a get-well card for Mommy."

"Cool!"

I peered over her shoulder.

"A pirate ship, huh? That's really good."

Abby grabbed a red pencil and began coloring what I had assumed was an oddly shaped cloud. Now I could see that it was a parrot. Nightmarishly large in comparison to the ship, but still recognizable.

"It's Vivi's ship," Abby said.

"So it is."

Now I looked, I saw that one of the figures on the boat had a lot of orange hair.

"I'm going to be a pirate when I grow up."

I smiled.

"I used to want that too. But wouldn't you miss your mommy?"

She raised her head from her paper and looked at me like I'd gone insane.

"No. She'd come with me."

I put my head on one side and pursed my lips.

"I guess she could. But what about Granny and Nolan and Alana and everyone?"

"They'd all come with me."

"Gonna get awfully crowded on that ship."

"Vivi's ship has lots of people on it."

"True."

I suddenly remembered a whole host of other characters from the books: Crawdad Jim, Eric the Pomeranian, Peg-leg Pauline, and Bananas the light-fingered monkey cabin boy.

"All pirate captains need a crew," Abby said confidently.

"I...guess they do."

"Granny said the best thing about Vivi is that she never has to leave her family behind. Every time she sets sail for a new adventure, her home and family go with her."

I sank down in a chair next to Abby and stared blankly over her head.

"Joel, are you sad?"

"No, kiddo. I'm not sad."

I'm just re-evaluating my whole life.

"I wish you and Mommy weren't fighting," said Abby quietly.

"Me too, kiddo."

"If you weren't fighting with Mommy, you could be a part of my pirate crew."

I leaned forward and ruffled her hair.

"Look," I said, "I don't know what's gonna happen between me and Mommy, but that doesn't mean I can't be there for you."

She looked at me uncertainly.

"Really?"

"Yeah, really. I'm not lucky enough to be your dad but I can still be your person."

She rested her chin on her hand and looked at me thoughtfully.

"Ok," she said. "You can be the parrot."

I stuck out my lip.

"Is my position on this crew up for negotiation?"

"Maybe." She shoved a piece of blank paper and the box of crayons across the table. "But you have to make Mommy a card too."

"You drive a hard bargain, kiddo."

I stared at the paper for a moment and then began to sketch.

CHAPTER THIRTY-EIGHT

Olivia

"Where's Abby?"

I'd been asking the same question since I came around. I was far more interested in the whereabouts of my daughter than in the details of what had happened to me. Terms like 'acute appendicitis,' 'peritonitis,' and 'emergency surgery' flew right over my head. The surgeon seemed a little offended, like I wasn't paying adequate attention to the impressive details of how he had saved my life. I was groggy, sore, and disorientated, but I needed to know my little girl was safe.

After an eternity of prodding and poking, the hospital staff were finished with me, and my grandmother swooped in. I let her fuss for a couple of minutes and then I hit her with my question.

"Settle down, dear," Granny said, rearranging my blankets for the third time. "Joel's been looking after her."

Joel?

Vague memories of Joel's face, his hand on my forehead, feeling warm and safe with his arms around me. I remembered him being there, but I was convinced it had been a fever dream.

"She's been with Joel all this time?"

My voice cracked and tears trickled from the corners of my eyes. I told myself I was being ridiculous, that it made no sense to be crying.

"He truly has been a gem," Granny went on. "Nolan had planned to go pick Abby up, but Joel insisted on bringing her in himself."

My heart leaped.

"When are they coming?" I asked eagerly.

"Really, Olivia," Granny scolded. "You must calm down and rest. You nearly died! If Nolan weren't so relieved, he'd be furious that you didn't let on how sick you were. We both would."

I shrank from her reproving glare.

"I didn't know."

Granny sighed and looked at me sadly.

"Would it have made any difference if you had? Honestly, Olivia, one of these days you'll learn to let yourself fall and trust that there are people there to catch you."

Guilt writhed in my stomach. I knew I found it difficult to lean on people. What I hadn't realized was that I'd fallen several times recently and someone had been there to catch me. At the school carnival, with Marsha, calling me an ambulance and taking care of Abby. Joel had caught me every time. He'd done it without being asked and I never really noticed. Instead, I'd pushed him away. Was it too late? Had I lost my chance? My face crumpled and fresh tears poured down my cheeks.

"Oh, come here, you silly girl."

Granny V came to the head of the bed and pulled me into a careful side hug. I buried my face in her chest and sobbed. We were still in that position when the door creaked open and a colorful bouquet of balloons floated into the room. They were followed by Nolan and Russ.

"There she is!" Russ said. "How are you feeling, honey?"

"I'm fine." I lifted my head from Granny's bosom and hastily wiped my eyes. "A little sore but the doctors say I'll be fine in a few weeks."

Nolan kissed me on the forehead and tied the balloons to the head of the bed.

"Sorry, the shop was out of flowers. You'll have to make do with these."

"We got this too."

Russ presented me with a stuffed bear holding a heart with 'get well soon' written on it.

"Aww," my grandmother cooed. "A bear from a sugar bear."

Russ went pink and cleared his throat.

"Thought it might amuse Abby if nothing else. We, uh, got one for Erin too," he said, holding up a paper bag.

Erin!

"How is she?" I asked anxiously. "How's the baby?"

"Both doing fine," Nolan said. "The OB-GYN said I can take them home tomorrow."

He'd just finished speaking when his phone buzzed.

"Ah. Looks like Abby and Joel just arrived. I'll go down to meet them."

He was only gone five minutes, but it felt like hours. Butterflies danced frantically in my stomach, and I couldn't focus on anything Granny and Russ said to me.

When the door next opened, Abby ran in with Nolan not far behind. She'd obviously been pre-prepped on my delicate condition as she skidded to a halt by the bed and planted a very restrained kiss on my cheek.

"Hi, Mommy."

"Hi, baby," I choked, fighting tears again. "Are you alright?"

She nodded.

"Joel took me to Loretta's for pecan pie and apple juice, and I made you this."

The pirate ship on the front of the card was violently colorful and I spotted a familiar figure with a mass of orange hair.

"I'm going to be a pirate when I grow up," Abby said. "Joel's going to be the monkey on my ship."

"The monkey?"

"Yes. He wanted to be the co-captain. But I said *you* were the co-captain, and he could be the parrot."

"Isn't he a little big to sit on your shoulder?" Russ asked.

"That's what he said," said Abby seriously. "So I said he could be the monkey instead."

I opened the card and smiled at her spidery message. Abby bit her lip and frowned.

"Are you better now, Mommy?"

"Getting better," I said, smoothing a hand over her hair. "Seeing you helps. It makes me feel 100 times better."

"How about the card?"

"Ooh..." I pretended to think about it. "At least another 20 times better."

"Mommy?"

"Yeah, baby?"

"Can Joel come in here? The nurses said he couldn't because you have too many visitors already. But he made you a card too."

"He did?"

My mouth went dry, and I didn't trust myself to say any more. There was a pregnant pause followed by Russ clearing his throat.

"You know, I think I'll go get a breath of air," he said.

"I'll join you," my grandmother agreed.

Nolan glanced at me and then at Abby.

"Hey, baby girl. Would you like to come and meet your cousin? Auntie Erin is probably feeding him right about now."

Abby's face lit up but then fell again. She looked at me uncertainly, as if she was worried I was going to disappear.

"Go on," I said. "I'll be here when you get back. I can't go myself yet, so I'll be counting on your elephant's memory to give me all the details."

"I'll send him in," Nolan whispered, steering Abby out of the door.

I lay staring at the ceiling, excitement and apprehension fizzing in my chest. I didn't have to wait long. In less than five minutes he was standing by my bed. His hands were in the pockets of his shorts and his stormy eyes peeked shyly from under his long black lashes.

"Hey. How are you feeling?"

Elated? Confused? Terrified?

"Pretty lousy."

"Well." He knelt by the bed and took my hand. My heart skipped. "You look beautiful."

"Liar."

"I never lie."

I raised an eyebrow. He put his free hand on his chest.

"I'm an artist. We take the whole 'beauty truth' thing pretty seriously."

I tittered. It was a bad idea. He squeezed my hand as I winced and clutched my stomach.

"Thank you for taking care of Abby for me."

"Of course."

He held my hand in both of his and kissed my fingers.

"You don't have to thank me, Vivi. You think I'd leave either of you hanging?"

The tears spilled over once again. Why was he being so nice to me? I didn't deserve it.

"Hey! What are these tears for?"

"I'm sorry. I should never have pushed you away like that. I just got so..."

"Scared? I get it. I'm sorry too. Shouldn't have acted like an ass. But I promise, there's nothing to be scared of. I'm here and I'm not going anywhere."

I shuffled as far onto my side as my stitches would allow and stroked his cheek with my free hand.

"I thought I dreamed you."

"Maybe you did. I've dreamed about you plenty of times. It's only fair I should drop into yours."

"You dreamed about me?" I asked, smiling through my tears. "What did you dream about?"

He flushed.

"Well, there was one involving donuts that I probably shouldn't tell you about until you're feeling better. And then there was one where you were a pirate and you made me walk the plank."

"What had you done?"

He gave me an injured look.

"Are you saying I deserved it?"

"Probably."

He rolled his eyes.

"You said your crew wasn't talking applications and you weren't interested in a drunken stowaway."

"Drunken?"

"Don't ask."

I ran my thumb over the back of his hand and cleared my throat nervously. It was time to take the plunge.

"Turns out you were misinformed," I said casually. "The crew *is* taking applications."

"I know. Abby made me the monkey."

I caught his eye, brought his hand to my mouth, and nipped the end of his finger. He groaned.

"A promotion opportunity just came up," I said meaningfully. "Why don't you tell me what you've got to offer?"

A grin broke slowly over his face.

"Well," he pondered, playing along. "I'm excellent at heroic rescues. I mean, seriously. You and Erin in less than 48 hours. Should probably hang fire on congratulating myself for that one, though. Fairly sure she doesn't know what I did to her kitchen yet."

"Is this another thing I shouldn't ask about?"

"That's probably wise. So, there's daring rescues. Then there's my prairie oysters; ask Jayden about those."

"Stop! You're going to make me laugh again."

"Sorry."

"No, you're not."

"You're right, I'm totally not sorry. Hmm, what else am I good at? Cuddles, foot massages—"

"A little bird tells me you also do an awesome line in 'get well' cards."

He closed his eyes and hid his face in our joined hands.

"Abby threw me under the bus, huh?"

"It's one of her talents."

He reached into his pocket and drew out a folded piece of paper.

"I'm not so good with words," he said. "So I decided to draw how I felt instead."

Heart pounding, I unfolded the paper. My breath caught. It was a colored pencil drawing of three bunnies in a woodland glade. One of them was me; I recognized myself from the tattoo—russet fur and a bright green eye. Then there was a smaller version of the russet bunny. The third bunny was the largest and it was the strangest bunny I had ever seen. Its fur was a patchwork of bright colors, and it sported a rakish eyepatch. They cuddled together on a bed of wildflowers, all different but quite clearly a family. My hand flew to my mouth and a sound that was half a laugh and half a sob squeezed from my throat.

"It's beautiful," I said hoarsely.

"That's the other thing I have to offer. I love you, Olivia."

"I love you too."

He leaned in to kiss me, a sweet peck laden with the promise of more.

"Did I pass the interview?" he asked, resting his forehead against mine.

I nuzzled him with my nose and captured his lips in another kiss.

"Permission to come aboard, Mr. Morris."

ABOUT THE AUTHOR

Monica is a writer of romance novels and short stories. After spending almost a decade in the postgraduate study of literature and earning her PhD, she left the world of academia to pursue her dream career as a novelist.

She lives in the heart of the Yorkshire Dales with her long-suffering spouse, their furry menagerie and far too many books.

When not writing, Monica can be found walking her dog, devouring romance novels and getting hopelessly lost down internet rabbit holes.

ALSO BY MONICA MYERS

The Tasty Temptations Series

The Sweet Spot

Indelibly Yours

Printed in Great Britain
by Amazon